HARLEM SUNSET

HARLEM RENAISSANCE MYSTERIES BY NEKESA AFIA

Dead Dead Girls

Harlem Sunset

HARLEM SUNSET

A HARLEM RENAISSANCE MYSTERY

NEKESA AFIA

BERKLEY PRIME CRIME
NEW YORK

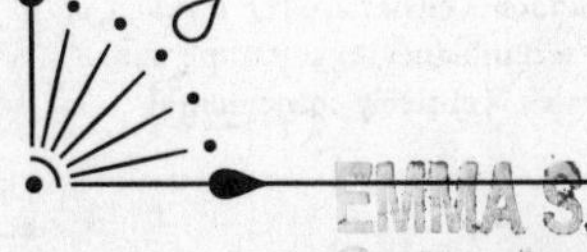

BERKLEY PRIME CRIME
Published by Berkley
An imprint of Penguin Random House LLC
penguinrandomhouse.com

Library of Congress Cataloging-in-Publication Data

Names: Afia, Nekesa, author.
Title: Harlem sunset / Nekesa Afia.
Description: First Edition. | New York : Berkley Prime Crime, 2022. |
Series: A Harlem Renaissance mystery
Identifiers: LCCN 2021061097 (print) | LCCN 2021061098 (ebook) | ISBN 9780593199121 (trade paperback) | ISBN 9780593199138 (ebook)
Subjects: GSAFD: Mystery fiction.
Classification: LCC PS3601.F455 H37 2022 (print) | LCC PS3601.F455 (ebook) | DDC 813/.6--dc23
LC record available at https://lccn.loc.gov/2021061097
LC ebook record available at https://lccn.loc.gov/2021061098

First Edition: June 2022

Printed in the United States of America
1 3 5 7 9 10 8 6 4 2

Book design by Alison Cnockaert

A little less thinking, a little more feeling.

—STEPHEN SONDHEIM (1930–2021)

HARLEM SUNSET

1

SUMMER 1926

THE OCEAN SPRAY hits her in the face. She closes her eyes against it.

She's been on this boat, this glorified dinghy, for the better part of a week. They were approaching the sunny island of Manhattan.

In the distance Lady Liberty stands, her torch held high, beckoning all toward her.

She has been constantly seasick on the passage but staring at Lady Liberty makes her feel much better.

The first thing she is going to do when she reaches New York is get something to eat.

She leans on the railing. Around her little girls and boys throw their hats and try to evade their chaperones. They yell and jostle one another. She grits her teeth against the noise. She can't stand children.

Still, there's something to be envied about them. They're carefree; the world is at their feet.

And they have no idea.

There're five of them. The oldest is a boy, about eight. He's clearly the ringleader. He wants all of the other kids to do exactly what he wants. She just barely remembers her brother like that, fearless and domineering.

She can relate to that. He has no idea how *lucky* he is, to have been born a man in this world. It's easier to be a man. He'll learn that soon. The boy pushes one of the girls, a true cherub with red cheeks and big brown eyes, to the wood of the deck. The girl automatically bursts into tears, her anguished wails ringing through the air. People turn to look, and one of the chaperones, a harried woman, comes and scoops her up, admonishing the girl quietly.

She turns her focus back to the statue and the task ahead of her. Soon enough she'll be back down in her cabin. Even the gentle swaying of the boat is enough to make her sick. She's barely eaten more than soup during this boat ride.

It's the first time she's felt the sun since boarding. She's trying to make the most of it. Every breath she takes shudders through her. She's not made for ocean travel. She's had nightmares of drowning in the cold, murky water. She hasn't been able to sleep very well.

But she won't let this distract her. Ocean travel is the smallest of the hurdles she's going to have to jump. She'll need to remain focused.

The children are still squalling, fighting. It's to the point now that other people have started to remark on the behavior of these children.

She's ignoring the kids around her as she leans her chin on the cool metal railing. She turns her face to the unblemished blue sky. She has missed this so much.

She's so close to all of her goals. But something still feels wrong.

And she can't put her finger on it.

Hopefully New York City is more welcoming.

IT'S SO EASY to find her. Louise Lloyd is wearing a bright red dress, a headband against her forehead.

This place truly is a dive, nothing like what she's accustomed to. It's a hole in the wall. It took a solid fifteen minutes of wandering around to find it, even though the taxi dropped her off at the right spot. New York City nightlife is different, louder. The entire culture is meant to be a secret, but the noise from various clubs is deafening.

The table is covered in alcohol, sticky. She's careful not to touch it. She's intently watching this Louise. Louise doesn't match up to anything she's heard. The woman is tiny, her skin a luminous shade of red-brown and her eyes a bright hazel; she's practically glowing under the lights. The dress is cheap but doesn't look it, and layers of chiffon are beaded and move as she does, dancing in the light. Her lips are dripping in red.

She's just not who she expected.

But somehow she's not surprised.

The music is deep and longing. Louise smiles as she's wrapped up in the arms of an unfamiliar woman. They're dancing an intricate dance, one that requires the woman to put all her trust in the one leading.

Louise is good. She considers this as she watches from the shadows. The tango is a strong, romantic dance, and the women make it look easy. Every dance step is deliberate, and while her tango is technically good, Louise manages to look at the woman leading her around as if she has loved her for her entire life.

It's almost *wrong*, watching this dance. It's not overly sexual, not really, but it's still perverse in a way.

And yet she cannot stop watching.

She's sizing Louise up, the way she's moving, deftly following her partner around the floor. She's heard that this woman makes a wonderful opponent.

The women here, the majority of whom are white, are watching too. Miss Lloyd and her partner stick out. The band is crying out behind them and Louise is making all of this look easy. It's a warm summer night, even warmer in the club, and it doesn't look as if she's broken a sweat. Almost simple, effortless.

She leans back against her chair. She swears that she saw a cockroach scuttle across the floor near her shoe and she regrets coming to this place.

But it is a necessary trip. She has to see what she is dealing with. She has to make sure she will have the upper hand. She sips from her glass; it's just water. She's going to need a clear head if she's going to do what she came to do.

Louise's head turns, and she swears those strange hazel eyes fall right on her. They go right through her. Despite the heat, she shivers. Eye contact is held for a moment when the world fades away and it's only them.

Then, as if it never happened, Louise turns away.

Game on, Miss Lloyd.

2

THEY MET AT a small café. Louise Lloyd sat across from Officer Andrew Martin. The summer sun drifted in from the window next to them. Louise concentrated on lighting a cigarette. She was exhausted. She crossed her arms over her chest and refused to look the officer in the eye.

"Miss Lloyd."

"Officer Martin."

His smile wasn't cold, but wasn't friendly either. The fact was that neither of them really knew what to say to the other. Louise kept herself still and straight in her seat.

"What is there to talk about?"

He had been her only true ally. It wasn't so long ago she was suspecting him of murder.

But that, and a little bit of blackmail, she hoped, was water under the bridge. Their working relationship had started with a violent punch from Louise outside a nightclub. Then, after Gilbert put her on the Girl Killer case, they had had no choice but to coexist.

Then they had had to work together when it became clear to both of them that Gilbert was the Girl Killer.

Gilbert had kidnapped her, had made her Harlem's Hero.

She would never be rid of him.

The officer's eyebrows knitted together in deep concentration. "You could have been killed."

"I'm the luckiest girl in the city."

They were having this conversation away from prying ears. She wondered what he would tell his superiors about the death of Detective Theodore Gilbert.

"You are lucky, make no mistake."

She knew Martin knew how close she had come to losing her life. Every time she closed her eyes, she saw the former detective lunge at her. Her heart constricted every time she blinked and relived that moment over and over.

"I know." It was supposed to be a joke—she tried to get out of too many things by joking—but the weight of the past few weeks hadn't been lost on her.

Martin looked around them, trying to see whether there was anyone nearby who might overhear their conversation. It was a habit of his and one that she had picked up. She could never be too careful. She never knew who was listening in.

Louise figured that she had a couple days of freedom while the impatient men at the precinct put the story of Gilbert's death together. Then she'd be back in the precinct jail.

She was going to make these couple days count. If she had learned anything over the past few weeks, it was that time was short, death was upon her. She should have as much fun as possible before she did die.

Maybe that wasn't the intended lesson, but it was the one she had learned.

Martin didn't say anything. They had had their differences and she wouldn't have imagined that they would be in cahoots now. He lit a cigarette. Every move he made was confident and assured, even in private company. He never let himself slip in any way. It was so annoying.

The daylight shone from the window into her eyes. Not for the first time, Louise wondered what she would do.

"You believe me, right?" Louise asked.

Andrew Martin was the only person Louise had told about the entire night in the Zodiac. She had had to; he had found her at the scene, her gun still in her shaking hand.

"Of course I do."

"What's going to happen next?"

There were so many things she prided herself on. The ability to spend all night in heels and never take them off. Her special skill of downing a bottle of gin and barely feeling it. She used to be able to add not being scared to that list, but that had changed so quickly.

"You are going to go home and sleep," he said with confidence. "You are going to go live your life until I decide otherwise."

She thought it was supposed to be a joke, but she didn't laugh.

"Do as you're told, Miss Lloyd. It'll only make things easier."

She couldn't just leave, could she?

It turned out that she could. She could step away from the building and head back to her home in the morning light. It was a brilliant summer day but she wasn't sure if she was sweating from the sun or from panic.

AFTER THE DAY—THE summer—she'd had, all she wanted to do was dance. The Gold Room in Harlem was nearly full, and much dirtier than where they usually went. But it was special. The Gold Room was for women like her: women who liked other women.

She was escorted by Rosa Maria Moreno, and they were on a mission.

A mission to spend every moment possible on the dance floor.

The band was playing and Louise felt more herself than she had in weeks. After everything, she wanted to be herself again.

This was step one.

The band was playing a waltz, and they had a plan. She and Rosa Maria ran to the bar, drank two drinks, and by the time the tempo had changed, they were ready to get on the floor.

"This place is nice," Louise said.

Rosa Maria considered it. "Not as nice as the Dove will be."

It was a moot point, considering the Dove wasn't open yet. Louise allowed her girlfriend to pull her onto the dance floor.

The music was tense and desperate. Louise let Rosa Maria hold her close. They were the only people on the dance floor. Everyone else was seated around tables, talking over the band, drinking.

It was any other ordinary night and they were going to make it good.

They began a tight tango. Her tango wasn't very good, but she trusted Rosa Maria to lead her across the floor. She trusted herself to listen to the music and react accordingly.

They could never go to a club and not dance.

She could feel eyes on them as they moved across the floor. At once, everything she had been thinking of, fearing, melted away. She concentrated on not falling over her feet. She concentrated on going where Rosa Maria led her.

But every time she closed her eyes, all she saw was the body of her dead sister lying on the cold concrete. She tried not to blink anymore. She tried not to sleep anymore.

Spending almost all night every night with Rosa Maria was a welcome distraction. Being on the dance floor was the only way she knew how to deal with this.

She was in uncharted territory, a pioneer of this grief.

How would she even begin to deal with it?

"You all right, Lou?" Rosa Maria asked. She could always tell if something was wrong. She said it was the way Louise held herself, stiff and tense.

Louise relaxed. "This place really isn't as good as the Dove."

Rosa Maria laughed. Louise always liked her laugh.

"People'll actually dance at the Dove."

It was hard to keep up a conversation, whispered in partial sentences between twists and turns and pauses. They managed it, though.

Rosa Maria, always able to do multiple things at once, was scanning the crowd. "I like the look of the singer."

Louise was staring into a pair of light blue eyes, a pair that seemed so familiar and yet so far away.

The world around her stopped functioning. The air was drained from her body and she nearly stumbled.

It was impossible for Theodore Gilbert to be in this club on this night. She knew that. She knew that because she had shot and killed him.

She blinked, and she realized the pair of eyes that seemed so distinctive belonged to a woman who was sitting alone at a table. As fast as it had come, her panic dissipated.

"Copacetic, babe?"

"Sure am." Louise looked around, trying to find the woman again. But she had lost her.

Maybe she had made the other woman up.

Rosa Maria righted Louise. It wasn't always easy to put all of her trust in someone else. But it was Rosa Maria.

Could she trust anyone anymore?

Her mind was playing tricks on her. She was exhausted. She was seeing things that weren't there.

She looked into Rosa Maria's eyes. Under the lights, the corners of her eyes crinkled. The music cried behind them, and when it finished, the crowd around them rather politely applauded.

Rosa Maria immediately left her to talk to the singer, a willowy woman with bronze skin who was standing next to the band.

And Louise tried to find that very familiar pair of eyes again. When she scanned the crowd, the band switching songs with the swell of a frenzied Charleston, she couldn't find them.

But she couldn't let herself believe she had made everything up.

She wasn't sure how she was going to survive.

3

SPRING 1927

FOR ABOUT THREE seconds, whenever Louise woke up with Rosa Maria's warm body next to her, she was blissfully unaware of everything that had happened. In those moments, Louise was the woman she had always been. She woke up in a tranquil state, completely at ease and happy with her life.

But she remembered. It hit her all at once. She remembered the dark of the Zodiac, the sheen of the metal barrel of the gun pointed right at her. Louise had had to act faster than she ever had in her life. It was him or her. And she was not going to lose. Louise Lloyd never *lost*.

The shooting was the first thing she thought about when she woke up. It was the last thing on her mind when she went to sleep. The ghost of Theodore Gilbert followed her around, weighing her down with misplaced guilt.

She had thought that ghosts weren't real. Now she knew the opposite to be true.

No matter the circumstances, she had killed someone. She had committed a mortal sin. No amount of praying would change that.

For weeks after the fatal shooting of Theodore Gilbert, she couldn't sleep, she couldn't eat, she couldn't do anything but pace and worry. She was irrationally scared that he was around every corner, waiting for her to let her guard down. She and Rosa Maria had still been living in Miss Brown's house then, and Rosa Maria refused to leave her side.

Louise would see one thing when she closed her eyes: Gilbert's eyes on hers, his gun aiming at her. She was lucky she had been fast; his bullet had just missed her.

Louise had withdrawn from her housemates, who, besides Rosa Maria, she didn't really like anyway. She had stopped eating, drinking, smoking. In the weeks and months following the Girl Killer case, the only thing she had wanted to be was not Louise Lloyd.

Louise would lie in her bed as the world moved on around her. Maeve Walsh had gotten engaged, and Louise hadn't had the heart to tell her that her fiancé had cheated on her and would do it again. Girls had moved out and gotten promoted. Their lives carried on, and Louise was rooted to her spot.

It felt like Harlem was choking her, suffocating her, squeezing the life from her one day at a time. For weeks after the news broke, she couldn't go down the street without being recognized; unflattering photos were put in the papers; murder magazines reported on the whole ordeal. She and Rosa Maria were planning to move out when Miss Brown kindly asked Louise to leave, as the publicity was too much.

Now she was older, exhausted, hungrier.

Theodore Gilbert had been playing her like a fiddle all along. And the worst part was that she had *trusted* him. His ghost would follow her around for the rest of her life. There weren't enough prayers for forgiveness she could say that could change that.

She tried to hang on to those three seconds for as long as possible. She woke up early after tossing and turning all night and getting little sleep, her head pressed against the pillow, eyes closed, chest heaving with her breath. Louise would think it was just a dream, some awful, horrible dream.

And in some way, she'd be right.

She was in the middle of a protracted nightmare. One day leading into another, they were always exactly the same.

Things had gotten better since they moved. A place of their own, no sneaking, no lingering looks over the dinner table. Louise was able to exhale for the first time in a while, and maybe she could move on. Gradually the stories slowed and the whispers stopped. She found a new job. But she still felt guilty. That was the only way to describe it. Guilt clawed at her skin, nipped at her heels, trailed her wherever she went. And there was no way she could escape it.

Louise had always tried to consider herself a rational person. She had faced these facts a long time ago. Theodore Gilbert had killed several girls, tried to kill her, wanted to pin her sister Celia's murder on her. She had had to kill him. She wasn't going to let him kill her. She had had no plans of dying in the dusty club she had once considered her home.

So she had shot, acting first and thinking second.

And she had won, but at what cost?

Rosa Maria turned toward her, an arm falling on Louise's stomach. "Hi."

Rosa Maria's voice was a whisper. She never liked to be loud in the morning. Rosa Maria thought that mornings were for quiet contemplation, coffee, and kisses. Louise kissed her nose.

"Did you get any sleep?" Rosa Maria asked.

"Just a little, but I'm fine," Louise said.

How could she tell Rosa Maria the truth? How could Louise let her worry after her? She couldn't do that, even if it meant hiding a large part of herself from the woman she loved.

"You never sleep anymore." Rosa Maria frowned, her perfect bow-shaped lips pulling down at the corners.

"That's not true," Louise said. "I sleep plenty."

She didn't. She wanted to linger in bed, but she worried that if she stayed any longer, Rosa Maria would start badgering her.

"Go get ready. I'll put the coffee on."

The two of them had settled into a routine since moving in with each other, and Louise liked sharing almost every aspect of her life more than she thought she would.

She just wished she could tell the truth.

THEY HAD THEIR morning routine down to a science. Louise worked nights. Rosa Maria worked days. As Rosa Maria bathed and dressed, Louise would make coffee and turn on the radio. Neither of them were big breakfast eaters, and Louise rarely ate throughout the day.

Louise would collect the papers from the threshold of the apartment and flick through the pages as Rosa Maria dressed. She usually danced through these tasks, doing a Charleston or a Baltimore to keep herself from getting rusty. She adored her job at the Dove, but she didn't spend much, or any, time on the dance floor.

That morning the papers were in an orderly pile: the *Tribune*, the *Daily News*, the *Negro Voice*. She read them all although she knew she shouldn't. She had tired of seeing her name grace the pages. It had just stopped. Harlem had moved on more slowly than the rest of the world, but with the new year, new stories had been found. Three months of quiet. Three months of peace. Louise could hear Rosa Maria humming as she dressed. She would come out from the bedroom with her blouse tucked into her skirt, hair still damp, in search of coffee. Louise sat reading the papers at the kitchen table, big enough for two, a lazy and rough wooden circle that didn't take up too much room in the combined kitchen and living room.

Rosa Maria stopped to kiss Louise before pouring the coffee. Louise would have to dress. She walked Rosa Maria to the subway every morning, and she had adopted a wardrobe of mostly black things made from crepe, linen, or wool, all the better to be invisible, and dressing was a matter that would take just a few minutes.

"What's in the news today?" Rosa Maria asked, placing a cup of coffee in front of Louise.

"Another marriage announcement," Louise said. "Truly scintillating stories."

Rosa Maria sat down across from her and leaned over the paper Louise was reading. Louise had grown rather fond of the *Negro Voice*—it wasn't all news, but also included writings and collections for Black people by Black people. She enjoyed reading the poems and stories when she couldn't sleep at night. Rosa Maria picked up the *Tribune*. It was the paper where she worked as a typist, writing and rewriting the stories that the men took credit for. Louise knew that Rosa Maria was intimate with every section of the paper and often glanced over the society pages before she had to leave.

"I suppose there can't be a murder at every turn," Rosa Maria said.

"I think we've had enough of that," Louise said.

They were able to spend twenty lovely minutes together, reading the morning news and drinking coffee, before they really had to go. And they managed to run the time out and rush through the door every morning.

They swapped papers; Louise searched through the crime section of the *Tribune*. She flicked through it, the ink staining the tips of her fingers. She scanned the stories. She was no longer taken up with the world of mysteries and solving them, but she still liked to read about them.

4

IN THE NINE months since the Dove had opened, it had become one of the hottest spots in New York City. It was a badly kept secret, and Rafael Moreno had worked so hard to make this place home.

To front the band, he had poached one of the best, Blythe Montgomery. She wore a headpiece of stars, and the light pooled on her bronze skin. She was breathtaking and her voice was amazing.

Behind the bar was Eugene Ross. He was sweet, a little dim. He never looked directly at Louise when he spoke to her.

Rafael was in tails; he dressed up for the Dove every night and encouraged all of his employees to do the same. Louise hadn't yet done that; her role as club manager required a certain level of maturity.

Rafael was showing a glowing, shining Harlem starlet to a roped-off table. She was all of seventeen and Louise was jealous of her youth.

And walking across the crowded dance floor was Rosa Maria. She was Rafael's twin sister, older by mere minutes. She wore a dark purple dress, and her hair had been dyed back to its original dark brown. Louise fought a grin.

Rosa Maria leaned on the bar, a coy little smile on her lips. "Happy birthday, mi amor."

The clock had struck midnight and it was officially March 5, 1927. Louise's twenty-seventh birthday.

She hadn't thought she would be able to survive being twenty-six. But everything in her life seemed to have quieted down.

And she now was twenty-seven.

"Eugene, pour some champagne," Rosa Maria said. "This is a special occasion."

"Happy birthday, boss." Eugene concentrated on putting two glasses on the bar.

Louise usually watched the night's proceedings from behind the bar. Her role as club manager meant that she was in charge of the alcohol supply. She also cut off anyone who had too much.

"I have a surprise for you when we get home." Rosa Maria raised one eyebrow.

"You don't have to do that."

"Well, I want to."

Working at the Dove led to very late nights. The club opened at eleven, the band started at midnight, and the place didn't close until three in the morning, Thursday through Sunday.

And there was nowhere else she would rather have been.

"You're an old lady now," Rosa Maria was saying.

"I'm still young at heart."

"Very funny."

Rosa Maria was squinting. She refused to wear her cheaters to the club on the basis that they made her look older. Louise made sure to carry them with her every night because, after a few drinks, Rosa Maria would always want them. Louise pulled them out now from where she kept her purse under the bar, and slid them onto Rosa Maria's face.

Eugene handed them two glasses. Rosa Maria picked one up. Louise had the other one. With a small, lovely smile, Rosa Maria tapped her glass against Louise's.

"I love you so much."

"Louise Lloyd?"

At the sound of her name, both she and Rosa Maria turned.

"You are Louise Lloyd, right?" The woman was dressed in dark blue. She seemed to be Louise's age. She clutched a paper from the summer, one that had Louise's photograph in it. "You may not remember me. I'm Nora. . . ."

"Nora Davies." Louise put her glass down on the bar and stepped out from behind it. "You're Nora Davies. I remember you. This is Rosa Maria Moreno. Owner's sister."

Sure, Nora was older, but her face was the same. She was taller now, taller than Louise, and she held herself with grace. She had the same small face and light brown eyes. She was one of the girls Louise had saved nearly a decade ago. It was strange seeing her as an adult. Louise had never met the other girls she had saved that day. Rosa Maria extended a hand and the two shook.

She had done what any other person would have done. She had always thought it unfair that she had been named Harlem's Hero.

"I didn't know if you would. But I saw your name in the papers. You're not easy to find."

That was by design. Privacy was the number one thing she valued now. For herself and Rosa Maria.

"I know."

Nora barreled on. She was a talker. "I just wanted to come find you. Say thank you. Ask you about the summer. What happened? Did you . . ."

Louise had made it her rule not to talk about the summer. She couldn't think about the summer. But Nora wasn't a reporter. Nora was a girl who had been through the same thing she had.

Louise picked her glass up again. Could she be honest? Blythe and her band struck up a new song, slow and longing. Couples moved around the shiny floor. Across the room was Rafael, still charming the Harlem starlet.

And in front of her was Nora.

"I can't believe this!" Nora was saying. "I can't believe you're right here. We have to catch up. We have to talk about everything."

"Now?"

"Now! Tomorrow. Whenever!"

Nora pulled Louise in for a hug. It was clear that she had been drinking.

Louise drained her glass and put it on the bar. "Eugene, three more glasses. I suppose we have something else to celebrate."

"Something else?" Nora asked.

"She's twenty-seven today," Rosa Maria said.

Yes, she was a year older. She had never looked at her birthday with any happiness or excitement. Had she not had to be at the club, she would have been in bed.

"Happy birthday!" Nora's voice went up an octave, and she pulled Louise into another messy hug.

There was something very interesting about turning twenty-seven.

THE DOVE CLOSED at three in the morning. After all the patrons had left, Louise, Nora, Eugene, Rosa Maria, and Rafael sat in a circle on the floor, drinking from a bottle of champagne.

They passed the bottle back and forth among one another. Suit jackets and shoes were removed; cigarettes were lit.

"What a night." Rafael was sitting next to Eugene. "A good night. Possibly our very best."

"Really? What made it so good?" Rosa Maria's pinkie finger was touching Louise's.

Louise had unclipped her hair. She'd started using a hot comb to straighten it and had let it grow past the current fashion and was rather liking the near-shoulder length. The only problem was that it constantly got into her eyes.

"It's Lovie's birthday."

"That doesn't make it a good night," Louise said.

The truth was that nights at the Dove were always more rewarding than those at the Zodiac. The Zodiac was where she had grown but the Dove was a place she had a stake in.

And the Dove was the best club in New York City.

Louise kicked off her shoes and took the bottle from Nora. The champagne was real and sweet. Rosa Maria took the bottle from her.

"Well, Louise, I still want to hear everything about your summer," Nora said.

"I can tell you about how we faked a séance," Rafael said. He was jealous that the attention wasn't on him.

"How do you fake a séance?" Eugene asked.

"Ghosts aren't real," Louise said.

"We used magnets," Rosa Maria added.

Nora watched them all. "Your lives sound so glamorous."

Oh, how Louise wished that were true. "What about you, Nora? What do you do?"

"Nothing very interesting." Nora smirked. "I work in a factory."

"How did you find me?" Louise asked.

"Pure luck." Nora winked.

They concentrated on passing the bottle back and forth for a couple of moments.

"Is it true he tried to blame your sister's death on you?" Nora asked.

"Yes." Louise thought about Celia every day.

Nora raised an eyebrow. "I can't believe it."

"I can."

Louise had lived it. And now she couldn't trust anything in front of her.

But she wasn't thinking about that now. She was drinking champagne with her friends.

"We never have to live through it again." Nora lit a cigarette. "I used to have nightmares of him grabbing me off the streets. I didn't leave the house for a year. I . . ."

"I know. Can we talk about something else now?"

Louise took another sip from the bottle, then passed it back to Eugene. A funny taste lingered on her tongue. She ignored it.

"And this place is amazing," Nora was saying, giving Rafael an intense look. She exhaled a plume of cigarette smoke. They had all taken off most of their formal wear, trying to get more comfortable.

"Is anyone else really tired?" Eugene asked.

He hadn't said that much all night. An hour had passed with them talking, telling stories, comparing lives. Louise nudged Rosa Maria, giving her a small smile.

And when Louise looked back on that night, that was all she could remember.

5

THE MORNING SUN spilled into the Dove, the stained glass window painting light blues and grays and yellows. As Louise woke, she found that they were all lying on the floor of the club. She didn't remember anything.

She pulled herself to her feet, feeling her body creak and moan. Her head pounded and her tongue felt heavy in her mouth. The room spun around her and she tried to get her bearings.

What time was it? How was it possible that they had all fallen asleep in the club? She began to look around, trying to figure out what had happened.

Rafael and Eugene had fallen asleep inches apart, facing each other. Rafael's dress shirt was partially unbuttoned. They were fine. They were *fine*.

Louise turned slowly, trying to make a timeline of the previous night in her mind.

The club had closed.

They sat awake drinking, as they were wont to do.

Then . . .

Louise woke up.

It couldn't have been later than ten or eleven in the morning. She couldn't remember anything after, roughly, four in the morning.

What had happened?

She rubbed the back of her arm, and when she drew her fingers away, she saw blood on them. Louise looked over to where Rosa Maria slept. She was still in her purple dress, curled up on her side. Louise could see the slow rise and fall of her chest, her lips moving on each exhale.

And three paces away from Rosa Maria was Nora.

She was lying on the floor on her back. Louise could see, even from where she stood, that Nora's chest and stomach were laced with stab wounds. A small knife, maybe five inches long, with a jeweled red hilt lay near her. Nora's brown eyes were open and she was in a puddle of blood. Blood that had seeped from Nora and was coating Rosa Maria's side.

"WAKE UP. WAKE up." Louise was shaking Rosa Maria, who was not the easiest to wake at the best of times. "Ro, please."

No one else was awake. If Louise could get her up and out of here, she could make sure Rosa Maria was safe.

But she wasn't that lucky. Would Louise *ever* be that lucky?

Rafael woke up first and let out a petrified scream, which woke his sister and Eugene.

Rosa Maria sat up. Louise helped her to her feet.

"What is going on?" Rosa Maria asked.

"I don't know, but, Rosa, Nora's dead and you're covered in her blood. I need you to take your dress off. Go into the bathroom and wash off as much of the blood as you can. We need to get home before anyone finds out."

Rosa Maria was looking over herself, her reaction delayed as she woke up.

"Give me your dress!" Louise said.

Wordlessly, Rosa Maria allowed Louise to help her out of the dress. It slipped through Louise's fingers and onto the bloody floor.

"Louise." It was Rafael, although he could go months without using her given name.

Louise turned to where Rafael and Eugene were. Andrew Martin was standing in the doorway with a group of officers behind him. Martin had been promoted recently. He was a detective now and wore plain clothes and a badge.

"Why don't we make this easy? All of you, grab some air. Even you, miss."

Rosa Maria was still trying to make it to the bathroom. She raised her hands. They were shaking.

"I'm going to need statements from all of you. Why don't we start with Harlem's Hero?"

6

THERE WAS NOTHING Louise could do except wait. The questioning at the club, and again at the precinct, had been brief and rife with confusion.

But the fact remained: no one could remember the night before.

She watched Rafael and Eugene leave the precinct. Louise perched herself on the bench that was for visitors. From her spot, she could see the closed door to the interrogation room that held Rosa Maria and the new detective.

She sat with her back straight. She wouldn't leave until Rosa Maria was beside her. She watched officers as they talked, compared cases. She had never seen the precinct like this; in her prior visits she'd been either in lockup or in the detective's office.

As Louise sat and waited, she tried to force herself to remember what had happened the night before. She tapped her fingers against the rough wood of the bench.

She was going to get Rosa Maria, they were going to go home, and they were going to figure this out.

The thing was, she knew Rosa Maria was a light sleeper. Years of sleeping next to her had taught Louise a lot.

She felt as if the memories were right there, stuck in her mind like a long-forgotten song lyric. She looked around. Even now, even when she knew no one was paying attention to her, she felt that somehow there was someone watching her.

She closed her eyes. She took three deep breaths. Her heart thrummed in her chest. She kept the gun Rafael had given her under the pillow. There had been three weeks in the fall when she had felt the need to carry it everywhere.

But she was fine. She was healing. She was twenty-seven.

That had to mean something.

She never thought she'd reach this age. She didn't think she'd be spending the morning of her birthday in a police precinct.

When would her life be normal?

She was going to lose it sitting here. She couldn't take it any longer.

She was up, and before she could think about it, she was pushing open the door to the interrogation room.

"This is a private discussion."

Martin didn't turn around. He was standing and Rosa Maria was sitting across the table from him. Someone had given Rosa Maria a jacket, and she sat with her arms folded on the table.

"I have this, Louise," she said.

Martin turned around and looked her over. "This doesn't concern you, Miss Lloyd."

"Let her go, Martin."

"Louise."

It was the tone of Rosa Maria's voice that almost made her relent. Louise was very aware of the fact that she couldn't do this without putting both of their lives on the line. And she didn't want that.

"Let her go, Martin. How much longer are you going to keep her here?"

"As long as I need to, Miss Lloyd. And I am again asking you to leave."

"I'll do it. I'll find Nora's real killer and you can leave us alone. Don't you owe me that?"

Louise had never known Andrew Martin to back away from a challenge. And she knew Andrew Martin loved to watch her fail. Martin sighed and pressed a finger to his temple. Louise crossed her arms over her chest.

"I owe you nothing." His voice was cool as ice.

"I believe it was me who put her life on the line with a killer." Louise was frantic and she knew he could tell. "You do owe me."

"And if you don't find Nora's real killer?"

Everything he said sounded so condescending. She couldn't believe that there was a time when they had willingly worked together.

Louise raised an eyebrow. "I will."

"In the very likely case that you do not succeed, I'll arrest you both." He was not very good at negotiating. "I'll be working this case from every angle. Don't let me catch you. Good-bye, Miss Lloyd, Miss Moreno."

THEY WALKED HOME in complete silence. Louise had chosen a unit in the most expensive and fanciest building that they could find and afford.

They still lived in Harlem, blocks away from their old boardinghouse.

"How do you feel?" Louise asked.

When they were in public, they were careful never to touch. All Louise wanted to do was pull Rosa Maria close.

"Tired." In the confusion, Rosa Maria's glasses had gone missing. She was pouting and squinting.

"We'll get you home soon enough." Louise just wanted to sleep.

She used her key to open the front door of the apartment building. The minute they were safely in the elevator, Louise pulled the other woman close. Tomorrow she could think of a plan. For now all they were going to do was sleep this off.

The unit was at the back of the third floor. The landlord, a crotchety old man who hadn't looked directly at Louise, had made it clear that he saved the shabbiest units for people he deemed lowlifes. The rent was also much more expensive than what he charged white people; with their combined income, they'd be able to remain there for only another couple of months.

It was nice feeling glamorous just for a little bit.

Louise always felt a small itch of longing. She lived in the same forty-block radius she had lived in all of her life. She didn't want to die without seeing something that wasn't New York City.

She loved the city; she did. But she wanted something different.

"Lou."

Rosa Maria was at their door. Her key was in her hand. But the door was just slightly ajar, only enough to be noticeable to someone who was going to slip the key into the lock.

But Louise had locked the door when they left for the night. She had double- and triple-checked. Louise was prone to forgetting to check that detail now that she didn't have to climb out of a window to exit her apartment.

"Get behind me."

Louise used her fingertips to push the door open. She stepped inside. The lights were off, and nothing seemed out of the ordinary. The sun was fighting its way through the dark curtains; she knew the layout of her apartment like the back of her hand. The kitchen wasn't much, more like a kitchenette. That was to her right. She grabbed a rather large knife she had left on the counter. If Louise took three steps forward, she would be in the little living room. To her left, the bedroom and bathroom.

Rosa Maria stepped in, turned on the overhead light.

On the wall of the living room, directly across from the door, written in dark red paint that looked unnervingly like blood, was one word: **GUILTY**.

THE WORD REMAINED on the wall when Louise woke up. Finding the apartment empty and that nothing had gone missing or was broken, she and Rosa Maria had gone directly to bed without saying anything.

Now it was eight in the evening and Louise woke to find Rosa Maria staring at the wall.

All of this was a terrible way to spend her birthday.

Louise pulled herself from bed, wrapped herself in her dressing gown, and went to where Rosa Maria was standing. Louise kissed her cheek, then pressed her forehead to the other woman's temple.

There were so many things she wanted to say, but she couldn't find the words.

When the knock on the door came, Louise was doing her best to scrub the writing off the wall. She didn't want to think about how she was guilty. Rosa Maria was sitting on the floor, watching Louise. She hadn't said anything at all since they woke. She must have been in shock.

Rosa Maria was the one who let her brother and Eugene in.

They'd have been to the club by now, making sure everything was set for opening. And now they were in her apartment holding gifts.

Louise stopped cleaning. She hadn't managed to get the accusation all off; it was still faint.

"Happy birthday, Lovie. How are you, older sister?" Rafael sat on the couch.

Louise jumped down and sat next to Rosa Maria. All Louise wanted was to be close to her.

"I'm okay. I keep thinking it over. I can't remember anything."

"Neither can I," Eugene said, helpful as ever.

"The champagne had to be drugged."

Louise looked at her friends. She wasn't in the mood to open anything, but she did need to know what they'd gotten her.

"How do you know?" Eugene asked.

Louise knew he hung around for one reason. Eugene was tall and his torso was shaped almost like a triangle, broad shoulders tapering into a smaller waist. His blond hair was slicked back from bright blue eyes, and he smiled with a deep dimple. He was very handsome, even if he wasn't very bright. Rafael had a crush. She was sure it was mutual.

"All of us drank from the same bottle and none of us can remember anything."

"Oh, that makes sense."

"And my darling Louise has yet to tell you the stupidest part," Rosa Maria said.

Louise rolled her eyes. "I made a deal with Martin. And now I have to figure out who killed Nora."

"Or . . . ?"

"Or Martin takes in both of us."

Hearing the words come from her mouth sounded insane. How

was she going to do this? She couldn't just try; she had to do it. Not just for herself but for Rosa Maria.

"Are you sure you can do that?" Rafael and Rosa Maria were making the exact same concerned face, although it was Rafael who spoke.

"I have a plan. I'm going to remember that night." It wasn't a very good plan.

"You know, I can help you with that." Rafael focused on lighting a cigarette.

"How?" Rosa Maria asked. She eyed her brother.

"I can hypnotize you, Lovie. I can hypnotize all of us. Then we can really get to the bottom of this."

"No." Louise and Rosa Maria spoke at the same time.

Louise thought that Rafael had matured in the few months in which he had been a business owner, but he still sometimes had some very bad ideas. She didn't even want to know how he had come up with this one.

"Oh, come on, Lovie. My ideas are always the bee's knees."

Rafael *loved* the occult, fancied himself a seer. Of course he thought he could hypnotize them.

"I can't think of anything worse," Louise said.

"It's duck soup."

"I'm sure I can think of something else."

How would Theodore Gilbert have handled this? She didn't want to think about him. Despite everything, she had learned a lot over the summer, and now it was time to use it.

She would go over this systematically. She would do this cleanly.

She would need a new notebook.

"Lovie, can you at least open these?" Rafael asked, onto the next topic. Maybe he was bitter about his idea being rejected.

Rosa Maria gasped and got up, running to the bedroom. She returned with an elaborately wrapped gift.

"Let's try to forget this for now, okay? Tomorrow, we can come up with a plan." She handed Louise the box.

Rafael had gotten Louise a shiny new gun, something she hadn't expected. But Rosa Maria's gift was the best. It was a new camera, dark red with an abstract lightning bolt design over the cap that covered the lens.

"I found the matching compact and lipstick."

Rosa Maria sat close to her. After years of living across the hall from each other, the novelty of being able to touch each other whenever and however they wanted had not yet worn off. The camera was probably wildly expensive, but Louise didn't care.

"It's perfect," Louise said.

The first photo Louise took with her new camera was one of Rosa Maria, Rafael, and Eugene in the apartment, sitting in a row on the couch, all three facing the camera seriously.

Louise would look back on that photo as a reminder of the day everything changed.

LOUISE COULD LIE next to Rosa Maria forever. Louise had thought about the future as lazy days and uncomplicated nights, lying next to her, watching her sleep, kissing the smattering of freckles that resided on Rosa Maria's left hip. Louise loved knowing the intimate secrets of Rosa Maria's body, the things that made her click. Louise was the only person on earth who knew that Rosa Maria went weak when she kissed those freckles. Her favorite thing to do was to kiss them one by one and feel Rosa Maria submit as she did.

They didn't often go to bed early, but with the Dove closed, there was nothing left to do. It was hard to believe that it was still technically her birthday. Rafael and Eugene had left early, possibly in the same mood Rosa Maria and Louise were in: wanting to go to bed early since they suddenly had no responsibilities. The Dove had gotten their exclusive patronage for months on end and going somewhere else felt like a betrayal. Even worse, they had to wonder if the Dove would ever open again.

But it was nice to have some time off. It was nice to be able to be in each other's company alone. So much of their time together was spent giving looks from across a room, keeping air between them, going out with Rosa Maria's brother and his crush to hide the truth. Louise had never really liked hiding the truth. She wished she could say it, stand on top of the roof and scream the fact that she loved a woman—she loved a woman who was brilliant and compassionate and beautiful.

But that wasn't possible.

"Are you watching me sleep?" Rosa Maria asked.

Louise knew that Rosa Maria wasn't actually asleep, because her breathing hadn't become regulated, and her hand flexed open and closed as if she was stretching it.

"What are you going to do about it?" Louise asked.

"Cash or check?" Rosa Maria's voice was husky and heavy, momentarily captivating Louise.

"I think you know the answer to that one."

Rosa Maria opened one eye, moving to kiss Louise deeply. Their bare legs were tangled in the sheets and Louise knew that, if they weren't careful, this could lead to something.

Louise had belonged to Rosa Maria, mind, body, and soul, for the better part of a decade. She thought their hearts were beating in harmony; she never felt completely whole without Rosa Maria by her side.

Louise leaned into Rosa Maria's kiss, feeling her tongue slide into the other woman's mouth.

She closed her eyes as Rosa Maria trailed a line of kisses from Louise's neck to between her thighs. She sighed as Rosa Maria pressed her tongue to the inside of her thigh. Louise ran her hands through Rosa Maria's hair.

They were one and the same. Louise was convinced of that.

This was the woman Louise knew intimately inside and out. This was the woman who could make the earth move and the sun rise. They were perfectly synchronized in every way.

"Are you okay?" Rosa Maria asked.

She laid her chin on Louise's stomach and looked up at her. Even in the dark, Rosa Maria's eyes were arresting, a shocking deep brown that made Louise look twice.

"I'm fine," Louise said. The truth was that her body just wasn't in it tonight. Maybe it was all the stress. "Come here."

Rosa Maria did as she was told, crawling into Louise's open arms. Louise kissed her once, then twice, realizing she no longer felt the butterflies and shyness of young love. Maybe this was maturity, in herself and in her relationship.

"I'm just thinking about Nora." She brought the woman up before she could stop herself. Almost immediately, she could feel Rosa Maria pull away from her, shut down a little. "I know. I just can't stop."

It had been a very traumatic day. She knew Rosa Maria would admit that. The day had seemed to go on forever.

"How about this?" Rosa Maria took Louise's hand in her own, using an index finger to draw on Louise's palm. "Next year, when you turn twenty-eight, we have a nice party with no murder involved."

"Just champagne and you and me," Louise said, and pressed her lips to Rosa Maria's.

Their relationship was so complicated, although she didn't want it to be. The keeping to the shadows, having to hide a significant part of themselves, having to be completely different people in public from those they were in private.

"I don't want anything else but champagne and you and me."

They had long dreamed of leaving New York City. They had long dreamed of a life lived as fully as possible. Louise just didn't know how it was possible.

"Sounds lovely," Rosa Maria said. She tilted her face toward the moonlight, which made her skin glow.

Louise ached to make her lie as still as she could while she captured Rosa Maria's simple beauty in the moonlight. Louise didn't move. If she concentrated, she could feel Rosa Maria's heart beat next to hers. "Next year, just you and me."

And Louise wanted to believe it. She wanted to believe it so, so badly.

8

LOUISE WOKE UP earlier than she normally would have. It was a Sunday, so Rosa Maria didn't have to work.

As Louise sat down at the kitchen table—it had come with the place, along with three almost outdated but still stylish dresses in the wardrobe—the remnants of the word **GUILTY** watched her every move. After Rosa Maria fell asleep the previous night, Louise's mind had moved in circles.

How could she not have known? In retrospect, had the champagne tasted funny? Was there anything wrong with the bottle? She knew there hadn't been.

And if Nora was dead, what did that mean for her?

All she wanted was a cigarette. She had been trying to cut back and was doing a rather good job of it, but she pulled out a pack and lit one as she got up to pour her morning coffee.

All she had to do was figure out the truth. She hated that Rosa Maria had been pulled into the middle of this. Louise had known the other woman for roughly nine years.

She didn't have the makings of a murderer. Louise knew that.

She often thought that she knew Rosa Maria better than herself. From the bedroom, Louise could hear Rosa Maria sigh, still half asleep. She needed something concrete, something that she could start with.

She sipped from her coffee mug, feeling the fog she had been in fade away as she did so. She closed her eyes, smoked her cigarette.

Why?

The knocks on her door interrupted her thoughts. For a moment, she thought they were gunshots. Her nerves were already frayed to the breaking point.

Even as she acknowledged the fact that she wasn't dressed and she wasn't wearing makeup, she opened the door.

It was probably just Rafael with a pocket watch and a big book of nonsense, ready to make good on his hypnotism threat.

But her visitor wasn't Rafael. He was a young man, probably Louise's age, maybe a little younger. He was dressed in brown, not a flattering color for anyone, crushing his hat underneath his left arm. His brown eyes looked her over.

"Miss Louise Lloyd?"

"Who wants to know?"

"I'm Walter Hart. I work at the *Tribune*."

"I'm not interested in giving interviews."

Louise froze. She hoped Rosa Maria wouldn't get out of bed, come to the door, and reveal to this man how many sins they were committing.

"No, wait! Please." His eyes widened. Over his nose and on his cheeks he had a smattering of light freckles that made him look younger than Louise suspected he was. "I really need this. I really, really need this. Just one quote, please. Unless you'd rather I put whatever I want in your mouth."

He raised an eyebrow. This stranger was testing her. Over the past eight months, she had managed to talk to the press only once, and that was one line full of very colorful language she'd truly rather not repeat.

And unfortunately, she couldn't have him put words in her mouth. She knew how powerful the papers were. She knew how important public opinion was. And while all of this was going on, she couldn't afford another mishap. She pulled her robe closer to her body, cinching the waist of it as tight as it could go. Then she stepped out of her apartment, closing the door behind her.

"One question. That's it."

He cleared his throat. He looked mildly surprised that his little plan had worked.

"Well, hurry up."

"What do you have to say about Rosa Maria Moreno's role in the death of Nora Davies?"

Typical. Louise lowered her voice. She was worried that if she was caught talking about murder to a member of the press, she and Rosa Maria would be kicked out. "Miss Moreno is innocent."

"What are you going to do about it?"

That was a second question, but Louise let it slide.

"Prove it."

THE GARBAGE BEHIND the Dove was where Louise began her investigation. The bins were located on the street behind the building; she sent the bartenders out there at the end of every night, and she thought if there was something to be found, it would be in there.

Luckily, it was March and the New York heat wasn't making the garbage smell.

Maybe she didn't have to jump in. She could just dig around the top layer of trash, see if she could find what she was looking for. Louise gripped the side of the metal bin, weighing her choices. She was doing this to clear Rosa Maria's name. She had to remember that.

She had seen so much worse. Why did some garbage scare her?

Louise made up her mind never to be scared about anything again. She plunged her hands into the bin, feeling the layers of trash give way as she did. She squeezed her eyes shut, trying to feel something, anything that would help her. She brushed past broken bottles, crumpled napkins, and other assorted items. She clasped onto a shoe, black and shiny, with a broken strap. Louise stared at it for a moment and then tossed it back into the bin.

How many secrets would one bin hold? Louise—her stockings and dress be damned—kicked off her shoes and pulled herself, with a Herculean effort, into the bin. Almost immediately, her stockings were ripped. She continued digging, feeling her hair fall from its pins. This wasn't solving anything. She was lucky that there were no nosy newspapermen lying in wait to find her in a compromising position.

And this position, with her torn stockings and hitched-up skirt, would have been worse than any other they could have found her in.

Well, almost.

"Are you okay?"

The voice was low, clean, and male. Too stereotypically American. It made Louise look up. She was faced with a tall man with thick walnut brown hair and a mischievous smile. His hand was extended, a small wad of bills in it.

"Please," he said, "let me help you."

She smiled. "I would be so grateful."

He lifted her out of the bin with too much ease, slipping the wad of cash into her hand discreetly as he did. She wasted no time slipping it into her brassiere.

"There you go."

His voice was kind, but there was something about it she didn't trust. He sounded as if he was trying to disguise his real voice. It annoyed her, reminded her of something someone from Jersey might do.

"You're my hero, Mr. . . . ?"

"Schoonmaker." Schoonmaker. It sounded like it was New York royalty up there with the Astors and the Vanderbilts. But it also sounded as if he could be pretending to be New York royalty. Exactly what someone from Jersey would do. "I'm here to serve, Miss . . . ?"

"Lloyd." She thought about giving a fake name, but her real one slipped out before she could decide on one.

Schoonmaker looked her up and down. "Louise Lloyd?"

She relaxed into a smile. "No, a different one. No relation."

"Ah, then that girl must be raising all sorts of hell for you."

"I'm sure she doesn't mean it."

Schoonmaker laughed as if what she'd said was funny.

"I'm sure she doesn't," he repeated when his laughter subsided.

She sized him up. Schoonmaker was taller than anyone she had ever met, even Gilbert, long and lanky. He was dressed almost too nicely. His suit was a perfect navy blue and everything he wore was coordinated. He looked as if he spent more time and money on clothes than she did.

"Why don't we get out of here, Miss Lloyd? I'll make sure you get home safe. Promise."

She didn't want to make a promise to this man. There was something telling her she shouldn't trust him.

"You know, I own half the places here."

She wasn't impressed. No true New York royalty would brag about their wealth, nor would they own illegal clubs. This man wasn't who he said he was, although he made a brilliant effort.

"Oh, like which ones?"

"The one whose garbage you're going through, for starters."

"The Dove?"

"Have I seen you there?"

Louise paused. She was careful not to let him read her. "I'm not much of a club gal."

This elicited his laugh again. She wondered what it was like to be so carefree as to laugh all the time.

"Anyway, I have another couple garbage cans to go through."

He stopped laughing, stared at her. His eyes were intense and dark brown. The way the sun illuminated them, she could see dark blue rings around his irises. She cleared her throat. She had been in the presence of this Schoonmaker for less than five minutes and she didn't know what to think about him.

"I mean it. You ask the bartender in there, tell him you know Schoonmaker. He'll treat you right."

Ah, yes. Schoonmaker still thought that she was down on her luck. She made a mental note to ask Rafael about him. As far as she knew, Rafael owned the Dove.

"Isn't it closed?" Louise asked politely.

"When it opens back up."

He kissed her on the cheek, rather bold considering they were perfect strangers. He tipped his hat and departed, whistling. Louise pulled out the cash he had given her and counted it. It was nearly two hundred dollars. She placed it back where she had put it for safekeeping.

That man wasn't who he had said he was.

LOUISE WAS STILL dizzy from her encounter with Schoonmaker. She was still trying to figure out who he was and why she had thought digging through the garbage was a good idea. She knew she was covered in the smell of it. All she wanted to do was go home. She picked a stray piece of lettuce from the sleeve of her coat and flicked it away.

She could make it to the subway. She could ride the subway home. She could get to her apartment and then take the world's longest bath.

She kept her head down as she walked, trying not to look anyone in the eye. This was Midtown, edging toward Broadway. She wasn't sure anyone around here wanted her to look them in the eye.

Louise could stay out, try to break into the club, and look for evidence, but she didn't want to get caught. The doors were padlocked shut, and she wasn't sure that she could crack the lock.

Rafael's hypnotism idea was looking better and better.

Louise, in her haste to get to the subway, bumped into a man. "Sorry, sir," she mumbled.

He looked at her, his sloped nose wrinkling in recognition. "Are you Louise Lloyd?"

"No."

She didn't know how many times that would work in a day. She wanted anonymity more than anything else in the world. She wanted to walk down a street and not be recognized. But it was happening more and more, and too many strangers had opinions about her and her life.

"You are."

He spoke slowly and with some recognition. Louise was sure that she had never met this man before in her life and that could only mean one thing: he had read the papers and had had thoughts about who she was and what she had done.

"Hey, I have to say something to you." His hand was on her wrist now. "You are going to stand there and listen."

Louise tried to pull her hand away, and his grip tightened. She had to play the next few moments very carefully.

"Sir, please let me go. I am not who you think I am."

"Yes, you are. I saw you in the paper. You're her. And I think you need to listen to me."

His grip was tight on her wrist. No one was stopping to offer assistance. Everyone ducked their heads, bumping into her as they passed.

Louise pulled herself up to her full five foot two. "Sir, you have to let me go. I'm not who you think I am, and if you try anything, I'll scream as loud as I can."

"No one's going to help you, sweetheart."

"Excuse me, sir. I believe the lady asked you to let her go." Louise's savior was a woman, just a little taller than she was. She was white, with her dark blond hair coiffed into a perfect bob. She wore a professional skirt suit and she looped her arm through Louise's free one. "We're going now and I will thank you to let go."

Stunned, the man did as he was told. The mystery woman pulled Louise toward a café, much like the one she used to work at, and over to a table.

"How thrilling." She removed her suit jacket as she spoke. "You are Louise Lloyd, though, aren't you?"

"I am."

"I'm Harriet. Harriet Sinclair."

She extended a hand. She was neat and clean and Louise felt disgusting sitting across from her. Louise took her hand and Harriet gave her a gentle shake.

"I'm new in town. I want to be a writer."

"My friend works at a paper. She's a typist at the *Tribune*."

It was the only thing Louise could think to say. She was looking into Harriet's milky blue eyes and she was lost in them. There was something so familiar about Harriet, but she couldn't place it.

"Ah, very nice. I was hoping you could do me a favor, now that I've done you one."

"I didn't need your help," Louise said, "but I'm glad I had it. Thank you."

"Men can be such brutes, can't they?" Harriet's oval face darkened as she frowned. "But really, Miss Lloyd, I hear you're a hot topic around here. I'd love for you to do me a favor."

This Harriet was bold; Louise had to give her that. And Louise always liked bold girls. "Depending on what it is."

"I've been over papers from the summer. You've never given an interview. I want one. Exclusive." Harriet raised one dark eyebrow. Now, in the café, her hair looked more copper than brown. Was there such a thing as too bold?

Louise weighed her options. She could get up and leave. She had the sense she wasn't welcome anyway; people were staring at her and not in a kind way. Or she could accept this woman's offer.

She could say no, but she needed public opinion on her side. Not for her, but for Rosa Maria. Their lives were so entwined that she could ruin Rosa Maria's with one wrong move. No one could know how intimate they really were. The world saw them as confidantes. Nothing more, nothing less.

She could still feel the folded bills against her chest, and suddenly she felt guilty about taking so much money from a man she didn't know.

"I want to make it in this city, Miss Lloyd. I want to be a force to be reckoned with. I'm sure you know how that feels." Harriet's eyes didn't leave Louise's face as she considered the request.

Louise did know what that felt like.

Maybe it was sympathy. Maybe it was gratitude, but Louise nodded. "All right. An exclusive story. I'll do it."

Harriet squealed and clapped. "Thank you! Thank you! How lucky it is I ran into you, hmm?"

Louise should have known there was no such thing as luck in that city.

9

THE BEADS THAT blocked the doorway clattered as Louise pushed them apart. She normally wouldn't have done this. She normally would have had a plan in place. But the fact that she still couldn't remember that night was scaring her.

Madam Colette was a legend in Harlem. No one knew how old she was; there was a rumor that she had occupied the same little efficiency apartment since before the turn of the century. It always smelled like sage and tea, it was always warm, and the little old lady was always seated at her kitchen table.

The story was that Madam Colette could read someone's mind, see into the future, do anything she was needed to do. Louise never believed it. She had had no reason to believe in the mystical or the occult.

But she was desperate. Not desperate enough to go to Rafael for help, not yet. Madam Colette's reputation was well known.

"Janie." For her age, which no one knew, Madam Colette was a spry lady. She moved with a deftness and diligent decisiveness that Louise envied. "Janie, you're here. You're here!"

"I'm Louise," Louise said. "Louise Lloyd. Janie was my mother. She passed away."

Louise was Janie's twin. She had a striking similarity to the mother she had barely known. Louise was never sure how to take it, but Janie had been beautiful and she knew the older lady meant it as a compliment.

Madam Colette blinked twice. Her eyes were so dark, it was hard to find her pupils. Her gaze was unnerving.

"Right," she said slowly. "Louise. You do look so much like Janie. I knew her when she was a little girl, you know. Sit down."

Louise did as she was told, settling down at the rough wooden table, hitting her knees on it as she did.

"I have a couple questions," Louise said.

The old lady impatiently shushed her, raising one finger as her dark eyes scanned Louise's face. "I know what you need, darling." Her voice growled with a mixed and unplaceable accent. Madam Colette squinted as she regarded Louise closely. "You need tea."

"Tea?" Louise asked.

She wasn't familiar with the old woman's methods, but success stories moved their way through Harlem like ivy on a building. Recently, Myrtle Collins had gone to Madam Colette for some sort of fertility potion that worked; she was expecting a baby in the winter.

Louise didn't care about any of that stuff. She knew that everything in the world had a plausible and rational explanation. There was no way this woman could tell her anything with tea.

Madam Colette got up, poured a cup of tea, and set it in front of Louise.

Louise took a sip; it was so hot, it burned her mouth. "What is this supposed to do?" Louise asked.

She was still feeling a little hungover from that poisoned

champagne on her birthday at the Dove. It wasn't in a good way either, not the kind of hangover that called for languid mornings in bed, reading a novel she wasn't paying attention to.

Louise did feel like she was in a dreamy state, but this state was much more like a nightmare. Madam Colette watched as she took every swallow, and when the cup was empty, she snatched it from Louise's fingers and took a look inside. Louise could do nothing but sit and watch as Madam Colette's lips moved in silent exploration. Louise wrinkled her eyebrows, too afraid of the old lady to say anything while Madam Colette turned the cup around.

"Dark past." When the old lady spoke, it was a surprise. "You have a dark past, Louise."

Madam Colette's eyes fell on her and Louise felt a little shiver run down her spine.

"There's a night I can't remember," Louise said.

"I know what you need." The old lady's tone was indignant at any suggestion otherwise. "The leaves know you better than you know yourself, little miss."

Properly cowed, Louise sat back in her seat until Madam Colette was ready.

"The answer you seek is inside of you, Louise."

Madam Colette's eyes were still on the tea leaves in the cup. Louise watched as she turned the cup.

"It's in your past. Look inside of yourself."

This sounded ridiculous, but Louise smiled. She placed a couple of dollars on the table and bade her good-bye.

She was still thinking about her visit to Madam Colette when she exited the building into the fresh and clean morning. She kept her head down as she trailed back to her own building. She had just paid to drink tea and have some batty old woman tell her to look inside of herself.

None of her questions had been asked or answered. She stopped by a drugstore and bought a bottle of Coke. She was craving one, after having to drink tea that was much too hot. She sipped it as she walked, letting people pass, walking home slowly so she truly could mull it over. She liked to be able to sort things out.

Louise was steadfast in her belief that Madam Colette was a fraud. Nothing about her visit made any sense. Her mind hummed in that dreamy state, possibly a long-lasting effect of being drugged. Seeing Madam Colette had been a bad idea. Louise wouldn't make that mistake again. She was going to start at the beginning.

"DO YOU EVER get the feeling you've made a mistake?" Louise asked.

Rosa Maria was sitting next to her on the couch. The two women shared a look and then turned to Rafael, who was holding a pocket watch. For someone who didn't know what he was doing, he looked very excited about this.

"Only when it concerns my brother."

Rosa Maria watched him intensely. She looked better today. She had taken the day off of work and was compulsively cleaning the apartment when Louise returned from her meeting with Madam Colette.

This was only step one of the plan. When this failed, not *if*, she was going to systematically go through Nora's life. She had bought a new notebook especially for it.

Eugene hovered over Rafael's shoulder. He had a curl falling into his blue eyes. His cheeks were flushed pink. "Don't hurt them."

"I'm not gonna hurt them. This is the easiest thing in the world."

Louise would have loved to have half the confidence Rafael had. Instead, she doubted every move she made.

"Who's first?"

"I'll go first," Louise said. She wondered briefly if she was being led to slaughter.

She stretched out so she was lying on her back, her feet in Rosa Maria's lap. Rafael kneeled down next to her, beginning to swing the pocket watch. Louise's brow furrowed as she watched him.

"Look at my watch, Lovie."

Louise did as she was told. She could feel her heart beating, stammering in her chest. The apartment was so quiet that the only things she could hear were her thoughts telling her that this was a bad idea.

Rafael did this with all the charm and pizzazz of a screen actor. "You are getting very sleepy."

His voice filled her senses, drowning everything out. If she turned her head and looked, Louise would see him right next to her ear. She was hyperaware of everything she could feel, from the hair rising on her neck to Rosa Maria's hand on her calf. She thought she could even hear Eugene breathing over Rafael's shoulder.

"I'm going to count backward from five, and when I snap my fingers, you'll be back in the Dove. Five . . . four . . . three . . . two . . . one." Rafael made his voice low and slow.

Rafael snapped and the world around Louise stopped functioning. But she wasn't in the Dove. No, she was in the Zodiac; it was dark and cold, nighttime. She gasped and her breath caught in her throat.

She wasn't sure what had happened. She hadn't thought this would work. She had been focused on the Dove, but everything she was avoiding had returned to her at once. This wasn't real. She had to tell herself that. None of this was real.

But then why couldn't she open her eyes?

"Where are you?"

She could hear Rafael's voice echoing away from her. She didn't answer. She couldn't say anything.

"Lovie, where are you?"

In front of her was Theodore Gilbert, deranged and angry, planning to kill her. And there she was, holding the gun she had used to kill him. This wasn't supposed to be happening. She was supposed to be reliving the night Nora had died. She wasn't supposed to be here again, stuck in an infinite loop of the worst night of her life.

She was guilty. She had tried to console herself by saying she had done what she had had to do, but that wasn't true. She knew that. Maybe she had always known it but she was trying to run from it. She was having a strange out-of-body experience. She was watching herself decide to take a man's life.

Her stomach curled. She watched as emotions ran through her, her own face drawn and tight, her hazel eyes blinking in the dark. It was strange seeing herself, seeing the situation like that. She was outside of it all. She saw the moment she pulled the trigger. She saw the moment Gilbert died.

Rafael snapped again, and Louise was brought back to the present. To her apartment. To her couch. She could feel the threadbare cushion on her back, Rosa Maria's hand still on her calf. It was as if time had stopped. She relaxed her body; everything in her had tensed up. She exhaled slowly, trying to bring herself back up to the here and now. She knew that this wouldn't help, but she didn't think it would go this badly.

When she opened her eyes, Rosa Maria, Rafael, and Eugene were all staring at her.

"What?" Louise asked. She pulled herself together.

"You were screaming." Rafael's dark eyes were wide and the color had drained from his face.

"No, I wasn't." Louise pulled herself up so she was sitting, looking directly at three worried faces. She cleared her throat. "I'm fine."

"Lou"—this was Rosa Maria—"what did you see?"

Louise had never told her friends everything about that night: how could she? She had done all she could to stop the truth from leaking out and she was still the villain.

"Nothing. Hypnotism doesn't work." She exhaled. "You two should leave. I think I'm just a little tired."

Rafael and Eugene shared a long look, but they did as they were told. The minute the door was shut, Louise turned to Rosa Maria.

"I am so sorry. I am so, so sorry." The words came rushing from her before she could stop them. "I know you didn't kill Nora. This has to do with me."

"Why?" Rosa Maria took Louise's hand in her own.

"I . . . I wish I knew," Louise said. "I don't know. I don't know who would do this to me or you. I'm so, so sorry." She looked into Rosa Maria's face, her brown eyes—the eyes she had fallen in love with so many years ago. "I was serious about my deal with the detective. I'm going to clear your name. You're not a killer. I'll do anything for you. You know that."

"I know, but, Louise, if you're right . . . you're playing a dangerous game. I can't let you do that for me."

Louise knew that. She knew it. She shut her eyes. She felt like she was going to cry. After everything, she was exhausted. She was so tired, she was convinced she could curl up in bed and sleep for a month or two. But she had to keep going.

"We have no other choice. I'm not letting you hang for something you didn't do. And I'll prove you didn't do it."

She kept saying it, but she didn't know how she would do it. She wished she could remember. She wished that someone hadn't tampered with her mind. She didn't know what to trust now. Was what she was seeing in front of her the truth? Or was someone playing with her reality as well?

She didn't like this feeling of vulnerability that followed her. As much as she tried to remember, nothing came up. The black void in her memory was an insult.

"I love you so much." Rosa Maria's voice was a whisper.

Louise moved to kiss her, feeling the other woman react almost automatically when she did.

This was the life she wanted. She wanted to keep it for as long as possible.

She just didn't know how.

LOUISE STILL KEPT a rosary in her purse. This one had been her mother's, one of the few things of Janie's she owned. It was something she didn't want anyone else to know about.

Not even Rosa Maria knew, and that woman knew all of Louise's secrets.

She waited until the service was over, middle of the day when no one else was around. She never attended services anymore. But this was so ingrained in her that she could never leave it behind.

Louise placed herself in the middle of the pew. She removed her coat, but left her hat. She knew she should confess, felt the old itch of Christian guilt running through her.

But she was praying. That was enough.

Louise could remember praying with her mother. Those were her earliest and probably her favorite memories of her mother. She remembered being two on the verge of three, Janie big and pregnant with the being that would become Minna. Louise's hair was in tight braids, her face clean and her clothes orderly. Janie always made sure that her daughters were an extension of her. They would kneel at Louise's bedside, candles on the table. Janie would take Louise's hands in hers and speak in her soft and melodic voice. "If you talk, my loved girl, He will listen." She took being a pastor's wife seriously, and she expected her daughters to as well. Louise had been late to talk, always preferring to watch and observe the world, then put her two cents in. Joseph had been concerned but it was Janie who spent time with her.

Louise never looked back on her childhood and adolescence as idyllic. She would have loved that: a childhood in which she had gotten to be a child, instead of a mother to her younger sisters, after their real mother died when Louise was ten.

She held the beads in her hands. She let the cross dangle between her fingers. She was glad of the warmth of the church. It was safe and familiar.

Her eyes flickered to the ceiling. She had always been taught that good people go to Heaven. Good people get rewarded.

But good people shouldn't have died so young.

Maybe Louise resented her father for the death of her mother. Even with her aunt moving in, it had been up to Louise to make sure her sisters, the twins being infants, were clean and cared for.

He had never remarried. He thought a person got one great love; Janie was his and now Janie was gone. And he took too much pride in being a widower with four daughters even though he had always wanted a son.

Louise leaned forward. This wasn't about her mother or her father. This was about who she was.

She wanted to believe she was good at heart. It all came back to what her mother had told her. No matter what the world tried to do to her, no matter what anyone said, Louise was deserving of love and respect.

And she had believed it. She had gone through life trying to demand that respect.

But now. She didn't know if she was right or wrong, and no amount of prayer was going to help her through this.

The truth was that when she killed Theodore Gilbert that night, she hadn't thought she was capable of killing someone. She had done what she thought was necessary.

She sat back in the pew. She could hear the quiet life of the church around her, other patrons whispering conversations and prayers, the quiet shifts of the floorboards underneath feet. She hadn't realized that the church was in need of some repair. In her memories, in her dreams, it always stayed the same. It never aged.

Louise stayed perfectly still. She closed her eyes, lifted the cross to her lips. She tried to think of the person she was and the person she wanted to be, and how they were different.

She tried to imagine what her mother would tell her. *My loved girl, you have been through so much. You have fought and come out stronger.* Louise could picture leaning into her mother and feeling the warmth.

Janie would believe in her unequivocally. Janie would fight for her innocence.

And Louise would have to fight too.

She wanted to be a person she could be proud of. And that meant not doubting herself or who she was.

Although that seemed easier thought about than done.

It scratched at her that while she was here praying for the absolution of her soul, she was wasting time.

Louise put her rosary back in her little purse. She slipped her sunglasses back on.

She had people to prove wrong.

10

LOUISE CLIMBED AN ancient set of stairs. She was visiting the factory where Nora had worked. She could hear the various clicks and whirs and thrums of factory life. Other than the mechanical sounds, the place was silent. Louise got to what she thought was the right floor; the door was closed.

She used the tips of her fingers to open it.

The employees were mostly Black and Asian, mostly women. They worked in complete synchronized silence, not talking or laughing. Louise swallowed hard. Every step she made was smothered by the machines.

"Miss, you can't be here."

The voice made her turn. Although some faces looked up, the noise and movement didn't stop.

The man was older than her, maybe by a decade. He was just a little taller than she was. He dressed like he had money. Black suit, shiny shoes. He had a bright red pocket square folded neatly. He wore wire-rimmed glasses that were supposed to lend him an air of maturity. But his boyish face, round and ruddy, ruined the illusion.

"I'm so sorry." Louise turned to him. "I'm looking for my friend. Nora Davies. She works here, right?"

He laughed, a genuine belly laugh. It knocked Louise off-balance. She hadn't expected anything to be funny. She stood in front of him until his laugh subsided. It was always awkward when someone found something very funny and no one else did.

"Look, doll. You see Nora around, you can tell her she's fired."

"Why?"

"She hasn't shown up here in three weeks. Marjorie took her table and was glad to do so."

It was so hard to forget that everyone was replaceable. That there were hundreds of people lining up, waiting for someone to fall so they could take their place.

"Why hasn't she shown up?"

"I thought you were friends."

That lie had gotten her in trouble before. She wasn't very good at it.

"Why?" She repeated her question instead of doubling down.

He looked her up and down. Louise held his gaze.

"I don't know why she hasn't shown up. But I can tell you that she would have been fired anyway. She's lazy and messy and I don't have time for that in my factory."

"Right." Louise shifted.

"Now you need to leave, doll." He walked away before she had the chance to say anything.

She hadn't gotten much information.

"Psst."

The sound came from a couple of rows away. It was very discreet, and it came from Marjorie, the worker the man had pointed out. She moved her hands as she motioned with her head for Louise to come closer.

Louise did as she was told.

Marjorie spoke with a thick and heavy Jamaican accent. She looked Louise over. "I heard Nora was dead. Is that true?"

"Yeah."

"You're not one of her friends, are you?"

"Not really."

Marjorie couldn't be older than Louise, yet she seemed so mature. Her hands didn't stop moving as she talked. "Listen, you won't find one person who's a fan of Nora in this place. Mr. Walker is right. She's rude and lazy and didn't want to be here. I don't even know why she was."

"What?"

Marjorie dropped her voice an octave, rumbling quietly. "She's known around these parts for gambling." The other woman lifted one dark painted-on eyebrow. There was something about her that reminded Louise of a distant aunt or cousin.

"Gambling?"

"Nora's running a numbers game. None of her customers seem too happy with her."

"Of course," Louise said. She rose to her feet, feeling a click in her knee as she did so.

She understood that: she also had done what she had to.

Marjorie was sliding Louise a scrap of paper, folded once in half. "If Mr. Walker comes back and sees you here, he'll throw you out by the window."

They were seven floors up. Louise didn't know if Marjorie was joking.

But she had gotten what she had come for.

And she thought that if she could figure out Nora's numbers racket, she'd have a whole host of suspects as well.

A NEUTRAL LOCATION. That was what Louise needed for her first meeting with Harriet. She chose a drugstore on the fringes of Harlem, not because it was where she would have taken her sisters, but because it was where she felt comfortable. And she wanted to have the upper hand. She hadn't told Rosa Maria about this.

Louise didn't know why she was doing this.

That was something she was having trouble making sense of herself.

With the pile of letters Louise had received from other reporters, Louise wondered why she hadn't sat down with one of them.

But she understood where Harriet was coming from. And Louise wanted to succeed too. Harriet came in like a little whirlwind. She was solid, with a dancer's sort of grace in the way she walked and moved her arms, but she wasn't thin like Louise was.

Harriet wore a rather stylish composé dress, a gradient of dark greens that hung just under her knees and went beautifully with her coloring. She made the spring fashion look effortless. Louise was still wearing summer fashions from the year before, albeit with a cardigan on top.

"Beautiful!" Harriet greeted her. There was something odd in the way she talked. Not her voice, per se, but the words she chose.

"Stunning day, isn't it?" It wasn't, really. It was on the verge of rain.

With a deft little hop, Harriet was on the barstool next to Louise. She gave the soda jerk a little wink. He pretended not to see. She placed the tools of her trade—a notebook and a rather fine pen—on the counter and turned to Louise.

"How do you want to do this?"

"I didn't realize I had a choice in the matter."

It was hard to keep up with Harriet, and in that regard, she reminded Louise of Celia.

"Of course you do. This is your story. I want to tell it right. Don't you hate when a story isn't told right? When everyone makes up lies about you and then they all become public?"

"Yeah, I do."

Louise got the feeling that this example wasn't necessarily about her. But she nodded and cleared her throat. The soda jerk placed two cool, tall glasses of Coke in front of them. Now Harriet paid him no mind.

Was this too much? Did Louise want herself out there? But this was better than the other option: to keep having men she didn't know make up stories about her.

"All right, Harlem's Hero, where do you want to begin? Your childhood?"

"No." Louise had little desire to talk about raising infants when she was ten. She thought about it for a moment. "Why don't we talk about the winter?"

Recounting the early winter of 1916, the winter she was kidnapped, was hard, but Harriet listened and wrote. She was a rather fast writer, recording Louise's responses in small print and half words, a code that made sense only to her. It was almost mesmerizing, the way she wrote.

"What? You stopped talking."

Louise had been in the middle of describing what that basement somewhere had felt like, but she stopped when she was watching Harriet write. "Oh, sorry."

"Did you think you were going to die?"

"Yeah." Louise closed her eyes. When she opened them, she was staring at herself in the warped mirror: hazel eyes, brown skin, eyebrows knitted together. Every time she looked in her bathroom mirror now, she saw what age had done to her. Lines at the sides of her mouth and her eyes, grooves in her forehead. She looked older than twenty-seven. If she wanted to, she could probably pass for a spry early thirties.

But she didn't want to do that.

Louise turned back to Harriet. "I did think I would die. It's weird thinking about it now. It's just a moment in my history."

"What about Nora?"

News of Nora's death had, of course, spread like lightning through Harlem and the surrounding areas. Her connection to Louise had quickly followed. Rosa Maria's innocence was being hotly debated.

Louise no longer read the papers. She couldn't handle it. "It was me and Nora and two other girls. I barely remember them now. It was a surprise when Nora turned up in front of me the other night."

Harriet put her pen down. "You didn't keep in contact?"

Louise shook her head. "I felt so bad about it, but my father controlled my life pretty tight."

"How so?"

"Wanted me to marry."

"Who?"

A small, despondent smile played on Louise's lips. "Someone who used to be a friend. I had thought I wouldn't mind marrying him."

"But what?"

"It wasn't where my heart was."

Harriet nodded in a way that maybe suggested she understood. She wrote something else down, then sipped from her glass.

Louise sipped from hers. She moved her head so she could hear the bubbles furiously and frantically pop in the glass, a noise that had always been a comfort to her. She wasn't sure what to say next.

"So, what did you do in the meantime?" Harriet asked.

She was fully facing Louise now, her notebook on her lap. Up close like this, Louise could see silver threads woven into the green on her dress. The effect was dainty and lovely.

"I worked. I lived in a boardinghouse. I tried to be a normal person."

Harriet was left-handed. Louise's aunt Louise would have said that was a sign of the devil. Louise ignored this. Harriet smiled.

"You know, I really appreciate you doing this. It's not easy, I know."

"I know what it's like to be a girl in this city." Louise picked her glass up again. "I'm glad to help."

Harriet looked down at her notebook, then up at Louise. Their eyes locked and it was three long heartbeats before Louise looked away.

11

THE LAST PERSON she had expected at her door was her sister. Minerva "Minna" Scott was her younger sibling by three years, and had turned out to be exactly the sort of woman her father wanted to raise. Louise was pretty sure she had been ripped off of the Lloyd family tree in favor of her younger sister.

"Lou." Minna was dressed smartly as always, matching hat, coat, shoes, and little purse in a shade of goldenrod that bounced off her dark skin. She shifted so she was standing against the doorjamb and Louise realized that Minna was pregnant again. "Are you at least going to invite me in?"

"Sure." Louise was too shocked to do anything but step aside and let her sister pass.

It was good timing: Louise had just come back from walking Rosa Maria to the subway station. She was about to change into something a little more lightweight than the dress she currently wore, and then was going to figure out something new about Nora.

Minna sat at the kitchen table. The two had been trying to repair their relationship recently. It had not been going well. In fact, Louise had just given her sister this address at the beginning of the month, despite having lived here for much longer. It was weird to see prim and pregnant Minna in her apartment.

"I need your help, Louise." Minna looked around the little apartment, her nose wrinkling. Minna's brown eyes, warm and sweet, took in the remains of **GUILTY** on the wall.

Louise cleared her throat. "I've been redecorating?"

"What have you gotten yourself into?" Minna looked back at her older sister.

"Just a tiny stitch. Nothing to worry your pretty little head about."

"Louise."

"I'll be fine." Louise leaned against the counter, crossing her arms over her chest.

Minna exhaled, pressing a hand to her stomach. At that moment, she looked older than Louise had ever seen her. She had a toddler son already, and frankly, she looked more exhausted than ever. "It's about Josie."

Louise hadn't spoken to her other sister in roughly seven months. That wasn't for lack of trying. Josie had effectively cut her out the day after they buried her twin.

And Louise understood. It was a hard thing to go through. Louise just wished Josie would open up. They had all lost a sister.

It was harder for Josie, though.

Josie and Celia had been together their entire lives. In truth, Josie had needed her sister in order to make it through the world.

Now Josie wasn't coping well.

Josie had always been a fighter. Their mother had died in childbirth, nearly taking Josie with her. It had been a long, complicated, horrible night.

But Josie had lived and Louise had no doubt that if she wanted to live through this, she would, without anyone else's help. She was a stubborn little thing. She took the lead from her twin, but she was brilliant and bold.

"What about Josie?"

"You need to talk to her. I'm scared she's gonna end up killing herself if she doesn't straighten up. Bring her here. Show her . . . this. She'll get it."

"So you want to use me as a cautionary tale?" Louise wanted to be indignant, but the truth was that if it would help, she'd try it. She was eager to help her sister in any way she could.

And she truly didn't want Josie spiraling down her difficult path.

"Not exactly . . ." Minna leaned back in her chair.

"You can say it, Minna."

"Look at your choices, Louise."

"Just because I wanted something other than to be tied to one man for the rest of my life, because I wanted to see the world, I'm the one who made all the mistakes?"

"How much of the world have you seen, Louise? I live twelve blocks from you. I walked here." Minna narrowed her eyes.

Louise was getting heated, her cheeks reddening with anger. She took a long, slow breath and collected herself.

"They've always looked up to you." Minna was glaring at her reflection in a little compact mirror so she didn't have to look at Louise. "Make it count. You were supposed to lead by example, and look at you."

Minna had never said it, but Louise was sure she blamed her for Celia's death as well.

And the blame fell squarely on Louise's shoulders.

If she stopped moving for a moment, she would be crushed under the pure weight of the guilt she carried.

Louise lit a cigarette, unable to respond until she inhaled

deeply. "Fine." She exhaled, closing her eyes. She didn't want to fight with Minna any more than she had to.

This was something she could do. Everything else in her life was up in the air. She couldn't trust anything in front of her. But she could support her sister in finding her way.

"Of course. I'll do whatever we need to do."

She took another deep drag on her cigarette. She wished it was the summer before that last one, when her big-sister duties included taking her sisters to the drugstore for Cokes and ice cream.

But time had moved on.

Minna relaxed into a smile. "I can't do this on my own, Louise. Thank you."

She did seem grateful. Maybe she didn't want to fight either. Louise really had to be nicer to Minna. There were only three Lloyd girls left.

She and her sisters had always been the sort to do things by themselves. They had been raised to be the same kind of stubborn. That had led Louise and her sisters down different roads in life.

Was she confident that she could help Josie? No.

Was it worth it to try? Of course.

IT APPEARED THAT unit 3I was full of visitors that day. Just as Minna left, Rafael showed up with a man in tow.

"Lovie. Lovie." Rafael had a key. Louise hadn't wanted to give him one. Rosa Maria hadn't either. "Was that your sister?"

"How do you have a key?"

"Hey, Lovie, is that any way to talk to guests?"

Rafael invited himself in and the man who was with him was familiar in a very bad way.

"Mr. Schoonmaker?"

He looked toward her, an expression of surprise covering his face. "Miss Lloyd? The other Miss Lloyd?"

"The other?" Rafael asked at the same time Louise said, "Call me Louise, please."

Schoonmaker laughed. It was his toss-his-head-back laugh and Louise crossed her arms over her chest.

"I should have known. Jolly good play, though. Can I have my money back?"

"No." Louise had already secreted the money he had given her in the apartment and she was not giving it back.

"Worth trying," Schoonmaker said.

"You've met?" Rafael asked. It was sweet that he was a step behind.

"Mr. Schoonmaker here caught me rifling through the Dove garbage," Louise said.

"Why were you in the garbage?" Rafael asked incredulously.

"Clues," Louise said.

"Oh, Lovie," Rafael sighed.

And what could she do? She seated them on the couch and handed out cigarettes and glass bottles with the deft politeness one would expect from one's host. Her raising and training hadn't been for nothing.

Louise pulled a kitchen chair to the living room and sat facing both men. Rafael leaned back on the couch with all the leisureliness in the world.

"Have I ever said that this apartment is better than mine? How did you get a better apartment?"

"Rafael, what are you and Mr. Schoonmaker doing here?"

"Schoonmaker, please," the other man interjected. "Mr. Schoonmaker was my father." He winked at her. Louise raised an eyebrow.

"Schoonmaker here is my business partner. We went in on the Dove together."

Rafael leaned forward as if this was some secret. And it really was some secret. Louise had had no idea how Rafael had pulled the money together for the club, and he had avoided telling her until right now. He had artfully managed to change the subject every time Louise brought it up, sometimes literally dancing away from her to avoid it.

"And I think he could be of some help."

Schoonmaker leaned forward as well. Up close his facial features were lovely: thick eyebrows set over dark eyes, a long nose over thin lips. He was always smiling and that made him look younger than Louise suspected he really was. He was dressed too nicely again. His suit was emerald green with a black waistcoat. His shirt was blindingly white against both colors. Louise felt underdressed for a meeting in her own apartment in her simple day dress of black linen.

His voice was still odd to her: smooth and satin and soft but with something off about it. Louise looked into his dark eyes.

"I've heard you've found some trouble."

"I don't find trouble. It hunts me down."

"Right," Schoonmaker said. He puffed on his cigarette. "I believe that."

He took a slow look at her and Louise realized the hem of her dress just touched her knees while she was sitting.

Louise clutched her bottle between both hands, just to have something to do with them.

"Schoonmaker just told me that he was in the office that night," Rafael said.

"You were? We didn't see you."

"I do my best to stay undetected. I'm Raf's silent partner. You get it."

Louise wasn't sure she did get it. "Did you see us?"

"I heard you," Schoonmaker said. He talked in a way that was oddly intimate, as if they were discussing something other than a night at the club. "You and Nora. You were fighting about something. Then the other girl joined in."

"Rosa Maria?"

"Mostly yelling in Spanish, but yelling all the same."

Louise looked toward Rafael, unable to say anything. His eyebrows were knitted together in faux concentration. Louise looked back at Schoonmaker.

"What was she saying? What were we saying?"

"Miss Lloyd, I may seem all knowing, but the fact remains: I don't speak Spanish. She sounded so angry, though. All of you did. You don't remember any of it?"

"We were all drugged," Rafael said.

Schoonmaker looked between them. He pursed his lips in thought. "Well, I didn't get all of it. But someone was really mad and someone else was jealous of someone. You three fought outside, but two of you went back inside." He smiled proudly, as if he were a child performing a trick for a treat. None of that was helpful. "Nora stayed outside. Talked to someone. I didn't get his name. She didn't say it."

"How did you hear it?"

"You girls get loud." His smile turned to something more lascivious.

Louise pulled her chair back a little bit. "Is there anything else? Anything that could be of use?"

Schoonmaker nodded. "Yes. In fact, Nora is—was—the Eye in the Sky."

"The what?"

Schoonmaker raised an eyebrow. "You've never heard of her? She's running a pretty lucrative numbers game. She and I have done some things sometimes."

Louise didn't ask what those things were.

"She's discreet," Schoonmaker said.

"You never told me that," Rafael said.

"I only thought about it now."

"The Eye in the Sky?" Louise asked.

"Because she sees all." Schoonmaker's eyes widened. "She was good at what she did."

"Right . . ."

Schoonmaker's casual, friendly persona dropped and he became serious. Louise was right: when he stopped smiling, he looked older. She was still unsure of who he was and who he was pretending to be. But his voice was intense when he spoke.

"If you look into this, be careful. I've heard that the only thing Nora was better at than making money was making enemies."

"She was one woman. How much damage could she do?" Louise asked.

In response, Schoonmaker smiled that smile again.

12

THE EYE IN the Sky. How had Louise not heard about Nora's work? According to Schoonmaker, who had overstayed his welcome after Rafael left, she had risen to prominence in the past couple of years. She was known for being strict and ruthless.

She had a small team. And all Louise had to do was meet this team.

Which was how she ended up sitting in a Harlem park, Schoonmaker next to her, waiting.

"Are you sure about this?" Louise asked, and not for the first time. Louise sat still and straight but it felt like ants were crawling over her body. Nervous energy raced through her.

"Of course, Lovie."

Schoonmaker had, unfortunately, picked up Rafael's habit of using her middle name, and that only. She should have nipped it in the bud; it was a move that was too familiar, too friendly for someone she wasn't on equal footing with, but it was sort of charming. Also, she was forty-nine percent sure that he was doing it to annoy her and she was not about to give him the satisfaction of getting to her. She recognized his type: he was much like Rafael in the way everything to him seemed relaxed.

He leaned back on the bench, a sigh escaping his lips.

Louise was unsure of why she had accepted his help. It came with too many strings, and it did mean that she was sitting next to this man she barely knew in the middle of the day. He had already made it clear that personal questions were off the table.

Roughly three minutes into waiting, Louise had asked, "So, where are you from?"

He had winked and said, "All around, Lovie." That had brought that line of questioning to a close.

And now they were twenty minutes into waiting and she was becoming more and more sure he had played a trick on her. But he never changed his demeanor. So Louise didn't change hers.

She had never been good at waiting. She always wanted things to happen immediately. It was one of her worst traits and she knew that. She was working on it.

"Drugged alcohol, huh? You think we'll get the Dove back?" This was the way Schoonmaker tried to make conversation.

"I don't want to talk about it."

"Mad, huh?" Schoonmaker turned to face her. "I get it. I'd be mad too. I think you have a lot more reasons to be mad than I do."

She sure did.

She didn't respond to that, mostly because she didn't know how and because she didn't want to give him the satisfaction of being right. She didn't want to know what that would do to his ego. But she was more scared than angry. How had she let this happen to her? She should have known better.

"Look." Schoonmaker pointed his chin in a general direction.

Louise looked to where he had gestured. "What?"

"There."

The man was dressed cleanly and casually. He was Black. His hair was cropped close and he adjusted his pair of sunglasses as he strode toward the bench. He sat next to Louise. She was in between two men, one of whom she didn't know and the other of whom annoyed her.

"Louise Lloyd?" The man's voice was low and deep.

"Yes?"

"Lawrence Wright."

"Who are you?"

He leaned back on the bench. "I'm Nora Davies' right-hand man."

"Told you, Lovie."

Smugness wafted from Schoonmaker. She didn't have to look at him to know that. She could feel it radiating from him in waves.

"Right," Louise said. "So, you were at the Dove the night she died?"

Lawrence took a moment. "You know I'm not doing this for nothing."

"Larry." Maybe Schoonmaker's whole thing was inappropriate nicknames. "We've talked about this. You're helping the lady out."

"I didn't realize you were dragging me in with Louise Lloyd."

"What is that supposed to mean?" Louise asked.

Lawrence looked at her. "I mean, you cause trouble everywhere you go." A popular opinion.

"Lawrence." Schoonmaker reached across Louise, his hand again full of cash. She wondered what it was like to be able to throw money at any problem. "Come on, we talked about this."

Lawrence's eyes didn't leave Louise's face. "Nah. I'm not getting into bed with a bitch like her."

Before Louise could react, Schoonmaker punched the other

man as hard as he could across the face. Then without flinching, he grabbed Louise by the hand and took off at a pace slightly faster than a leisurely walk.

"Don't look back."

Schoonmaker didn't even seem out of breath. Louise's heart was racing. Once they were away from the scene of the crime, he let go of her hand.

"Why did you do that?"

"Bastard had it coming."

"That *bastard* was one of the only people who could help me and you."

"He wasn't going to help you." Schoonmaker leaned against the wall, his long body folded in half as he exhaled. He smiled at her. "Nothing better to make you feel alive, huh?"

Louise wanted to yell at him. She realized that her first impulse wasn't very good, so she steadied herself and turned away from the man.

"Listen. I'm sorry. But there has to be a better plan."

"There isn't a better plan," Louise said. "I have no idea what I'm doing or how to do it."

Schoonmaker looked her right in the eye. He didn't say anything. Just looked right in her eye. His face was blank, totally unreadable.

Louise kept eye contact. She knew that she could never try to understand what he was thinking.

"You're right. I'm sorry. I was rash." Schoonmaker lit a cigarette. "We'll find a different way."

"You're not part of this," Louise said. She was surprised that she'd gotten an apology from him.

"Yes, I am."

“No, you’re not.”

“We’ll see, Lovie.”

THE NOTE MARJORIE had given her was an address. And it wasn’t of an apartment. It was a small office in a small building in South Harlem. The doors were locked, but Louise had never met a lock she couldn’t pick. Her mind was still occupied with Lawrence Wright.

A few months ago, she had at least been able to bank on the goodwill of others.

And she had been working with the police.

Louise should have been aware that now she was working against the police. She had the stink of scandal on her.

And she wished Schoonmaker hadn’t overreacted. She also wished, oddly, she had brought him with her. There was something daunting about entering a place and not knowing what she would find. She wished she had thought to slip Rafael’s birthday present into her purse. She hadn’t been spending as much time at the gun range, and her shot might be off, but she would have been safer with it.

The lights were off in the office, but enough sunlight streamed in for Louise to keep them that way. She closed the door behind her. The window was open and a stiff breeze blew in.

The office was tiny. One desk, two chairs, and a coatrack. The entire width of the room was Louise’s wingspan, the ceiling just out of her reach. It was small enough to be absolutely claustrophobic.

Her first move was to the desk. She sat down in the chair, moving as fast as she could, although she wasn’t sure who would come in.

The desk was old and wooden. She rifled through the papers

on top. There was nothing of great importance: a couple of letters addressed to a woman named Pauline, a couple of scrap pieces with numbers, all written in gorgeous slanted handwriting. She folded them and put them in her purse, just in case. She wondered why Nora chose to rent this place. She opened the one drawer, to her left. It was empty.

Louise wasn't surprised. Gently, she pried the drawer from its hinges, and knocked on the base. Of course there was a false bottom in the drawer. She couldn't get it to open.

The wind whistled by the window and Louise looked up. Cool sweat ran down her skin. She looked up at the door. It was still closed.

It was very odd, though, because she felt there was someone in the office with her.

She rationally knew it wasn't possible. She was alone. She heard the busy midafternoon noise on the street; the office was on the first floor. She moved to the window and peeked out. No one was there. She looked back at the desk.

Her heart raced, skittering wildly while she tried to collect herself. This wasn't real and she had to focus. She pressed a hand to her chest, trying to get herself to calm down.

Once it seemed like the threat had passed, although she wasn't entirely sure what the threat was, she kneeled down by the drawer, feeling for the latch that would release the false bottom. She had to give Nora points for style. She loved a false bottom in a drawer. She loved hidden *anything*, like the hidden staircase in the Dove that led to the office above the dance space.

The latch released with a strained, strangled squeak, the bottom flipping up.

Louise didn't know what she had expected to find. What she

did find was bundles of cash, all neatly lined up like little soldiers marching to war. There were also three very large bags of what looked like cocaine.

Louise stared at the drawer for a moment. She had a sinking feeling that Nora had been knee-deep in things Louise had no idea how to handle.

13

IT TURNED OUT that after nearly a decade of constant working, Louise wasn't too good at sitting around and doing nothing. Now that she had no real job and nothing to do but stare at her ceiling and try to remember, she didn't like being idle.

She sat crossed-legged on the bed while Rosa Maria got ready in the morning. They'd have a small breakfast together and Louise would walk Rosa Maria to the subway.

They didn't talk about the case and investigation. In fact, they were both aggressively avoiding it, pretending that if they didn't talk about it, it didn't exist.

Then at night, Louise would read and Rosa Maria would write and they'd go to bed together.

It was the sort of quasi-domestic bliss Louise had longed for as a child. As they crawled into bed, Rosa Maria turned and leaned into her. "What if I did it?"

"You didn't do it," Louise said. "I know that for a fact."

She had never once doubted Rosa Maria's innocence. They were going to bed earlier than they would have with the Dove open, but still late in normal society. The time was ticking past one as Rosa Maria took off her glasses and turned off the lamp. They lay there in each other's arms, clutching each other as tightly as they could. Something Louise didn't miss from the boardinghouse was having to wait until everyone was asleep, then sneaking from room to room.

Now they had the freedom to just be.

"I keep having these nightmares."

Rosa Maria wasn't sleeping well. Louise knew it; the bed wasn't very big and every shift and change echoed through it. She also looked strained. Her hair was greasy; bags were under her eyes. She just seemed exhausted.

"Try to sleep, love."

"Tell me how it's going."

Rosa Maria closed her eyes. Louise began to braid her hair; it was too fine to hold a curl but the motion was soothing.

What could she tell her? "Nora was running a numbers game."

"Really?"

"She was called the Eye in the Sky."

Even saying Nora's title was weird to her. Louise wondered what else Nora had been hiding. She told Rosa Maria about the meeting in the park, Schoonmaker's rash actions, and breaking into Nora's office.

"Schoonmaker is strange, right?"

It was always funny to Louise when Rosa Maria couldn't find a meaner word to call someone.

"Definitely a very specific sort of man," Louise said.

"I can't believe he punched someone." Rosa Maria pulled her dress on over her head.

Louise leaned over and lit a cigarette. Almost immediately, Rosa Maria took it from her. "I can."

Rosa Maria puffed on the cigarette. She could blow smoke rings. It was maybe the first thing that had drawn Louise to her. Even in the dark, it was overwhelmingly attractive.

"What about you, Louise?" Rosa Maria's voice creaked with cigarette smoke.

"I don't know."

They were living in some sort of purgatory, waiting for something to happen.

"Your sister is coming over tomorrow, right?"

"Yeah."

There were so many things Louise pointedly wasn't mentioning. The fact that she was giving Harriet her life story. That she had met up with the reporter over the past couple of days. That Harriet was funny and interesting and they ended up trading stories in the café near the hotel Harriet was living in. Every moment she spent with Harriet felt like an insult to Rosa Maria.

Louise took her cigarette back, placing it in between her lips. She shut her eyes, allowing herself to relax just a little bit. She wasn't ready to face Josie. At least Minna wouldn't be there to judge them both.

"Martin brought me in for questioning yesterday," Rosa Maria said lightly and casually. "He wanted to go over everything again. I suppose he'll be calling you in again soon too."

Louise closed her eyes. Sometimes she wished she'd wake up and be twenty-one again. She'd spend the whole winter indoors and her life would be forever different.

"Of course he will." Louise swallowed a pang of guilt.

That was all she felt these days: guilty.

14

IN THE FEW months since Louise had seen Josie, she had grown from being a sixteen-year-old kid to being an almost adult. She'd gone through a growth spurt, her hair was shorter, and her lips were redder. She wore a rather edgy outfit. She looked as if she hadn't slept all night.

"Josie," Louise said. She had been expecting her sister at the door, not this person who was a very good imitation of her sister.

"What?" Josie's voice was a raspy bark, one Louise knew all too well. She was hungover.

"Come in." Louise pulled the door open. Maybe she had underestimated what Minna had said.

Josie slumped into a kitchen seat.

"Josie!" Louise said. "Is that any way to greet your sister?"

Josie looked up at her. Her eyes were hard and cold. This was a far, far cry from the Josie she had known. "Can I have a glass of water or something?"

"Manners, Josephine." Louise regretted saying it the moment

she did. She sounded too much like her father and that wasn't the point of this. "Come on."

They sat together on the couch, facing the door. They didn't say anything for several minutes. Louise used this time to ponder what she should say to her sister.

"Josie, I know this is hard on you. It's hard on me and Minna and everyone."

"No, it's not."

"Yes, it is."

"Minna's having a new baby. You live here. Everyone is pretending Celia never even existed. It's not hard on anyone. It's hard on me."

Despite Josie's protests, Louise pulled her close, laying her sister down so her head was in Louise's lap.

"It's hard on all of us, Sunshine." Louise could feel Josie start to relax. "But you have to try. She would want you to try."

"I don't want this anymore."

Josie sounded exactly like she had when she was a child, angry and overtired. Her voice was soft and strained, as if she was trying to hold back tears. She moved so she was lying on her back over Louise's knees. Louise was aware that this wasn't her best angle.

"I don't want this at all."

"Why don't we think about something we can do together?"

"Like what?"

Louise paused. "I don't know. But you have to make me a promise, Sunshine. It's time for you to return to the world."

Josie pulled herself up. Even with her hangover, she seemed like the little girl Louise had left behind. Louise could see the fear and worry in her little sister's eyes.

"What if I can't?"

There were so many things Louise could have said. She hated the fact that she never knew what the right words were.

"I can't do anything without her."

"Yes, you can. And you will."

It was times like this when Louise had so desperately wanted a mother. Someone who would have known what to say. But she was the mother. She got Josie a glass of water and Josie quietly sipped it.

"Minna hasn't told me everything but you have to stop drinking and dancing all night."

"Really, Lou? Coming from you?"

"I have a job, little miss."

It was mostly true. She would have a job if the Dove opened back up, if she could clear Rosa Maria's name. But she thought about what she told Minna.

"Okay, how about this: If you clean up your act, we'll take a trip together." It was feasible, yes. It would be an adventure.

"Where?" Josie asked.

"Why don't we sail to Paris over the summer?" Louise asked. "I'll tell Father it's for your ladylike education, and when you come back, he can marry a neat young lady off."

"Really?" Josie asked.

"Yes, but you have to do something. Find a place to work and stop this spiral, Josie. Please." Louise placed a hand on her younger sister's cheek.

"Okay. I promise."

Just like when they were younger, Louise extended a pinkie finger. Josie wrapped her own little finger around her sister's.

"Thank you, Sunshine."

IN THE EVENINGS, Louise would meet Harriet at some previously agreed-upon neutral location. She was aware that she couldn't bring Harriet anywhere near her current life. In fact, it was nice having someone on the outside of everything. Someone to help her see clearly. She always chose someplace outside of Harlem. She didn't want to be seen or recognized. This evening, the location was in the middle of Central Park. Louise didn't go through the park as often as she would have liked.

Louise sat patiently. She was learning that Harriet was several minutes late to everything, but she brought a tornado of energy with her and it was hard to be mad at her for that.

"Darling!" Harriet exclusively talked like a fifty-year-old woman.

She was wearing dark pink today. She was always perfectly coordinated with her hat and coat and purse and shoes, and Louise got a shock of her perfume when Harriet kissed her cheeks. Harriet lingered for a moment past what was really appropriate, and when she pulled away, she had a small, sad smile on her face.

"Well, shall we?"

"I suppose so."

Going over every intimate detail of her life was strange. It made Louise feel too open. But Harriet was a good listener. She was not judgmental. She just nodded, wrote, and asked necessary questions.

They sat a respectful distance apart, facing each other. Harriet flipped to a fresh page in her notebook and wrote the date in her gorgeous script.

"Where were we?"

"Girl Killer investigation."

"Of course. Are you okay? What's wrong?"

To be fair, Louise had thought about nothing but Josie all day. What was interesting was that Harriet could tell something was wrong just by looking at her face.

"Don't write about this?"

Harriet closed her notebook and inched closer.

"It's my sister, uh, the youngest. I'm really worried about her. I'm worried she's gonna kill herself."

All at once, Louise realized that tears were starting to fall. She closed her eyes but didn't try to fight them. She was tired of being strong all the time. She was tired of being the one everyone could lean on. Not that she was ungrateful. Just tired of it all.

She wondered what it was like to have a normal life. She wondered what it was like not to be constantly needed. She shut her eyes and tried to push it all back down but that was a battle she was losing.

"I can't imagine how hard it must be," Harriet said. She had moved closer and allowed Louise to put her head on her shoulder. The move was comforting. Harriet was focused on rubbing Louise's shoulders. "You must be so tired."

Louise didn't say anything. She wondered what life would have been like had Minna been older than she was. If Louise were second in her family lineup. Minna was more suited to be the eldest anyway. There were so many things Louise could have hoped and wished for. But that wouldn't do her any good.

With a snap of sudden realization, Louise remembered where she was. She cleared her throat and pulled away from Harriet. "I think we should focus on the story."

"Right, of course." Harriet managed to make those words sound very distant. She opened her notebook, picked up her pen. "You're right."

She paused, as if she wanted to say something else. Louise couldn't think of anything rational to say. She was all caught up on her sister, her family, Rosa Maria.

"You can always talk to me," Harriet finally said. "I know we're whatever this is."

"I think we can call it friends."

The words slipped from Louise before she realized what she was saying. But they had the intended effect: Harriet grinned and she was so lovely, with the evening sun hitting her face, making her glow.

Louise looked away and focused on the map of Harriet's face: her nose, which was almost too short, her cheekbones. She had a large forehead but she covered that with perfectly curled bangs. Her blue eyes were round and her face was perfectly symmetrical. There was something about those eyes that Louise found soothing. Everything about Harriet was clean and effortless.

"So, tell me about Maggie's."

15

PAULINE MOORE WORKED in a dress shop. She had been Nora's right-hand woman. Louise had found her information in the empty little office. Pauline was like Louise in the way she wore black from head to toe, a strict and severe look on her face. Louise realized they must have been the same age but Pauline looked years older.

But her dark brown face was perfectly smooth and angular. She was stunning and currently moving at a quick pace across the floor. Louise hadn't yet been helped, but she knew that she wouldn't take precedence over the four white women currently milling around the store.

She had been distracted for days. Her focus wasn't where she wanted it to be. And she had no one to blame but herself. She was hoping that she could get herself back on track. Louise flicked past racks of sample dresses, almost all of them placed on order and sewn by an army of women on the floor above. The rattling of the sewing machines followed her as she moved through the store.

This rack held composé dresses, ones of seafoam to mint, royal blue to cerulean, amethyst to onyx. They were simple and pretty. Louise would have to order a couple. And while Pauline measured her, they'd have to talk.

Louise had taken to looking over her shoulder everywhere she went and she always thought there was someone behind her. She felt like someone was copying every move she made. But when she turned, no one was there. Louise exhaled. She tried to focus on the color gradients of dresses she didn't need. She missed buying pretty things just because she thought she wanted them. She fingered a red satin dress.

"Can I help you?"

Pauline had a bit of a Southern drawl. Louise wondered if it was natural or if it was an affectation. She wondered where Pauline had moved from. It was odd hearing a Southern drawl come from another Black woman.

"Yes, I'd like to order a few new dresses."

Pauline smiled a thin customer-service smile that was all-around pleasant. "Of course. I'll have to take your measurements."

In the little fitting room, Louise stripped down to her slip. Pauline unwound her measuring tape from her long neck.

"How are you today?"

Louise remembered this kind of pleasant conversation. It all ultimately meant nothing. She decided to get on with it.

"I want to talk to you about Nora Davies."

"I don't want to talk about her."

"I need to know more about her business."

Pauline had been taking Louise's measurements with quick-fire accuracy and she stopped now, standing up. They were chest to chest, or chest to stomach, in the tiny fitting room.

"I know you worked together."

"We were best friends."

Pauline didn't look at her. Suddenly something on the dusty floor was much more interesting.

"My best friend is going to hang for her murder unless I prove who actually did it."

Pauline closed her eyes. Louise recognized this; Pauline was saying a quick prayer. Louise said one too.

"All right." Pauline draped her measuring tape back around her neck.

"Explain it all, please."

"We'd take bets and pay out to the winner." Pauline made the numbers game sound far less complicated than Louise knew it was. "But she was always getting into trouble. She was getting in with Frank Lister's men. Selling drugs. Doing all of these things that we agreed not to do."

"Can you get me a customer list?"

"I could, but I suspect the problem isn't with our customer list." Pauline had dropped her voice to a whisper, and it was as if they were sharing a secret. "Lawrence was unhappy with the way she ran things. They never saw eye to eye. He was gonna confront her that night. . . ."

Pauline trailed off. She had just realized she was betraying the secrets of her friend. She pressed a hand to her mouth.

"Confront her about what?"

"Being dirty. Skimming off the top. Cheating people. Nora always said that's how we had to make a profit. That was the only way we were going to make any real money." Pauline bit her lower lip.

"And you didn't like it?"

"I thought we were doing a disservice to our customers. But she was good with numbers. She was convinced no one would find out."

"And what about Lawrence? What role did he play in all of this?"

If Pauline and Lawrence had talked, he hadn't mentioned the fact that he had refused to help Louise. But she was going to try again.

"They were always on-and-off. If they weren't fighting, they were . . ."

"Making whoopee?"

"Yeah." Pauline frowned. Louise got it. "If they weren't fighting, then they were going at it in different ways. Did you really want to make an order?"

The idea of buying dresses was far from Louise's mind, but she nodded.

Pauline smiled, something verging on an actual smile, not a pleasant customer-service one. "I know Nora was a lot to deal with. But she was tough. She wanted something better than this." Louise understood.

"What are you going to do now?" Louise asked.

Pauline began taking the rest of Louise's measurements. She focused on that for a moment or two, and when she looked up, her eyes, which were a stunning dark shade of brown, were filled with tears. "I don't know. It's silly but me and her have been friends for years. I miss her."

"I'm so sorry for your loss," Louise said. She meant it. She really did. Those six words were right only if she meant them.

Pauline pulled herself back together. She resumed her thin, polite smile. "I can take you to set your order now."

Louise ended up spending fifteen dollars on dresses. She hoped the expense would be worth it.

LOUISE STAYED OUT after dark so rarely now. Since the club had closed, there was no reason to do so. And crossing the Harlem streets to her apartment suddenly felt like an impossible feat.

How was it that she was a lifelong New Yorker, and yet she was afraid to be outside?

She could have rationalized that monsters didn't exist. She knew that. There was nothing waiting for her, hidden behind corners, to steal her away.

Except there had been. When she was sixteen, she was taken from these very streets. And now, weaving through the throngs of people, keeping her head high, she was scared.

She didn't want to be scared; she had grown up on these streets. Harlem was part of her and she knew that. And she couldn't be scared of something that was a part of her.

Her walk home from the dress shop wasn't long, but it was made so by all of the people milling around.

She couldn't shake the idea that someone was following her. She moved as fast as she could, looking over her shoulder every few paces.

She was being irrational. Everyone in her life would tell her that. But she wasn't afraid of just being followed. She was afraid of being followed by Theodore Gilbert.

She was sure he had died. She had watched the blood seep from his body onto the floor. She had waited to make sure he was dead.

And he was.

She was his killer.

The world was a lot grayer than that; she knew that. But it

still felt as if she needed to be punished for her sins. It wasn't even him she was seeing, not really. It was an indiscernible tall figure that could literally be anyone in the world.

Sometimes, Louise felt like she was dreaming. Like maybe she was the one who had died instead and now she was stuck in the echoes of purgatory. Maybe she deserved all this. She wasn't as good of a person as she thought. She knew that too.

Was her mind playing tricks on her? That was possible. She had been surviving on little food and sleep, all the cigarettes and sham alcohol she could get, for months, trying to forget. She wished her fear were tangible. She wished she could turn and face it head-on.

But she *had* done that. And now she had this.

She thought she heard her name. Not very strange. Louise was rather a common name, and she was lucky to be one of a million Louises. As she moved through the streets the voice got louder, then ebbed away. The thing about living in New York was that she was completely invisible until she wasn't. She could picture herself grabbing onto people's arms, crying out, asking if they were hearing something that was all in her head.

And she knew it. It was all in her head. She was imagining it, from some guilty place that couldn't let go. She hadn't told anyone about how she felt.

The thing was, she knew that Harriet would eventually ask. And she had to decide what to say when she did.

"Lovie!" It wasn't Rafael. It was Schoonmaker.

"Were you following me?" Louise asked.

"No. I just saw you. Is someone following you?"

Schoonmaker looked around. His impressive height was something Louise didn't have. It was very easy for Schoonmaker to take a cursory glance around the streets and shake his head.

“I was just coming to see you. I feel rather bad, you see. I shouldn’t have punched that man.”

“It’s fine.” Louise wanted him to go away. Her heart was racing and she wasn’t sure she could trust him. She looked up at him and frowned. “Did you kill Nora?”

“I had no reason to kill the Eye in the Sky, Lovie. I made a tidy profit with her. She was rather helpful.”

He was grinning. This was a joke to him. Louise turned and he moved to grab her arm.

She dropped her voice and narrowed her eyes. “Let me go.”

Schoonmaker did as he was told. His eyebrows knitted together. He was the very picture of concern.

“I’m fine. I just want to go home. Please. I just want to go home.” He didn’t say anything else. Just nodded and let her go.

She moved through the throngs of people, knowing he was watching her as he disappeared. She could feel his eyes on her; she was sure of it. But when she turned around, Schoonmaker was gone.

16

WHEN LOUISE WOKE up, Rafael and Eugene were in her apartment. It was early, or maybe it was late. She knew Rosa Maria was awake too.

"How did he get a key?" Rosa Maria asked.

"I thought I took it back," Louise said. The two men were anything but subtle.

"Eleven thirty," Rosa Maria said.

"How early did we go to bed?"

They had, in fact, gone to bed way earlier than they usually did. Both of them cited long days of being on their feet and they had turned in at half past nine. There was nothing in the world that could have made Louise feel older.

Rafael shouted in rapid-fire Spanish. Rosa Maria exhaled, closed her eyes, and pulled herself from the bed. She began to yell back as she put her dressing gown on and opened the door to the bedroom. Louise was nearly perfectly fluent in French and rather good in Spanish, but even after dating Rosa Maria and existing around the twins for years, she couldn't keep up when they began to argue.

Rafael was pacing the little living room, his hat in his hands. Eugene was behind him. There was a vague aura of worry about them both.

"Good, you're awake."

"We need that key back," Louise said.

"We need to talk to you. Martin brought us in for questioning today." Rafael was still moving, tracing the same path, a tight little box.

"Key."

Louise held her hand out. Eugene handed it over without looking at her. Louise took it; then she looked at Rosa Maria.

"Tea, I think."

"Something stronger," Louise countered. They did keep a couple bottles of gin in the icebox, just in case.

And they would need it right now.

"Let's take this from the beginning. What happened?" Louise asked.

She sat down on the couch next to Eugene. He stayed facing forward. His elbows were braced on his knees and he pressed the flat sides of his fists to his forehead. Louise leaned forward too, placed a hand on his shoulder. He didn't move away from her touch.

"They brought me in first."

Rafael lit a cigarette. Glass in one hand, cigarette between his lips, he didn't stop moving. He was about to make Louise dizzy. He turned, and in the light, Louise realized there was a fresh bruise on his cheek.

"What did he do to you?" Louise asked.

"Louise." Rosa Maria had placed herself at the kitchen table. "Let him continue."

They were all spread out through the little living room and kitchen. Louise was aware that this was how they had been just a week ago on her birthday.

"He threatened me. Told me to tell him what happened or I'd never get the Dove back. I said I didn't know." Rafael took a long sip from his glass, coughing a little as he swallowed. "He said that we'd have to stop this game."

"Raf, sit down." Louise rose from her seat.

He ignored her, pacing the same little path he was on.

"If you don't stop moving right now, I'm going to get sick."

"Sorry, Lovie." Rafael collapsed onto the couch. He and Rosa Maria shared a long look. "You may be next."

Louise didn't want to think about that. She couldn't think about that.

"What did he ask you?" Louise said. She cleared her throat. Then she went to pour herself a glass.

"About you. About that night. About Rosa Maria."

For a moment no one spoke. The reality of everything was hitting her. How could she keep them safe? She breathed in and out, slow and steady, until her hands didn't shake and she felt a little stronger.

"What did you tell them?" Rosa Maria asked.

"Nothing. I didn't say anything."

"I don't believe you. You think only about yourself."

Louise had never seen Rosa Maria angry. She didn't have an angry bone in her body. She didn't have the disposition. But now it was smeared across her face, her lips in a deep frown and her eyes flickering with fire.

"You know that's not true."

Rafael stood. They were twins, yes, but Rafael had four inches on his sister. Rosa Maria stepped up so they were eye to eye.

“Fighting isn’t solving anything.” This was Eugene, surprising them all. His eyebrows were knitted together in his signature look of tender confusion. “We have to end this.”

Louise lit a cigarette and exhaled. “I will.”

LOUISE WAS ALREADY awake and it was thirty-seven minutes before Rosa Maria had to wake up. Louise was making coffee and smoking a cigarette. She hadn’t gotten enough sleep; she was stuck thinking about Rafael and Eugene.

And Detective Martin.

And the fact that she was going to be arrested, as she had no idea who had killed Nora. She was sitting at the table, pressing her chin to it, staring at her coffeemaker when the envelope was pushed under the door. Louise stared at it for a moment, then opened the door. There was no one around. It was too early for the rest of the building to be awake.

But who had left it?

The envelope bore her name in messy, scratchy writing. She stared at it, trying to discern who it was from. The envelope was thick and bulky, and she wasn’t sure she wanted to open it.

If she left it, she could just ignore it.

But she couldn’t do that.

She used a knife to break the seal, a dark red stamp that reminded Louise of blood. She dumped the contents onto the table, and after pouring herself some coffee, she prepared to go through them. The first sip of coffee was the electric jolt she needed. The envelope had contained pictures. Pictures of her and Rosa Maria taken over the week since Nora’s death.

There were several intimate moments of her life all laid out in front of her. She could track the days the photos were taken by the dresses she had been, or had not been, wearing in them.

Louise stared at the photos of her and Rosa Maria kissing, her and Rosa Maria in an embrace. One of them in bed together. They slept with the curtains pulled back and Louise's face was turned toward the moonlight. She stared at herself in the photographs, trying to see if this really was her. Of course it was. The photos were taken from outside their street-facing bedroom window.

She put all the photos facedown. She felt bile rise at the back of her throat. She was no longer scared or worried. She was just angry. She was furious, a white-hot ball of rage. The very idea that someone was watching her and her life, targeting her, made her angry.

But she couldn't act too rashly.

There was someone watching them. Someone invading their private space. No matter how careful they were, they had lost.

There was a little handwritten note hidden among the photographs. Her hand shook as she reached toward it. It was a scrap of paper haphazardly torn from something else. The jagged edges were fine. The writing matched that on the envelope and was nearly illegible in its short missive.

Get out while you can.

She stared at the five words until they began to swim in front of her eyes. She packed everything back up and shoved it all into a random drawer she hoped Rosa Maria wouldn't check.

"What's going on?"

She hadn't heard Rosa Maria come from the bedroom. Louise looked up. Rosa Maria had wrapped her robe around herself; one shoulder of the robe was falling off. She blinked sleepily.

"Just making some coffee."

The lie came quickly, before she decided to lie about what she was doing. She should have said something about the photos.

"Why are you awake so early?" Rosa Maria sat down at the table.

Louise cleared her throat. "I just couldn't sleep."

"Yeah." Rosa Maria had signs of sleeplessness as well. She had dark brown circles under her eyes; every move she made was slow, as if she was so tired, she could barely think straight. "Me too. Have to get ready."

"I'm going to look for real work today," Louise said. She had enough in savings to be okay for a while. But she needed something more. "It'll work itself out."

Rosa Maria didn't look convinced. She rubbed her eyes and poured herself a cup of coffee. Now they were inches away from each other.

"Lou, why are you awake?" Rosa Maria turned to her. The space between them was inches, and yet it felt so wide.

"I really just couldn't sleep."

It wasn't a lie, although it felt like one. She tapped her fingers on the countertop. They rarely cooked. They rarely ate, actually. The kitchen was more of an art installation in the apartment. Rosa Maria pressed a hand to Louise's forehead.

"I'm not sick."

"I know." Rosa Maria didn't say anything else.

Louise thought this would be different. A year ago, lying in the pink room she had rented, feeling Rosa Maria's slow breathing under her. Those moments had been stolen. They were so precious to her. She was wondering if their relationship would survive all of this.

Sometimes she missed Miss Brown's house. She had hated living with all the nosy, busy girls. But she thought their relationship was stronger and better when it was lived in the late hours of the night and early hours of the morning.

Rosa Maria squinted. Her eyes were brown and bright. "You can talk to me, you know."

It wasn't a question. It was a statement. They had been each other's rock for years now. There was no one Louise would rather have been with.

But relationships were hard.

The world they were in was harder.

"I know," Louise said. The arrival of the envelope was on the tip of her tongue. She swallowed it back down as Rosa Maria poured her coffee. "Have a good day today."

"You'll walk me to the subway?"

There were so many things she wanted to say. So many things she could have said. But Louise just nodded. "Of course. Just like always."

17

ONE THING LOUISE hated was having to beg for help. Lawrence Wright worked in a barbershop Louise had never dared to enter. She had had to press Schoonmaker for this information. First, he hadn't wanted to give it to her; then he had wanted to go with her, which she was not going to allow.

She was starting to think he was seeing this as a game. He also seemed rather bored.

When she pushed the door open, all the chairs were filled with men. The radio in the corner was blasting loud but the multiple conversations drowned it out.

Lawrence had a customer. He smiled as he worked, talking with the other man as he leaned back in his chair.

Louise stood, nearly frozen to her spot, watching her surroundings. She waited until Lawrence was finished with his customer and was sweeping the hair trimmings from the floor. He looked her in the eye, then quickly looked away as he recognized her. She stepped toward him.

"See you didn't bring your friend with you. Get out," Lawrence said. His face was drawn and serious.

"No." Louise narrowed her eyes.

"Miss Lloyd, please."

Louise stood her ground. She wasn't going to let anyone push her around. "Ten minutes. That's all. Ten minutes."

They spoke in low voices so they didn't attract attention. It would have been rather hard to be noticed here. Louise raised an eyebrow. He wasn't going to back down either.

"I'll just wait here until you're ready. No rush." She could see him debate it.

He exhaled and smoothed his hands over his shirt. "Sit down."

Louise did as she was told. She closed her eyes rather than look at herself in the mirror.

He began to comb her hair. "What do you want to know?" He sounded resigned.

"I want to know about you and Nora," Louise said.

"That's none of your business."

"Were you angry with her?" Louise asked. She knew from experience she had to be persistent in her questioning techniques. "I've already heard about your *relationship*."

"I can't describe it."

Lawrence was still working on her hair. She had just washed and redone it that morning. It had been forty minutes in front of the stove with a hot comb, and she thought she looked all right.

"I hated Nora. I couldn't stand her."

"You know she's dead? She was murdered. You saying you hated her?"

"I know how it looked. It was a mutual hate."

Louise opened her eyes. She locked eyes with Lawrence in the mirror.

"She hated me too. We did everything we could to undermine each other."

"But?"

Lawrence exhaled. "I can't explain it, but I can say I didn't kill her."

"Not very convincing. Schoonmaker saw you."

"Schoonmaker was drunk. Can't trust everything he says. Can't trust anything he says."

Louise narrowed her eyes. Lawrence picked up a pair of scissors.

"What are you doing?"

"I'm at least going to fix your hair."

"It's fine."

Lawrence raised one eyebrow. Louise didn't meet his gaze. This was the price she had to pay. He stood in front of her, happily blocking her view of the mirror.

"But you were there that night?"

He didn't respond for a moment. He focused on brushing through her hair one last time. "Yes, I was. I was passing through and I saw you all outside, and I asked if I could talk to Nora alone. You two went inside, and me and Nora . . ."

He trailed off. Louise held perfectly still as he did so.

"We did talk. I wanted out. I wanted her to drop all of this. But she said she couldn't go back."

"But do you know who killed her?"

Lawrence paused again. "We ended up, well . . ."

"I get it. You made whoopee. Where?"

"Behind the club."

"Let's move on." Louise exhaled.

"Nora went back inside. I left. That's all I know."

Louise closed her eyes as he snipped away. The movement of the shop hadn't stopped around them. And it was strange, having their conversation among all the others.

"I didn't kill her. I couldn't have. I was at home, and you can ask my sister."

"Maybe I will," Louise said. Her suspect list was growing narrower and narrower.

"Listen, Nora had made a bunch of enemies. Finding the killer would be impossible."

He stepped away from Louise so she could see herself in the mirror. Her hair, previously a little too long, had been cut to her chin, setting off her face and eyes.

"Happy?"

"Yeah." Louise touched her jawline. She looked back up at him. "Could you get me a list of Nora's enemies?"

"I suppose so. But, baby vamp, that list is longer than my arm."

Louise got a particular sense of foreboding, something settling deep in the pit of her stomach. She had to look at her options, look at everything she had.

And she didn't want to doubt herself.

But she had nothing else.

If Rosa Maria hadn't killed Nora, then who had?

18

BY THE TIME the sun set, Louise was pacing near the Dove. She had asked Harriet to do this with her. It made sense to her: she didn't want to go into the club alone, and Harriet wanted to see the crime scene.

She had told Rosa Maria she was having dinner with Josie. She'd have to make up some lie when she got home.

Hopefully doing so would be worth it.

Louise clutched her purse to her chest and tried not to fidget. It was only ten minutes past the designated meeting time. She did have to wonder how Harriet managed to do anything when she was so late.

She watched as people passed her by. She was leaning on the club door, trying to quell the sea of discomfort inside of her.

"Darling!" Louise had to appreciate how Harriet, today neatly dressed in shades of purple, changed her greetings. "I'm sorry. I got caught up. It's been a busy day."

"Yes, it has," Louise said.

"So this is it, huh?"

Harriet eyed the door. She had a keen sense of distrust; she was never going to settle for what she saw. She always had to investigate.

"Sure is."

Louise had spent so many nights at the club, behind the bar, greeting people. It had been her life. She kneeled down and dug in her purse, pulling out a couple of long pins. Harriet bent down to watch. It was an impeccable, graceful move in which she kept her knees together.

The lock was as tricky as Louise thought it would be. It took her a couple of moments, but she cracked it. Rafael's teaching had never steered her wrong. Louise took the lock off and pushed the door open. They ducked under the rope marking the building a crime scene and entered.

She had seen the club like this one other time: the day Rafael told her he had bought it. There were overturned tables, dust on the floor and the lights. If she looked carefully, she could see remnants of Nora's blood.

Louise would admit to being glad she wasn't alone. Harriet was right next to her as they entered the space. It was funny how she had built it up in her memory. The Dove wasn't half as glamorous as she thought it was. It was small, and in the evening light that streamed through the windows, the space seemed a bit sad.

"Where do you want to start?"

Harriet had wandered around to the bar. She had removed a glove and was running a finger over the bar top. It came away covered in dust.

"The office, I think. But hold on."

Louise stepped behind the bar. She knew all the secrets of this place. She turned toward the wall, and used her fingertips to press until she found the hidden door concealed among wood panels.

"Whoa." Harriet had watched in mild confusion as Louise did this.

This was the place they used to store extra bottles. Louise had kept a rather strict inventory. The little room was also accessible by a back staircase coming down from the office above.

"I think whoever killed Nora stayed in here. Maybe all night."

Harriet stepped past her. The room wasn't big, but there was space for the average person, taller than Louise and shorter than Schoonmaker, to stand or sit. It would have been impossible to hear someone in there over the noise of the club. She rarely used the room while they were open for business. It would have been so easy.

Louise stepped inside of the room. She and Harriet were chest to chest. There was a little light. Louise pulled the cord to turn it on and let it hum to life. Boxes were stacked haphazardly, tossed against one another.

"From here up to the office?" Harriet asked. She had dropped her voice so it was low and breathy.

Louise nodded, barely getting herself to form words in the space between them. In the low light, Harriet's hair glowed and her eyes danced. The base of the stairs was behind Louise and she knew that she should go upstairs, go look in the office she so rarely spent time in.

"This is a little romantic, isn't it?" Harriet continued. Her tone wasn't subtle at all.

"I guess so." Louise knew what Harriet was doing.

And in a second, one that passed all too quickly, Harriet's lips were on hers.

In another second, Louise remembered where she was and stepped away, feeling her heart beat fast.

Harriet's eyes slid over her face. "What's wrong?"

"I can't do this. . . . We shouldn't do this."

By instinct, Louise looked around. There was no one else. Her thoughts stuttered and stammered. But her mind was blank. Louise leaned forward and kissed Harriet again.

They leaned into each other, the moment expanding for them to explore each other.

Louise pulled away again. She inhaled, letting everything in her body settle before she spoke again. There were so many things she could have said. But she just pointed to the staircase. Louise took one look around at the crates she kept in this little room.

Then something caught her eye.

It was the sheath to the knife that had killed Nora. It was nestled behind the crates, glinting its sinister shine, small rubies embedded in its surface, visible even in the low light. She kneeled down and picked it up.

This was easy to miss. She never would have given the police the location of this little cellar and it seemed they hadn't found it.

The idea that someone waited here to pounce when they were all asleep terrified her. She stared at the sheath, looking for initials, something that would crack the case.

Of course, it wasn't that easy.

"Louise."

Harriet was still standing there. Louise's lips were throbbing with her kiss. The time that had passed was roughly one minute.

"Office is upstairs. Let me go first." Louise climbed the stairs without looking back at Harriet.

LOUISE KNEW THAT Rafael had had the building changed to suit his needs. The staircase in the hidden cellar led up to a bookcase in the office on the floor above. It was a tight squeeze with Harriet right behind her. The design was almost ingenious. Louise had to wonder how Rafael had thought of this.

And then she wondered if there was anything else hidden in the club.

Louise used an elbow to open the door. The lights of the office were off. She had always appreciated this space; the windows made the light dance in a myriad of colors on the scuffed wooden floors. Louise went over and turned the lights on. She sat at the desk. Harriet thumbed through the books on the shelves on the wall. The bookcase really was a distraction.

When Harriet's back was turned, Louise pressed a finger to her still-buzzing lips. Harriet had tasted like candy, and in the moments they were entwined, Louise had felt desire rush over her skin.

She looked at the desk, trying to remember the task at hand. She was lucky to have known Rafael for so long. He really had a one-track mind. She opened the two top drawers. These contained the official club records, haphazardly piled on top of one another. There were some bills, maybe totaling two or three hundred dollars. Rafael had wanted a club; he hadn't wanted to do the day-to-day chores. That was where Louise came in. She picked up the bills and stuffed them into her brassiere.

The next drawer was bigger; the only things in it were a bottle and a couple of glasses stained with alcohol. Louise picked the bottle up. It was half empty and warm. She put it back down.

What was she trying to find here? She knew that Schoonmaker had been in the office around the time Nora had died. She stepped to the window and pushed it open. She could hear the noise of the streets surrounding them. If it were quieter, she could have heard people talking.

She looked toward the bookcase. She knew, by experience, that it took only a couple of moments to get from the office to the main floor of the building.

Louise descended the staircase. It was old metal and loud. It would announce the arrival of anyone, and with enough speed, anyone could hide behind the crates.

She got the distinct impression that Schoonmaker didn't notice many things around him.

And more, she knew the boxes had been in neat stacks. She was always careful with the glass bottles, and she and Eugene made sure everything was orderly before they opened for the night.

And now the boxes were displaced from their usual stacks.

Louise moved behind a pile, some boxes on their side, some boxes on their lids. She crouched down. The placement meant that she was totally hidden, and even *if* Schoonmaker had been looking, she wouldn't have been seen.

Had someone been there all night? Waiting?

The thought disturbed her. She looked at the dusty floor. In the low light, the knife sheath glinted. She could hear Harriet shuffling around above her. The little cellar was cold. The hair rose on her arms. She was standing on a length of blue ribbon just under the toe of her shoe.

She recognized it; she knew it was Rosa Maria's. How was she able to identify a length of blue grosgrain ribbon? Rosa Maria compulsively stitched little things into her ribbons. This one had a little red heart.

Louise couldn't remember if Rosa Maria had been wearing a ribbon that night. But then again, she couldn't remember anything.

Louise thought she heard a creak from the dance floor. Was someone else there? She had remembered to bring her gun this time. She pulled it out of her purse and lifted it in front of her.

Louise felt her eye twitch. She was nervous. She was doing something illegal but for a good cause. She wondered if that would balance itself out. She knew that anyone could come in, even though she had been careful to lock the door behind them when they entered.

She hadn't been to the range in a while. In her defense, she had thought she was done with this. Her hands shook a little as she stepped out from behind the bar.

But the dance floor was empty. She was alone. Maybe it was the wind. It was a windy night. She could hear it howl and rage outside of the door. The sun had set and now the moon spilled onto the floor. If she stood in the right spot, she could see Harriet still in the office.

She lowered her gun. She felt foolish, like a child playing pretend. There was nothing there. She was fine. It was all she had to do, repeat those three words to herself over and over. *I am fine. I am fine.* She closed her eyes and took a deep breath, waiting for the echoes of terror in her body to subside.

Louise was standing right where Nora's body had been found, the toe of her shoe touching the dried blood.

Louise knew she had to talk to Rosa Maria.

19

ROSA MARIA WAS home by the time Louise returned. She was sitting at the kitchen table, typing at the typewriter. The good part about living alone was that Rosa Maria no longer had to restrict her typewriting hours. There were many nights over the winter when Louise had fallen asleep to the gentle sounds of the machine.

"How is Josie?"

Louise bit her lower lip. She placed the ribbon on the table without saying a word. Rosa Maria picked it up, running her thumbnail over her tiny stitches on the end.

"I found this in the cellar," Louise said. She sat down, not even bothering to take off her coat.

"You were at the club?"

Louise had spent her entire trip home trying to think about what she was going to say. There was a large part of her that couldn't believe she was going to do this. There was a smaller part that needed the reassurance.

"I had to go look. I had to see."

Louise's eyes flicked to the stack of neatly typed pages next to the typewriter. She never asked Rosa Maria what she was writing. She wrote in Spanish and Louise thought it was private. And it always felt so personal. Rosa Maria never talked about it.

"Listen." Louise cleared her throat. She had to ask. She knew Rosa Maria couldn't have killed Nora. But that meant someone was trying to set her up.

The words stuck. "Did you kill Nora? I just need to know."

The moment the question was out of her mouth, she knew she couldn't take it back. The words hung in the air. She knew, in that moment, that she had said the wrong thing.

"I thought you believed me."

The things Louise would remember were the hurt and anger in Rosa Maria's tone. Her eyes started to well with tears and she shut them before any could leak out.

Louise felt guilt sit in her stomach like a brick. This wasn't how this was supposed to be. They were supposed to be happy and those moments were few and far between now.

"I do."

"Then why are you asking me?" Rosa Maria's eyes were still closed. Her tone had dropped to quiet anger.

"I just need to know." Her reasons didn't seem as strong as they had when she was on the subway. She regretted bringing it up. "Your ribbon . . ."

"My ribbon means nothing. You just don't believe me. Of everyone, *you* were supposed to believe me."

"I just need to hear you say it."

"Of course you don't believe me. Do you know what I'm going through?"

"Yes, I do." Louise could feel panic rising in her body. They had had fights before; what couple hadn't? But this was different. She could already tell that this would be very different. "I know what you're going through."

"I was fired." This clearly wasn't what Louise thought Rosa Maria was going to say.

"What?"

"I was fired. Two days after Nora's death. Too much speculation around me. I don't know what I'm going to do next."

"What have you been doing all this time?" Louise asked.

"It's not important."

"What's important is that you're keeping secrets from me and I'm trying to protect you."

"Maybe I don't need protection. I'm not some helpless little girl. You don't have to save me."

Louise stood, moving away from the table. She leaned against the countertop, taking several deep breaths to try to mitigate her anger. Rosa Maria got up as well, moving away from her. Any thought Louise had had of a relaxing night with her girlfriend was dashed.

"Maybe I have this all handled," Rosa Maria said.

"I'm doing this because I love you."

"You're doing this because you have a pathological need to save everyone around you."

"That's not fair." Louise was yelling and she couldn't stop herself. "I kissed someone else. Or she kissed me. I don't know." She didn't know why she said it. She was adding fuel to this fire. But if they were going to fight about it, she was going to get it out in the open. "I have been thinking about her for some time now."

"Who?"

Rosa Maria wouldn't look at her. It was then that Louise knew that she had made a mistake by mentioning Harriet at all.

"It doesn't matter," Louise said. "It's no one you know."

"But you're thinking about her," Rosa Maria said.

"I am, but I love you. You know that," Louise said.

Even saying the words felt hollow and empty. The atmosphere in the apartment was tense. The two women faced each other. Louise tried to get ahold of her temper before she said something she regretted. She wondered if she was in love or if she was just comfortable.

"Yes, I have been thinking about her but it's not serious or anything." Maybe this would help them in the long run. "I would never want to lie to you."

Louise swallowed hard. There had been so many instances when she had lied, and she was sure that Rosa Maria had lied to her as well. She didn't want to open any of those old wounds. All Louise wanted to do was move past this. She didn't know if that was possible.

"Oh, *really*?" Rosa Maria pulled one drawer open. She picked out the envelope with the pictures Louise had received that morning and placed it on the counter. "What the hell is this?"

"I was going to tell you."

"When?"

Louise didn't have a good answer for that. Their tempers were flying. Louise knew that the best thing to do was to take a step back, maybe go outside. She was desperately craving a cigarette.

"When was I going to tell you? When I thought it would be relevant."

"It's relevant now." Rosa Maria's voice was thin and quiet.

The two women faced each other, eye to eye.

"I was handling it."

"No, you weren't."

"I was trying."

"Why don't you try being normal for once? Normal girls don't go around solving murders. They leave that to the police. You're just a child playing a game."

The words were a slap. Rosa Maria knew she had hit Louise where it hurt. Louise took a step back.

"Is that what you think?"

It was hard for Louise to control her tone when she was seething. They had been together for so long. She didn't realize how easily they could crumble.

Louise also knew Rosa Maria well enough to know that she was lying when she spoke next. "Yes. I do. I think it's time for you to grow up and realize you will never be one of them."

Rosa Maria's dark eyes narrowed. Louise could see the storm raging inside of her.

Louise ground her teeth together. The photographs of them caught her eye. She took a step away from Rosa Maria, trying to calm down. She pressed a hand to her forehead.

"I'm not trying to be anything. All I've ever wanted to do was help."

Rosa Maria didn't say anything for a long time. It felt like both of them were winding down from their anger. Louise focused on putting the photos back into the envelope, feeling her cheeks burn as she did so. Rosa Maria lit a cigarette. They both needed some time to catch their breath.

"I wish you'd ask if someone wants your help before you try." Rosa Maria gathered her pages up and entered their bedroom, slamming the door behind her.

Louise would sleep on the couch that night.

THEY DIDN'T TALK the next morning. In fact, Rosa Maria was gone by the time Louise woke up, and that was a welcome change.

She made a cup of coffee and sat at the table, trying to smoke her anger away.

She hadn't done the right thing. She knew that. She would take it back if she could.

What if that were possible? To take back something she'd said, making it so she had never said anything at all. She wondered what the world would be like if she could.

By the time the night rolled around, Louise was antsy. She wore an iridescent midnight blue dress, with her favorite red choker necklace, then dabbed makeup on her face.

She hadn't been to Heaven on Earth in months. With the Dove open, there had been no need for it. But she went alone. Not a very proper thing for a young lady to do, but she didn't care.

And besides, she wasn't a young lady, not really.

The club was full when she got there. It was nice to be a patron for once, not having to worry about stock or selling or making sure young girls didn't drink too much. She had two glasses of terrible bathtub gin, letting the alcohol burn as it slid down her throat. Then she found a table and sat down.

The band was playing Irving Berlin's "Blue Skies." Louise would recognize that smoky, throaty voice anywhere; Blythe Montgomery and her band of men were on the dais. The lights shone off her purple dress and there were flowers in her hair, which was in an intricate braid down her chest, ending just above her navel.

For one moment, Louise was breathless.

"He's a maharaja."

"No, you're confused. He's a sheikh. But he's also a duke. A British duke."

Two women in beaded dresses and with darkly lined eyes were near Louise's table. Even over the noise of the band, their frenzied conversation was radio clear.

"I have never seen a man that tall." The first was a redhead wearing a fiery dress that matched her hair. She was sitting casually in her seat, leaning back as if this were an art salon. Her legs were long and Louise had to guess she was tall as well, cold and statuesque. "Me and him were necking in the rumble seat of his car."

"Ha." The blonde sitting next to her barked a harsh laugh. Her dress was so blue, it was almost black, and it shone dangerously in the lights from the club. This one was maybe not attractive in a conventional sense, but she held the attention of her companion. She was magnetic. "You and Schoonmaker? The Club King of Manhattan? Elsie, gimme a break."

Louise pulled her gaze away and back to the dais. Blythe was still singing away, and for a moment, Louise longed to be back at the Dove.

Elsie was enjoying holding court, even if her subjects amounted to one. She tilted her head and pressed a finger to her neck. Louise could see a small love bite on her neck. And the blonde whistled.

Louise wished the band would speed up a little. She didn't like to be alone, but she didn't want to be in her apartment. And just being around the things she loved helped.

She couldn't help but think about Rosa Maria, about Nora.

She couldn't help but focus on how her life could be different.

There was a part of her that wished she could be one of those girls on the dance floor whose only worry was getting back into her house without being detected. She watched as people danced on the floor slowly and longingly. She watched as a girl with starry eyes kissed her man like there was no one else in the world. She had spent many hours watching lovers kiss, and the pang of jealousy, of anger, never changed.

She wanted the world to be kinder. She resented the fact that she had been born into a world that was cruel. She resented the fact that she was one the world was cruel to. Louise knew what Janie would have said if Janie were here. Louise had to focus on the things she could do. She had to focus on the things she could change, since there were so many things she couldn't.

Louise wished she had drunk a little more that night. Months of trying to abstain had only made her crave the liquor. She lit a cigarette, and closed her eyes as she inhaled. Then she looked around, trying to figure out if someone was staring at her.

But no one even knew she was there. She was as invisible as she could be, and there was something so wonderful in that.

It occurred to Louise that she could do whatever she wanted. The thought to her was freeing but full of panic and terror.

Who was she when no one was looking?

Blythe and her band changed gears, to a faster song meant to get the crowd up from the seats. Louise could feel the tempo increase as people grabbed one another and ran to the dance floor. These were the moments she loved and the ones Rosa Maria loved too. Louise wished that she were next to her now. Even Elsie and her friend dropped their little beaded purses on their table and ran toward the dance floor, which was quickly filling up.

But it was better that Rosa Maria wasn't there. They both needed space. That was what Louise thought. She knew if she left now, she could get back before Rosa Maria went to bed, but she stayed in her seat. She was still seething from their fight, seething from everything they had said.

She wasn't so sure they could survive this.

Louise looked out to the dance floor. She thought she heard her name whispered in low tones near her ear.

When she looked around, no one was there.

20

"HAVE YOU STOPPED to consider this may not be about Rosa Maria?"

Somehow, the drugstore was the most private place they could think to meet. Louise had not wanted to sit across from Harriet, not since their kiss, but there was nothing she could do about it.

Louise was Harriet's story.

She didn't know if she liked that, but at least she was able to tell her own story. She focused on the glass in front of her, the radio playing a baseball game in the background. Anything to distract herself from Harriet's lips. Harriet was wearing a dress of dark blue, one Louise thought she might have already seen on her. Harriet's lips were painted a dark blood red, and when they parted as she wrote, they looked as inviting as ever.

Louise never thought she'd be a person who'd conduct an affair, and actually, she wasn't. It was one kiss. One kiss could be a mistake, and that was all it was.

Sitting near Harriet made her heart start to race. She thought about pressing her body against Harriet, running a hand through her hair, exploring her body. A heat rose to Louise's cheeks. Had she and Rosa Maria just been . . . tolerating each other?

She didn't want to think about it.

"It's about me." Louise placed her straw between her lips, leaving a smear of her own lipstick behind.

"I took the liberty of looking into your kidnapping case." Harriet flicked through her notebook, passing through her pages and pages of written information. Louise wondered how she kept it all organized.

"Aha." Harriet tapped on a page with a nail that was varnished royal blue to match her dress. "Here. Charlotte 'Lottie' Haynes and Etta Hall. The girls you were with a decade ago."

"How did you do that?"

Harriet's smile was just on the right side of smug. "I looked it up," she said as if that remark explained anything. "Lottie lives in a hotel now. I can't find Etta. It seems worth a shot."

From the radio, cheers exploded as a ball was hit well, Louise assumed. Louise stared at the names in front of her. She tried to picture the girls they had been, but she had barely met them.

"How odd," Louise said.

They'd be young women just like her, edging onto thirty and old age, in that order. It was hard to think of them as adults. She permanently saw them as crying girls in that cold basement.

She had been so brave then. She had had to be just as brave for the past year.

Louise was eager for her life to settle down.

That was all she wanted: a calm life where she didn't have to be anything to anyone.

While Louise was thinking, Harriet was writing. She tore the page out and handed it to Louise. "This is where Lottie lives."

Louise stared at the numbers of the address, then tucked the piece of paper into her purse.

"Is it okay if I try to make some contact with your family? Your friends? The story would be so much stronger if I did, you know." Louise recognized Harriet's casual tone.

"Have you done so already?" Louise asked.

"I talked to your father on the phone." Harriet began flipping through her notebook again. She stopped on a page titled *LLOYD FAMILY*. "He insists you were a troublemaker from the beginning."

"Impossible. I had to be a mother at ten years old." Louise rolled her eyes.

"I'm going to talk to him at your house. I'm so sorry—I just have to. Actually, a little later today." That explained Harriet's demure dress. "And don't worry. I'll give you a chance to dispute everything he says about you," she said.

Louise didn't like the idea of it. Even the image of Harriet sharing tea with her father that flitted through her head. This was her story. She was supposed to be telling it. But there was no point in saying what she wanted to say. It was done. Harriet had already made contact and had set her plans in motion. So Louise said nothing instead.

She took another sip from her glass, then moved to hear the bubbles pop furiously.

Harriet closed her notebook. She always did so with a little bit of a happy sigh, as if telling stories made her feel content.

Louise picked her glass up, feeling the cold on her fingers. "We don't need to . . . talk, do we?"

"Do we?"

Louise raised an eyebrow. Maybe Harriet was playing dumb. Maybe they had nothing to talk about. "I suppose not."

That would have been true if she could forget about the kiss, forget about Harriet's warmth, forget about their bodies pressed together in a desperate attempt to get closer.

But the memory would fade.

She loved Rosa Maria.

She knew that. They were going to grow old together. But the more she thought about it, the more it felt as if she was convincing herself of something rather than just knowing it was true. She didn't like that feeling at all. The guilt she had felt since the kiss sat in her stomach, a constant reminder that made it hard for her to eat.

The radio again brought her back to the present. Harriet was concentrating on emptying her glass; she had gotten a shake even though it was a cold March evening outside. They dug through their purses, placed their change on the counter, and exited the drugstore.

It was a windy evening. The two women linked arms as they fought against the Harlem foot traffic.

"Good luck tomorrow," Harriet said when they parted.

And Louise would think Harriet had actually meant it.

HAD SHE GONE to the wrong place? Louise was standing in the middle of the street, clutching the piece of paper Harriet had given her the previous night. She looked at it, and now she wasn't sure she was reading the address correctly. Over her shoulder was the Kodak that Rosa Maria had given to her for her birthday. She had taken her time, taking snaps of the city, as she made her way downtown.

She had taken the train down to the Lower East Side, and the numbers were melding together on the paper, not making sense to her.

Had she gone the wrong way? She was standing in the middle of the Lower East Side, trying to find the hotel where Lottie lived. She stared at the piece of paper, wishing there was some sort of device that she could hold and it would guide her to where she needed to be.

She prided herself on having a very good sense of the city. Louise was a city girl through and through but she was realizing how much of that was based around Harlem.

She was lost.

She resented the fact that her people had been shoved into Harlem, and they were barely wanted there. She wondered if there was a place in the world for someone like her.

She pulled her coat closer around her shoulders. She could give up, take the hour-long subway ride home, and call Harriet from the phone in her apartment. But she decided to back up and try it again. The sun was setting. She had spent all day trying to find a new job, and she had learned that with her name constantly in the papers, she was too much of a liability. Then she had gone to church to hope and pray that her life would turn itself around.

And all day long, she had thought about Lottie Haynes and Etta Hall. Had they been searching for her? Had they seen her in the paper as Nora had? It was weird to have a shared experience like that and not remain in touch. Louise lamented the fact that she had barely gotten to know Nora before she was taken away from her.

The night, which should have been the best of the year, the night she turned twenty-seven, was a black hole in her memory.

And every time she thought about it, her fear of the world was renewed.

Louise didn't know how much longer she could wander around this part of the city, one she didn't know very well. She was hyperaware that she was the only Black person on the street and that meant she had to be more careful. A couple of women—older than her, rich enough to hire one or two someones like her—sneered at her as she passed. She wasn't used to feeling so exposed. She missed the easy comfort of Harlem, the familiar streets.

But she had to get used to this.

Louise raised her chin and continued down the street. She thought she was hearing her name, but she knew that there was no one around her who knew her.

Her nerves were frayed. She was tired of living every day in fear. It was now something she couldn't get rid of, as if it was an essential item she needed to have with her. She was looking around every corner, leaving a light on at night.

She didn't like this feeling. It felt as if something was going to happen to her and she didn't know when. She wanted a strong drink and a good night's sleep.

"Hey! Lovie!"

That was real. At the sound of her middle name, she turned. She knew it wasn't Rafael who had called her, so it had to have been the only other person in the world who would use her middle name.

Sure enough, Schoonmaker ambled toward her. "I thought that was you," he said gaily. "Isn't it a wonderful evening?"

Before he could do anything, she opened her camera and took a photo.

It had been raining most of the day and the evening hung on to the angry storm clouds. He extended an arm, and being too shocked to do anything else, she took it.

"Are you following me?"

"Just a happy coincidence, Lovie. I'm thinking about expanding. I was looking at a building or two."

"The Club King of Manhattan, huh?"

He gave her a bashful smile. "That's what they call me." He almost preened at her use of the nickname. "Have you gotten anywhere with the Eye in the Sky?"

Louise exhaled. There was a part of her that was grateful to see a familiar face, even if she wasn't sure how she felt about him yet. "Nowhere. I have no idea who killed her."

"Can I give you some advice?"

Louise knew from experience that he would give it anyway.

"I think you need to change your direction. Nora had a lot of enemies, but what about your friend?"

It wasn't even good advice. She blinked as she took it in.

"She has no enemies."

"What about you?"

"My only enemy is dead."

Schoonmaker laughed. "Come on, Lovie. You don't have one enemy? Not someone you kicked out for being too drunk? Where can I take you?"

"The subway. I need to go home."

Schoonmaker began to whistle.

She could feel heads turn as they passed. "Did you have a good day today?"

"Everything is coming up roses, Lovie."

21

GETTING JOSIE BETTER wasn't an easy road. Josie was sitting at Louise's kitchen table, surly and hungover, her arms folded over her chest and her face folded into a scowl.

Louise was exhausted, and on the long list of things she wanted to do, she would put fighting with her sister right under having a tooth pulled out.

"Josie, come on."

They had been in these positions for forty minutes. Josie was still too hungover to form comprehensible sentences. Louise was tired of having to be the disciplinarian. Her job as the eldest sister was supposed to be teaching her sisters how to do their makeup and helping them sneak out of the house.

She would never admit when she was in over her head, but she was in over her head.

"I just wanted to have some fun."

Josie's jaw was set. Louise recognized her own stubbornness in her sister.

"I never get to have fun anymore."

Josie was still dressed for going out. Louise had found her, drunk and exhausted, in a spangled gold dress and matching heels, outside of her door at four in the morning.

"That is not true and you know it."

Louise leaned against the counter. She was furious, but was trying to talk quietly. Rosa Maria was still asleep, and the last thing Louise wanted to do was wake her. Things were still tense between them but they were in a much-needed quiet period in which all they did was exchange pleasantries. She didn't see things warming up between them anytime soon.

And she had bigger things to deal with. She had called Minna, who she knew woke early. They were planning a two-pronged defense attack. And Louise was a little anxious to see how Minna would blame her for this current situation.

Louise sipped her coffee. Truly, she was too tired to put together sentences and to figure out what she should say so her sister would hear it. Maybe she should stop trying. Maybe she should withdraw all support and let Josie figure it out herself.

She poured a glass of water as she considered this. She couldn't do that. It went against everything she knew. They had been raised under the creed of "family first." That was important to her. She couldn't leave Josie out in the cold, not when she needed help more than ever.

So Louise decided to say little until Minna arrived.

She placed the glass of water on the table in front of Josie. Her sister eyed it, then leaned her head on the table, closing her eyes. "Can I please just go home?"

"No." They had been through this four times now, and every time, Louise felt a little bit more discouraged. "Minna will be here soon and we just want to talk to you."

"I just want to go home."

Josie's voice was soft, and for a moment, Louise remembered the baby she had been.

"I know, but this is important."

Louise pulled a chair to the table, placing her cup of coffee in front of herself. Josie watched her do so, then closed her eyes again.

"Come on, Sunshine. You and I had a plan."

With that, Josie sat straight up, her eyes narrowed in anger. "I don't want to be in your shadow all the time, Louise."

"I never said that," Louise said.

"I don't want your stupid plan. I don't need you to take care of me."

Louise could feel her sister's temper rearing up. It was like a kettle, slow to simmer but once she started, she couldn't be stopped. Josie rose from her spot, angry flames in her eyes.

"I never wanted any of this. And I'm not supposed to be here without her. I don't deserve to be here."

In one fluid motion, Josie smashed the glass of water on the floor, nimbly picked up the biggest piece of glass she could, and with one millisecond's worth of hesitation dragged the glass over the skin of her wrists, closing her eyes against the pain.

Louise acted before she could really process what was in front of her. She grabbed a towel, maybe dirty but better than nothing, from the kitchen and wrapped her sister's wrists in an attempt to stop the blood from flowing.

"Help! Help me, please!" She was screaming the words over and over, hoping that someone would hear, hoping that someone would help her. She screamed until her throat was raw and then kept screaming.

Rosa Maria came rushing from the bathroom. She kept a cool head in an emergency, and Louise was grateful for that. Rosa

Maria took one look at the scene in front of her and, barefoot and in her bathrobe, she rushed to the street to call for help.

"Let me die," Josie wailed. "Why can't you let me die? I want to die. Let me die."

Louise was still screaming over her sister's pleas. She squeezed as hard as she could, trying to stop the blood flowing from her sister's wrists. She held Josie close, rocking back and forth, unable to stop screaming until her neighbors were at her door, hovering, wanting to help.

One woman who lived a few doors down kneeled next to Louise and took over holding Josie's wrists still and tight. She calmly directed a bystander to get Louise a glass of water.

The commotion around 3I continued until an ambulance took Josie away. Louise wasn't allowed to ride with Josie; she'd have to follow after calling her father, a task she dreaded.

Just as Josie was being taken away, Minna appeared at the door, breathing heavily and clutching her swelling stomach. She didn't say anything, just took one look at Louise sitting among broken glass, blood, and spilled water on the floor, and kneeled down, wrapping her arms around her elder sister.

It was that touch that made Louise begin to cry.

LOUISE HAD BEEN to this hospital only once before. But she recognized the nurse on the ward, Cristina, as a woman who had helped her the previous summer. Nurse Cristina was coming off of a twelve-hour shift—the only thing giving that away was an errant curl that had escaped from her little cap—but she still showed Louise to Josie's room before she left.

"She'll be fine, but she needs rest. You all have an hour."

Louise had missed Cristina's brisk and sensible tone.

Josie was lying on the bed, her eyes blinking sleepily. She was surrounded by Minna, their father, and their aunt. Louise hovered at the door, removing her hat and gloves.

She should have given it a couple of hours. She should have stayed at her apartment, cleaned the glass and water and blood.

But she had to be here.

She stepped into the room, not wanting to disturb the family moment going on. She hadn't seen her aunt or father in months. Minna noticed her first. A hand on her stomach, where it always was, Minna reached toward Louise with her free hand.

Josie's wrists were bandaged. The fingers of her right hand opened and closed slowly, and her eyes were glued to the window. She looked so small and so frail in the bed. No one said anything. There was nothing left to say.

Louise was grateful help had arrived in time. She couldn't have been the reason she had lost another sister.

Josie looked toward her, saying nothing, a little grimace on her face. Louise could feel her father staring at her, fury on his face. She couldn't look at him. She had been so careful not to do anything that might lead to seeing him. She changed her church times; she moved. She didn't want to see him, and she knew he didn't want to see her.

She always felt awkward being near her father.

But she also couldn't stay away forever.

She avoided his gaze for a long time. She went over to Josie's bed and kissed her sister's forehead. She squeezed Josie's hand gently. Josie watched as she did so, not saying anything. It was as if no one wanted to say a word. What was she supposed to say to the sister who had just tried to kill herself in front of her?

And Josie, still surly, still hungover, in insurmountable anguish, had nothing to offer.

It was something of a stalemate.

It was Minna, predictably, who broke the silence. "Josie, love, you have to be more careful. We can't lose you too."

Louise wondered how her family would spin this. There was the family truth and the public truth, and she knew this family truth couldn't get out. Most of her didn't want to know it.

She stayed near Josie's side, making small circles on the back of her own hand. She resisted climbing into the bed with her sister to stroke her hair, like she had when they were kids. She swallowed hard.

She had the faintest inkling that she could have prevented this.

"Louise, may I please talk to you outside?"

Her father's voice was cold. She didn't have to do what he asked her to do, but she did, pulling herself up, dusting off her skirt, and following him out to the hallway.

She was grateful for the fact that her father would *never* make a scene in a public place. He grabbed her by the wrist and pulled her into an empty room. She yanked her wrist away and crossed her arms, rising to her full five foot two.

"What?"

She was going to make this as quick as possible. She could tell he wanted to make it quick too. It was in the way he looked at her. His stare was full of anger seething just below the surface.

"You know that's not how you address me."

"If you were my father, I wouldn't. But you disowned me and made it clear you're not my father. I'll address you however I want." Louise couldn't believe she had talked to him like that.

He grabbed her by the shoulders. She pulled herself away. He was scowling, and she saw so much of Josie in him. Louise knew that she was a dead ringer for her late mother, down to the odd muddy hazel of her eyes. She knew that was why her father resented her. He cleared his throat. She was not going to let him intimidate her.

"You need to stop seeing her. After your mother—"

Joseph never called Janie by her name. If he mentioned her at all, it was as "my late wife" or "your mother." Louise had always thought that was odd.

"What about my mother?" Louise asked.

She was on high alert. He rarely mentioned her, and every time he did, she learned something new. Joseph swallowed and actually managed to look contrite.

"She didn't die in childbirth."

He didn't look at Louise as he spoke. She felt her entire body go cold with this realization.

She had blocked out her mother's death so long ago. Those days following the birth of Josie and Celia, the hazy summer days that turned into nights while Janie fought. She didn't know? How could she have known? She had a sister and two infants to care for. She had been busy.

"She did it to herself."

Louise shivered, unable to process the information she now had.

Louise cleared her throat and changed the subject back to the present. "Josie is going to get better. Then I'm going to move her in with me. She doesn't need your brand of help." She glared at her father, the man she had come from, with renewed anger within her. "You'll never see either of us again."

It would be easier said than done, but she wanted the best for her sister.

And it was something she should have done years ago.

"I'll need her things packed up."

"How are you going to support her?"

She didn't have an answer for this. She inhaled. "Better than you could."

MINNA AND LOUISE stood side by side long after their father had left. Josie was curled up in the bed. The nurse on shift had tried to convince Minna and Louise to go. Louise wanted to stay. She would stay with Josie for as long as she could.

Ultimately, the two elder Lloyd sisters decided to switch shifts. Minna had a husband and child; Louise had an investigation. But none of that mattered.

Louise turned to her sister. Minna was the prettiest Lloyd sister: she had wide brown eyes fringed with impossibly long lashes set in a heart-shaped face. Even months pregnant, Minna carried herself with a grace and poise that Louise never could muster.

"Did you know?"

"Know what?" Minna asked. She kept her voice low.

They weren't actually sure Josie was fully asleep, but her eyes were closed and her breathing was even. Louise took Minna's arm and pulled her from the room, closing the door so there was no chance Josie would hear.

"That Mother killed herself," Louise said.

Of course Minna couldn't have known. She was all but seven or so when Janie had died.

"That's what he just told me. How could he not say anything?"

"He probably didn't want to hurt us," Minna said.

That was something else Louise couldn't fathom: Minna had a good relationship with their father. It stung, knowing that Minna was the daughter Joseph always needed, whereas on the Lloyd family tree Louise was the black mark relegated to cautionary-tale status.

"You know how you get."

"If you're saying I'm acting irrationally, I will slap you," Louise snapped. She regretted the threat the moment she made it.

Minna took a small step back, frowning at Louise. "I can't remember much about then."

"We didn't even see her. I tried. I wanted to get into bed with her," Louise said.

The memories hurt. She couldn't remember her last time with her mother alive, but she remembered the gale-force screaming and heartbreakingly eerie silence that followed.

Louise tried not to think about Janie's death. If she focused on it for too long, she would find herself resenting the woman for not wanting the life she had chosen.

But maybe it was more complicated than that.

"All I wanted to do was see if the twins would squeeze my finger. Aunt Louise wouldn't let me get close." Minna frowned.

"Aunt Louise wasn't there," Louise said. "Didn't she come later?"

The events of the summer of 1910 were long ago and hazy in Louise's memory. But she was never going to say that Minna was right about something. That would go against everything she stood for.

"Yes, she was," Minna said. She inhaled as if she were about to give a ten-minute speech about why she was right, but stopped herself. "It doesn't matter. What matters is Josie right now." It was hard to focus on anything else. "We can't lose Josie too."

Louise nodded solemnly. "I know."

This was their job as older sisters. They were protectors; they were caretakers. And Louise wished she had done a better job with Celia.

Every day, she was reminded that Celia's death had been directly her fault. Josie's state was her fault too, a direct result, and she knew it.

Sometimes when Louise couldn't sleep, she thought about the woman Celia would have been. She was always charming and boisterous. She would have made the world bend toward her every whim. Josie had the same fire, although it was unused in the other twin.

Louise needed a cigarette, but the last time she had tried to smoke in the hospital, Nurse Cristina had yelled at her. It had been traumatizing enough to almost make Louise stop for good.

"I'm not letting her go back to that place, that house."

"Do you have a plan, Louise?" Minna asked.

Stupid question. Louise never had a plan. She, in fact, prided herself on moving from impulse to impulse like some toddler who was easily distracted.

"No, but she's not going back to him."

This was something she should have done ages ago, but up until the past few months, she had been living in a boardinghouse with no space and not enough money to take care of both of them.

"He's not that bad," Minna said.

"He is killing her." Louise's voice dropped to a whisper. "She isn't flourishing. She can't go back."

She knew that they shouldn't be discussing Josie's fate and future without the girl in question. Louise should have asked Josie what she wanted. But she wanted to make her own stance clear.

"I don't care if you're with me or against me, but I am not losing another sister."

Minna looked taken aback. She didn't reply for a moment, but she swallowed hard, placed her hand on her swelling stomach, and nodded.

For once, Louise was right. She fought the urge to smirk in the same condescending way Minna did. "We are going to see her through this, no matter what."

For the first time in about a decade and a half, they were working together instead of against each other. They were united in their cause, for their sister, as they should have been.

Josie was lying on her back, staring at the ceiling when they reentered her room. "Thought you left." Her voice cracked on the sentence.

Louise looked at her sister's bandaged wrists.

"We're staying here with you." Minna moved closer to the bed, and sat on the one uncomfortable chair. "You'll be better soon."

Louise hoped that was true.

22

LOUISE STAYED BY Josie's side as she recovered. The doctor wanted her to stay a little longer, until he was sure Josie wouldn't try something like this again.

She sat by Josie's side for hours, long after visiting hours were finished, long after her family left. She wanted to prove to her sister that she would always be there for her.

Josie didn't say much of anything while she was in the hospital. Nurse Cristina checked in on her multiple times a day, bringing contraband sodas, makeup, and candy for Josie to entertain herself with. Louise loved watching the nurse interact with her sister; they laughed and talked as if they were old friends.

And she realized that she missed having that relationship with her sister.

At night, Louise climbed into bed with Josie, wrapping her arms around her sister's little body. She hadn't realized how little Josie was until she saw her in the hospital bed. Even more, she looked frail. Her hair was stringy, her skin greasy. And she had never seen Josie be this unnervingly quiet.

Two nights after the incident, Louise was still thinking about what her father had told her about her mother. The thoughts only made her want to hold her sister closer. Everything could be put on pause, the case, her relationship.

She missed her mother, and now she was angrier at Janie than she ever had been. Louise knew that it was unfair to be angry at the person who was dead, but she had needed her mother.

"Hey, Sunshine?" Louise's voice cracked.

Josie rolled over so she was lying on her back. That was as much of a response as Louise was going to get. She did have to wonder what Josie was thinking about. Josie had always been a thinker; Celia had always been the talker. Celia talked enough for the two of them. Josie was still getting used to having to speak up.

"I'm gonna tell you something, but it's a secret."

"What?" Josie asked.

"I want to tell you this because I trust you."

"Tell me." Josie's voice hissed out into the quiet room around them.

Louise closed her eyes. She buried her nose in her sister's hair. If she could tell her sister this, she could feel better.

"You know why I never got married like Minna?"

"Because men don't like you."

"Yes, but more important, I don't like men."

She thought she was being overheard as she said it. The idea was ridiculous; it was past midnight and everyone else was asleep. There were nurses on the night shift; one passed by every forty minutes to make sure Josie didn't need anything.

Louise took a deep breath, closing her eyes and pulling Josie as close as she could. "I love women." Saying it out loud was facing something she never had before. She knew this about herself; she had recognized it early on. "I love Rosa Maria the way women are supposed to love men."

Josie turned to her. In the darkness of the room, her green eyes seemed electric bright. She curled into Louise's torso. "Why are you telling me this?"

Louise rested her chin on Josie's head. For a moment, they didn't say or do anything; their breathing fell into sync. The moonlight spilled into the room from the little window on the wall near the bed.

"Because I want you to know that whatever you choose to do, whoever you choose to be, I will not love you any less. Ever, Sunshine. I promise."

She could have been a better sister. She knew that. There were so many things she could have done better. But the past was the past, and she had to focus on the future.

Josie didn't say anything to this. Louise felt as if she had ripped out her own heart and laid it on the table.

But if Josie was surprised, she hid it well. "Why are you here, then?"

"I am spending time with my baby sister. I'm gonna move you in with me, okay? You don't need to be in that house anymore."

Josie exhaled, a long, deep breath with which all the air left her little body. Louise had never felt closer to her sister than she did now.

"You love her?"

What a loaded question. If only Josie knew. Louise closed her eyes and tried to get herself to relax. "Yeah, I do."

"Good."

That was her younger sister, nonjudgmental. Louise thought about when she had moved into Miss Brown's house, across from

Rosa Maria's room. She thought about how her heart had fluttered in her chest the moment they had met.

And now look at them.

"Louise, I don't wanna die." Josie's voice was so quiet, her lips didn't move.

It was strange, being awake when everyone else was asleep. Even the normal bustle of the city had dulled down to a small murmur of activity. Louise would usually be out at a club now, but she couldn't think of anyplace more important to be than here with Josie.

"I know, Sunshine."

"I don't want to be here anymore."

"Only a little longer." Louise was reminded that when the twins were children, they were champions at whining to get their way.

But now Josie just seemed scared, and Louise couldn't blame her.

This world was big and Josie was so small. There was no way Louise was going to be able to save her sister from everything horrible in the world.

Josie fell into a soft sleep, one in which she snored lightly, and her side rose up and down.

Louise was going to have to try to protect her from everything.

"WE NEED TO talk," Rosa Maria said.

Louise was pulling late nights at the hospital. By the time she got back to the apartment the next morning, Rosa Maria was awake, smoking and drinking coffee. Louise's dress was crinkled from sleeping in it. She could feel her breath and knew her hair was out of place. She was exhausted; the hospital bed really wasn't made for two people. She had been awarded a couple of strange looks on the route home. But she didn't care. *We need to talk* were the four words that set panic through her body. But she was too tired to defend herself. She didn't want to spend the day screaming at Rosa Maria.

"I don't want to fight." Louise closed her eyes.

"I don't want to fight either," Rosa Maria said.

Louise sank into the chair opposite Rosa Maria, pressing her cheek to the table. It was cold and she felt as if she could fall asleep right on the table, right there. She propped her chin on her fists and looked up at Rosa Maria. All at once, she swallowed her fear and doubts down. She got up and pressed her lips to Rosa Maria's, lingering for as long as she could.

"I love you," Louise said when she pulled away.

This was who they were. They had functioned for years without grand declarations of love. And they didn't need them anyway.

"You can never lie to me again."

"I won't." She meant it. She really, really meant it.

"You have a telegram. Looks official."

Louise picked it up. It was her police summons. She was due in two days at ten in the morning. She stared at the typed words. She didn't want to face Detective Martin.

She knew what this meant. She was falling behind. The police knew something she didn't know. She was going to be arrested. She had failed herself and Rosa Maria.

And she was convinced that someone was watching her.

She hadn't been able to think about the case in days. She hadn't been able to think about anything but Josie.

"You haven't seen anyone around the apartment, have you?" Louise got up and poured herself a cup of coffee. She took a long sip, and let the caffeine do its thing.

"No." Rosa Maria drew the word out as if she was unsure of something.

"What?"

"There was a call last night, and I picked up, but the person hung up."

Not suspicious on its own. The phone was one they shared on a party line. Their ring was two long, two short, and people very rarely called their apartment.

Louise flicked through the rest of the mail. It was mostly bills and rather persistent interview requests. One was from the *Tribune*. She felt she owed the writers at the *Tribune*. If she had been more careful, maybe Bernard Thomas would still be alive. She often thought of his widow, not enough to go visit but enough. She knew that she couldn't have seen his death coming, and yet she felt responsible for it. She had put the deaths of all of the Girl Killer victims on herself, and that was no way to live. She stared at the paper, a young writer begging for her story. She almost threw it out, but then put it back on the counter with the other letters for her. She didn't know why her address was public knowledge, and right now she wasn't grateful that it was.

The phone rang.

They both stopped and stared at it on its special little table near the door. Louise let it ring twice before she went to pick it up. She placed her hand on the receiver, then lifted it to her ear, clearing her throat.

"Hello?" A pause. She could hear heavy breathing on the other end. "Hello?" she said again.

"Guilty." The word was whispered; the voice was deep.

Louise felt her blood run cold before the voice continued.

"You, Louise Lloyd, are guilty."

The use of her name sent shivers down her spine. But she didn't respond. She didn't bite her tongue and didn't say anything.

"Louise Lloyd, you are going to hell."

She slammed the receiver down onto its cradle, breaking it. She and Rosa Maria would have to pay for that, but she didn't care. She placed a hand on her chest. Then she opened the door to see if anyone was there. There was no one. She didn't know why she thought someone would be standing there. But the hall was empty. She raced to the window that looked onto the street to see if she could spot anyone by the pay phones. There was no one near the phones. Louise exhaled and pulled the curtain shut.

"Who was it?"

"Wrong number."

"Louise."

"I'm certain it was a wrong number. It's not a lie."

But if that were true, how had the caller known her name? She wasn't going to think about it. She needed to not think about it. She needed to sleep. That was all this was, exhaustion. She closed her eyes and tried to take a couple of deep breaths to steady herself. All she wanted to do was rest, then go back to the hospital. It was funny how quickly her priorities had changed. Now what she cared about was being with her sister.

"Go get some sleep," Rosa Maria said softly. She was flicking through the newspaper.

Louise didn't want to know if there were any new mentions of herself or Rosa Maria in there.

Rosa Maria folded the paper back up. "You have too much on your mind."

Louise wrapped her arms around Rosa Maria's shoulders, kissing the crook of her neck. "You're right." She closed her eyes, smelling the other woman's perfume. It had been so long since they had been close, physically and emotionally.

But Louise had the sense that things were changing.

23

THE RADIO HAD gone staticky. Louise was lying on the couch, flipping through the *Negro Voice*, trying to listen to the radio. But the radio wasn't working. It was old, seven or so years at this point. She and Rosa Maria had bought it because it was cheap, and she knew how to deal with it. Louise often played the radio when she was home by herself. It was so much better than being alone with her thoughts. Louise got up and smacked the radio as hard as she could, a hollow noise sounding from within. She turned it off and turned it on again. The static continued. She squinted at it, knowing that her knowledge in fixing the thing was limited.

She flicked it on again. She looked toward the wall. Faint red letters still showed there, no matter how hard she scrubbed. And Louise had scrubbed until her fingers were raw and bleeding.

She was *guilty* and she knew it.

The radio still fussed. She thought she heard the serious voice of a newsman break through. Louise flicked the knob, changing the station. The static died down and she could hear what was being said.

"And in other news"—the voice was stunning and clear in its diction—"famed murderess Louise Lloyd is scheduled to hang later today. Miss Lloyd, as everyone knows, is the Detective Killer. She was convicted of the murder of former NYPD detective Theodore Gilbert—"

When Louise awoke, she was covered in a thin layer of sweat. She was lying on her bed, on her back, her heart beating. She had been dreaming. It was a dream. It wasn't real. Rosa Maria was lying next to her, snoring lightly. It was about two in the morning. After the Dove had closed, there was no reason to stay up to all hours.

Tea. Louise needed tea. She pulled herself from bed, wrapped her dressing gown around herself, and put water in the kettle. She and Rosa Maria weren't tea drinkers, but there was always a package or two in the cupboards to be offered to visitors. Louise pulled out a tea bag, put it in her cup.

She often thought about how things would have turned out had Detective Gilbert not been the man he was. And in spite of everything, he had been her mentor. She could picture him sitting across from her in his impeccable suit, waistcoat unbuttoned. He would look at her, discerning blue eyes trying to figure out what she knew.

"What do you know, Miss Lloyd?"

He would ask the question after taking a moment to light a cigarette. She could see it so clearly: him sitting at his desk in the little office, the summertime Harlem sun streaming through the window, all of it idyllic and lovely.

"I know that someone is trying to set me up, and I don't know why. Someone killed Nora to frame Rosa Maria to get back at me." Louise said the words out loud, although she was alone. "I know that someone wants to see me fall."

"Why?"

She had hated his constant questions, the needling, his drive and desire to get to the root of every problem. But that trait had made him ruthless and skilled in what he did. And she had to remember that that was murder.

"I don't know," Louise said. "I don't know."

That was the piece to the puzzle that she was missing. When she closed her eyes, she could see the case mapped out in front of her.

"But why?"

Why Nora? Why wait until everything had died down and everyone had moved on?

"You're smarter than this, Miss Lloyd." Imagination Gilbert leaned back in his chair, now eyeing her with derision. "I picked you for a reason."

"You picked me because I was a stand-in for something you couldn't have," Louise said.

"I picked you because you had potential, Miss Lloyd. You were supposed to be part of my legacy."

"Your legacy of death! Of course I didn't want that."

Imagination Gilbert narrowed his eyes, a frown on his face. "You and I are alike, Miss Lloyd. Two sides of the same coin. You'd do well to accept your fate."

"Louise!"

This voice was real. Rosa Maria was rushing from the bedroom to the kettle on the stove, where it was whistling away. Louise hadn't noticed. Rosa Maria swore in Spanish and moved the kettle from the heat.

"What are you doing? You're about to burn down the building!"

"Oh, I . . ." Louise couldn't formulate an answer. She blinked.

Was she living in a dreamworld? "I'm sorry. I guess I just got distracted."

"This isn't like you," Rosa Maria said. She used a tea towel to clean the spilled water. "What is going on?"

She wasn't about to admit that she was just having an imaginary conversation with the man she had shot. She blinked. "I don't know. Nothing. Go back to sleep. I'll handle it."

Rosa Maria exhaled, pinching the bridge of her nose. She was exhausted, as Louise was, with all of this. "Louise, you can't keep doing this."

"Just go back to bed."

The words were harsher than she had intended. Rosa Maria recoiled from her, but did as she was told, shutting the bedroom door behind her. They rarely closed that door. They liked to be able to see each other virtually all of the time. It made Louise feel safe.

Louise refilled the kettle to try again. She watched it this time, sitting at the table to do so. Now she didn't even want to drink anything; her stomach was as unsettled as her mind was.

She had an overactive imagination. That was all it was. She had scared herself; she was overthinking and overtired. She needed to get some sleep.

Louise turned off the kettle, poured the water into the sink. Instead of going back into the bedroom, she fell asleep on the couch, the lights on to dispel any ghosts.

"YOU KNOW, LOVIE, you may want to ease up on this." Rafael was lying on the couch, smoking a cigarette.

Rosa Maria was sitting at the kitchen table with her typewriter, not really paying attention. But she stopped typing long enough to add, "I agree."

Louise should be with Josie, Minna was already there, and yet she was so numb, so scared, she could hardly move.

And she had more pressing business.

Rafael sat up. It was strange seeing him without Eugene beside him. But Louise wouldn't have been able to take Eugene's sweet, stupid questions that morning.

"Lovie, are you ready?"

"I have to say that this is ridiculous."

Rosa Maria never stopped typing as she spoke. She was trying to reach some ridiculous, self-imposed deadline. Louise admired the fact that she was of two minds when she was writing and talking at the same time.

Rafael slid a look to his sister. "No one asked you."

Rosa Maria let out a string of curse words in Spanish. Rafael didn't give her the satisfaction of replying. He moved to sit on the floor across from Louise and lit a cigarette for her. She inhaled, letting the smoke calm her down. She had been a nervous wreck all morning.

And she had to concentrate.

"I can't ease up on this. It's my fault Nora's dead."

"How?"

This was a genuine question, one Louise couldn't really put an answer together for. She felt the guilt weighing on her body and mind until she was sure it was doing physical damage, but she couldn't say why.

"Everyone who's close to me dies."

"I'm still alive," the twins responded at the same time without missing a beat.

"I wouldn't be so sure you'll stay that way," Louise grumbled. She inhaled from her cigarette, feeling the smoke fill her body. "Nora would still be alive if she hadn't actively sought me out."

"That doesn't mean Nora's death is your fault," Rafael said.

"Besides, you're not on the hook for her murder." Rosa Maria kept typing.

She would not stop writing for love or money, Rosa Maria couldn't do anything but wait. And hope. Maybe that was the source of her writing anxieties.

This was getting to all of them. Louise knew it. Their fears were manifesting in different ways. Rafael could barely go a day without visiting the apartment, and Louise was scared that someone was going to get her. And maybe Nora's death wasn't really her fault, but she had to solve it.

That was on her.

"And it's not your club on the line."

"You can give up," Rosa Maria said.

Louise hated when Rafael and Rosa Maria agreed on something. It was rare, and it was annoying. They got the same smug tone of voice and the same haughty look on their faces.

And they seemed to agree on matters relating to Louise only when they were sure they were right.

Very annoying.

"Okay, Lovie. We need to concentrate."

Rafael turned Rosa Maria's and Louise's attention back to him. To be fair, he didn't have that much time this morning either. He had already told them that he and Schoonmaker had a series of important meetings that afternoon. He refused to say what they were about, but Louise knew they were for the Dove.

"I'll be straightforward," Rafael said.

This might have been unnecessary, but Louise had gotten Rafael to go over the questions Martin threw at him during his interrogation. She hoped Martin would be more gentle on her, but she couldn't be sure. She needed all the preparation she could get. She wasn't going to let Detective Martin get the better of her. She would destroy him if she got the chance. And she really wanted the chance. She knew where her friends stood on this: she should proceed with more caution than usual. But there was a part of her that wanted to throw caution to the wind. There was something she was missing and she wasn't sure what.

"He'll start with asking your name and occupation and where you were on the night of March fifth."

"Those are all things I can answer."

Louise exhaled, blowing smoke out as she did so. She squeezed one eye shut while she used the butt of her old cigarette to light a new one. She tapped her fingers on the floor below them.

"Very good. I'm very glad. It's going to get trickier once he starts asking about Nora," Rafael said. He gritted his teeth; his jaw tightened. "He's going to get a little tough with you."

She swallowed hard. "I can handle it."

"I know you can, but be careful. Do not do anything to rile him up."

Louise had heard that many times in her life. There were so many times when she had had to try to make herself more invisible, more inconspicuous for the egos of men, especially white men. She was not going to do that anymore. She didn't want to.

"I'm not going to do that. But I'm going to tell the truth."

They all shared a look. They knew the truth was a weak story. They hadn't stopped to discuss it, not really. What was there to discuss? All of them had been drugged.

She focused on tapping a little rhythm on the floor with her fingers. *Index, index, middle, ring, index, index, middle, ring.* That was soothing; concentrating on a pattern helped her focus.

"And when he doesn't believe me?" Louise asked.

Eugene's and Rafael's sessions had both gotten physical after Martin accused them of lying.

And the same thing would happen to her.

"Stand your ground." Rafael's eyes narrowed.

"And when that doesn't work?"

Rafael didn't have an answer for that.

Rosa Maria got up from the table and wrapped her arms around Louise. "You'll be fine, mi amor. Just tell the truth, and you'll be fine."

Louise wanted this to be true, but she just couldn't believe it.

She knew she was missing something right in front of her.

She owed it to Nora to figure it out.

HEAVEN ON EARTH wasn't a particularly good club. But Louise and Rosa Maria went anyway, if only to get their minds off the present. It was one of those clubs that didn't have anything special about them. It was a dime-a-dozen spot that had popped up in an effort to capitalize on the lawlessness of young adults and the rather profitable alcohol trade.

The tables were full. Louise and Rosa Maria clutched their glasses in the center of the dance floor. Louise had perfected the Charleston steps, while not spilling a drop from her glass, by the time she turned twenty. It was a skill she had found she would always need.

She missed this, and being there alone a couple nights ago hadn't been a replacement for dancing with the love of her life. They seemed fine now; they were on track to be better than ever.

They wore the dresses Louise had impulse bought, and although they weren't evening dresses, Louise thought they looked fashionable and unique.

And she didn't want to think about Nora. Or her impending police interview. She pushed all of that to one side to be addressed later.

She drained her glass, feeling the familiar shiver run up her spine as she did so. She'd have to get a refill. The bad thing about no tables was she was stuck clutching an empty glass.

It had been a very long time since she had graced the dance floor. Her body remembered the steps she had taken such care to learn. She was grateful for that.

Louise wondered, as the subpar band changed the song to a waltz and she took her leave, if this was a place Schoonmaker owned.

Now that she had met him, it felt as if he was everywhere. He owned *everything*. How could she not have known that?

Rosa Maria joined her at the bar. Her skin was dotted with sweat and she looked more beautiful than ever in the pale blue of her dress. Louise felt her heart skip as their arms touched. They had to be more careful now; they both knew that.

But no one in this shitty club was watching them. They could have kissed if they wanted.

They didn't but the thought was exciting enough to get them by. Louise paid. It stunk not owning the club or being at a club where Rafael tended bar. She had forgotten how expensive drinks were.

But they drained their glasses as a new, faster song started up.

It felt . . . normal. Strikingly normal. Really normal. This was what she had been doing before the Girl Killer murders, before her life had totally changed. She missed the old Louise, the dancer

Louise. The fun Louise. She had had to be serious for too long. She wanted to be young again. She missed the Zodiac. The Zodiac Club was the place where she had done all her growing up, where she had met Rafael and learned to dance. It was unfortunate that she had had to leave that part of her life behind. She didn't even like to pass the place where the building had been. It was ten months and the loss still hurt.

Was it silly to mourn a club? Yes. But she felt very justified in being silly.

She and Rosa Maria threw their arms up in an effortless and elaborate Charleston. They were able to clear the dance floor with their quick and synchronized moves. They were so close, Louise always knew what Rosa Maria would do next.

They complemented each other perfectly.

How could she throw this away for Harriet? The thought sank her good mood like a stone in a river. She had to talk to Harriet still, but that was something that could wait until tomorrow. She could forget about all that for one more night too. All she wanted to do was think about dancing, drinking, and Rosa Maria in her dress. Louise could see, at the right moments, the strip of flesh underneath Rosa Maria's garter strap, and that flash of skin drove Louise wild.

She was sufficiently drunk, floating on a cloud of alcohol. Everything seemed good now. Everything seemed rosy. Without throwing off her steps, she leaned over to Rosa Maria and yelled, "I'm so glad we're here."

It was up to them to create the fun everywhere they went.

And luckily that was a challenge they were up to.

They danced to every song. Fast songs, slow songs. They danced until Louise's body hurt and she could feel her shoes giving way. Her dress was covered in sweat, *she* was covered in sweat, and she hadn't felt this good in months. The band got better as the night went on, or maybe she just got drunker and looser. Even with multiple drinks, she was sure of her footing. She was certain that dancing was the only thing she was good at. And when Heaven on Earth closed, at two in the morning, Louise and Rosa Maria linked arms and hailed a taxi to take them back to their apartment. It was a perfect night. In the elevator, up to their door, it felt like they were floating on air.

Then Rosa Maria unlocked the door to 3I, and everything came crashing down.

The apartment had been broken into and totally trashed: windows broken, glass scattered on the floor, dishes smashed, the bedroom decimated. Louise kneeled at the wardrobe. Every last cent she had compulsively saved was gone. She didn't want to think about how much money she had lost. She turned on the lights, assessing everything in the apartment.

On the wall, above where the couch was, across from the door, was one word written in red paint:

MURDERER

24

THE PAPER CAME early, and neither of them had slept that night.

Rafael and Eugene brought it in when they arrived. It took Louise a moment to understand what she was staring at. It was the *Tribune*, and her name was in bold across the top of the current page. She stared at herself. She stared at herself and Rosa Maria, at photos she had seen before, photos she had stashed in a kitchen drawer. She didn't have to read the article to know what it was saying. Next to that was a picture of her and Harriet, taken surreptitiously from the front door of the club, the door of the cellar open and Louise totally exposed. Harriet's light hat was visible.

There was nothing she could do but stare. Her entire body stopped functioning. She felt her knees give out and she sank to the floor. She could feel the blood running through her body; she could feel herself start to shake. But she couldn't say anything.

This was only the start. She knew that. It was already noon and any chance she had of controlling the rumor, controlling her own story, was already gone. She couldn't do anything. "Rosa Maria." Instantaneously, she regretted everything she had ever done. Rosa Maria was in this position—*they* were in this position—because of her. Rosa Maria wouldn't look at her. She was crying noiselessly. "I am so sorry."

Louise wished they weren't doing this in front of Rafael and his dim-bulb boyfriend.

But beggars couldn't be choosers.

Louise stood, clearing her throat. She didn't want to think about what would happen to them. She didn't want to think about how everyone would know, how her and Rosa Maria's lives would change from this moment on. She stepped toward Rosa Maria.

Rosa Maria took a step away from her. "I'm staying with Rafael until . . ."

"I am so sorry," Louise said again.

She couldn't think of anything else to say. She could barely think at all. The only thing she could really feel was the anger that was pulsating through her body. Years and years of being careful, of being discreet, had led to this.

"I didn't want any of this. I didn't mean any of this."

"Lovie." This was Rafael. "Eugene's gonna help Rosa Maria pack, okay?" He was speaking in a calm voice, one he would use interchangeably on angry children and guests who had drunk too much.

She couldn't argue. There was no way in the world for her to argue. She nodded numbly and let Rafael lead her to the couch, where they sat side by side. He didn't say anything. Rosa Maria closed the door behind her and Eugene.

Louise stared at the photos of herself in the paper. She pinched herself, trying to determine if this was a dream. She started to read the companion article, then stopped. She didn't need to read the slurs and insults that were being hurled at her. She closed her eyes, wishing everything in the world could stop.

"Lovie." It was minutes of staring at a closed door before Rafael attempted to speak. She had never seen him at a loss for words, but now he opened and closed his mouth three times before ultimately not saying anything.

"I didn't mean this. I didn't want this. Who would do this?" Louise asked.

Rafael put an arm around her, pulling her close. She blinked dully in the ether.

"Louise, you have to pull yourself together."

It wasn't that long ago that they were eighteen, going to the Zodiac, dancing the night away before sneaking back home. It was easy to feel indestructible, especially if they knew a good Charleston. She wanted those days back. How was it possible that time had passed so quickly?

"I . . . I can't. I'm done. I can't do this anymore."

Louise exhaled and leaned into Rafael. She was tired of pretending *not* to be tired. She had been through the wringer in the last year. If anyone deserved a break, it was her.

"You don't mean that, Louise."

"Yes, I do." She pulled herself away, sat up straight. "If I keep doing this, then everyone I love is in danger. I should have known that. I should have been smarter."

After Celia, Louise had to be wiser about protecting the people she loved.

But she hadn't been, and now she had to pay the price.

"You can't blame yourself." Rafael was keeping his voice soft and calm.

"But who else can I blame? I seek danger. I seek it out for what? For this? How would you feel? What would you do?"

He didn't say anything. Louise got up and poured herself a drink. She drained it in one large gulp. She exhaled and poured another glassful. She closed her eyes against the burn of the illegal alcohol.

"I did this." What a terrible realization. She hadn't even been that careful. She had kissed Harriet, although her face wasn't visible in the photo.

And Louise's world would be different. She mourned yesterday, when none of this had happened yet. Sitting in the Gold Room having the time of her life. And she wanted it back.

"I would be angry," Rafael said.

"Of course you would," Louise said. "I can't be seen with you. In case people find out." She had never been a very public person and this was the worst thing that could have happened.

She crossed her arms as Rosa Maria emerged, Eugene behind her carrying two large suitcases. Rosa Maria didn't look at her. Louise stepped toward her.

Rosa Maria stepped back and said, "I did love you, you know."

SITTING ON THIS side of the table was peculiar. There was no other way to describe it. Detective Martin was standing across from her, his sleeves rolled up to the elbows, his wide, flat hands on the table. She knew he was trying to intimidate her.

She had already decided she wasn't going to let him.

Louise focused on lighting a cigarette, getting the match lit before lifting it to the cigarette between her lips. She made sure that every move was decisive and confident, although she could feel herself shake like a leaf in the wind. It was hard to try to be cool when she wanted to scream out of fear. She hated this little room. It dawned on her that this was the spot where Bernard

Thomas had been sitting when she unknowingly gave him poisoned tea.

"Drop the act, Lloyd." Martin's voice was an angry hiss.

"What act?" She raised an eyebrow. This was going against how she was raised. The Lloyd girls were raised to be polite to everyone. She tilted her head up, looking directly into Martin's eyes.

"This *bullshit*."

It was hard to imagine that they had once worked together. She watched as his scowl relaxed.

"What?" she asked again. She was toeing the line and she knew it. She removed her cigarette from her lips and exhaled as much as she could as slowly as she could.

She had known this was coming. Only a fool couldn't have seen it. She had been called into the station, formally, for an interview at ten a.m. It was now ten thirty-five and they hadn't done much but stare at each other in contempt. She was all bravado, and she knew it.

"Where were you the night of March fifth?" Martin asked.

"I was celebrating my birthday with my friends."

"Where?"

"The Dove Nightclub."

She hated saying it. She knew he already knew about the club; he had arrested her there. But it was sacrilegious to mention the club when she knew it was against the law.

Not that she cared much.

"And the club closed around . . . ?"

She could tell he was restraining himself. There was no part of her that wanted to answer these questions. There was no part of her that thought this would help.

"Three in the morning. Some friends and I stayed in and we spent time talking after we closed."

"And at what time did Rosa Maria Moreno murder Nora Davies?"

"She didn't." The answer tripped on her tongue. She stuttered over it. "She never would."

He paused. About sixty-five percent of these interrogations were dramatic flares. Martin pulled out his notebook and flicked through a couple of pages until he settled on one. "Fox Schoonmaker says that you all were fighting in the early hours of March sixth."

"That doesn't mean Rosa Maria killed anyone."

Fox. Fox Schoonmaker. What a ridiculous and pretentious name. If Louise had merely suspected that Schoonmaker wasn't who he said he was, it was all but confirmed now.

"That doesn't mean anything. People fight."

She was managing to stay calm and cool but her nerves were running her ragged.

Martin looked her over, the lids of his eyes flickering as he did so. In the months since they had worked together, he had gotten bigger, broader. She could tell he was stronger. He could, if he wanted, strangle her until the breath stopped in her body.

"You two are close, aren't you?"

She didn't like the way he said "close." She kept eye contact, but didn't respond. She didn't want to give him anything.

"I know Rosa Maria told you. Just tell me what she told you."

He lowered his voice so he had to lean in close. His mouth was near her ear and she shivered, feeling the hairs on her arms and neck rise in protest.

Louise swallowed hard. She focused on staring straight ahead. "I can't remember the night."

He slammed a hand on the table and Louise bit the inside of her cheek so she wouldn't cry out.

"Bullshit! You all are hiding something. Whose idea was it to kill Nora? Was it yours, Miss Lloyd?"

"I would never—"

The sentence was halfway out of her mouth when Martin laughed in response. "Are you forgetting that you have killed before, Miss Lloyd?"

He said her name with so much ire, she didn't look at him. She trained her sight on the closed door in front of her. She refused to look anywhere else.

"I had to kill him."

"You wanted to."

He was echoing the thoughts that had plagued her for months. Was there a part of her that had wanted to pull the trigger? Wanted to get revenge for every girl that man had killed?

And if so, why wouldn't she admit it to herself?

"No, I had to. You know what he was."

"What about Nora? Did you have to kill her too?"

Louise drew in a breath, trying to keep herself calm. "I didn't kill her. My friends didn't kill her."

He narrowed his eyes, leaned on the table. "I'd be so careful if I were you, Miss Lloyd. You're treading on thin ice. I always knew there was something off about you."

She had never seen Martin so smug and sure in his belief that he was better than her based on arbitrary traits like his white skin and his penis.

Louise was not in the mood to play these games with him. He wanted to get inside of her head and she was not going to let him. She raised an eyebrow, keeping eye contact. She was tired of these men.

He placed the newspaper in front of her. She didn't look at the photographs printed inside. She kept her eyes on Martin's face.

"What do you think about this?"

"Nothing." Louise's heart pounded in her chest. "I think nothing about it." She tried to keep her breathing steady, tried not to betray her true emotions.

"Do I have to explain these photos to you?" Martin asked.

She certainly would have liked to see him try.

"I think you're blowing all of this out of proportion. This isn't evidence of anything."

She had to be careful how she chose her words. If she said the wrong thing, she would be shipped off to jail or worse. She had to protect what was left of her reputation. She crossed her arms over her chest.

"I don't need to spell it out for you, do I?"

"No, and you can't hold me on anything. I would like to leave." She wouldn't have put it past Martin to do all of this to keep her from the case.

"You're not going anywhere yet, Miss Lloyd."

His tone was cold and measured. He fell into silence as he glared at the newspaper in front of him. She stared straight ahead, still and quiet. She wasn't going to let him bait her into anything. She knew this was all part of an act; he was going to be silent to goad her into talking. She knew better. She was not going to let him win. Louise waited, trying to turn his game on him.

"I always knew." His words were quiet and thoughtful when he spoke again. "What type of woman wouldn't want to fulfill the duty she was put on this earth for? What woman would frequent those dens of sin, live with other women, wasting the best years you could have as a wife and a mother?"

Louise gritted her teeth, not buying into it. "I hope you know the world has changed," she said. "It doesn't make me ill or stupid not to want to be a mother."

It was rich of him to be talking. It wasn't so long ago that Martin had been in a serious relationship with one of her former housemates while conducting an affair with a sixteen-year-old girl. He didn't realize the hypocrisy coming from his mouth.

"Did you kill Nora?" Martin asked.

The way he asked the question, so casually, nearly made Louise snap. She had to hold on to her anger. She knew that her temper was her least attractive trait, but she could still use it.

"Were you having some type of disgusting affair with her and killed her when it went wrong?"

"I would never do that," Louise said.

"Did you owe her money?"

"I didn't even know her," Louise said. "I want to leave. Now."

She put as much venom in her voice as she could muster. Martin raised an eyebrow. He knew he couldn't keep her, not on some photographs in a paper.

"Fine. But I can't release you on your own."

"What do you mean by that?"

Perfect timing. There was a knock on the door, and when the detective opened it, her father was standing there. Martin smiled, cool and collected. "You're free to go, Miss Lloyd."

25

FOR A MOMENT, when Louise woke up, she thought she had been in a horrible nightmare. But then she opened her eyes, realized that she was in her childhood bedroom with her father down the hall.

This was worse than a nightmare.

She dressed in the dress she had worn the day before, the only thing she had with her. She had a headache. Being released into her father's custody meant that when they arrived home, he had yelled at her for hours. He had threatened to have her committed.

She wished he would. An asylum would be an awful place to live but it would be an end to this torment. It was funny how he still had so much power over her. Louise sat on her bed. The door was closed, but she could hear her aunt singing church songs from the kitchen. Her father would be in his office. She knew this routine like the back of her hand.

Louise blinked twice and pulled her curtains back from the window. It was midmorning, and the sun was washing over the street. She considered climbing out of the window, but then she realized she was twenty-seven years old. She had a right to use the front door and leave.

Besides, she had a job to do.

Louise wasn't lucky. Her father was waiting for her when she opened the door. He moved before she could anticipate it. He struck her across the face, almost knocking her to the floor.

"Get back in there." His voice was full of ice.

Louise did what she was told without thinking about it. She had been raised to obey every command.

Louise sat back down on her bed, the bed that had very recently belonged to Celia. She watched as her father looked around the little room. She realized now that the silence was being used as a power move, used to intimidate her.

"My life is none of your business."

"I made so many mistakes with you. You're stubborn and ornery. You have no sense of decorum. And now . . . this."

He wasn't yelling. Louise was grateful for that.

"You are a mistake, Louise. I want you to know that. When I got the phone call telling me where you were? What people are saying about you? I am ashamed you are my daughter."

The words were worse than a slap. She had complicated thoughts about her family, her father in particular, but she wanted him to be proud of her. She wanted him to love her and she was worried that that feeling would never go away, no matter how old she got. Louise couldn't let herself look at him. She kept her gaze fixed on the wall.

"What would your mother say?"

"I hope she'd be proud of me, despite everything. She actually wanted me. You just wanted someone to continue your legacy."

"Your mother would agree with me." Venom hissed from his voice, causing Louise to physically recoil. "You have strayed from the light of God. I wanted a daughter who would behave, and look what I got instead."

Louise's stomach turned. She knew he was glaring at her; the hairs on her bare arms rose.

"You are going to stay here until I figure out what to do with you."

Her father slammed the door with such force that the window-pane quaked in its frame. This was all part of Martin's plan. She had to hand it to the detective; it had been a smart move calling her father.

Louise lay down on the floor, on her stomach, reaching under her bed. She had a sparse few possessions still in this house and they were hidden there: old lipsticks, a couple of coins, scraps of paper with her faded writing, and a bottle of perfume that had long since soured.

Celia had mixed in some of her own possessions: cigarette stubs with red lipstick, little love letters, and the writings of a sixteen-year-old girl. Louise felt a pang wash over her. This was so typical of her sister and it made Louise miss her even more.

She was aware that she could kiss her life good-bye. There'd be no saving Josie, no moving her into the apartment. Louise shifted so she was lying on her back, staring up at the ceiling. She could hear her aunt and father having a conversation, obviously about her, in curt tones. There was nowhere to hide in this brownstone. There was nowhere she could go.

Louise craved a cigarette and a stiff drink. She let her eyes close, blinking slowly. She had never thought she would be here again. She lay on the floor, counting as seconds drifted by, transforming a beautiful morning to a lovely afternoon, to a rather brisk evening. She was starving, but couldn't bring herself to leave her bedroom.

What would he do with her?

The door opened again and Louise sat up. Her aunt Louise looked down at her, a firm frown on her lips.

"Dinner. You will join us. You will not complain."

Louise stood up. She followed her aunt to the dinner table, where they all sat in silence.

THE LETTERS BEGAN at midnight. Midnight, when Louise was the only person in the brownstone who was awake. She thought she heard the metallic flick of the mail slot. When she convinced herself to get out of bed and walk to the parlor, she saw the envelope on the floor. It bore her name. She picked it up and opened the door. The streets were bathed in the pale light of the streetlamps. The air was stiff and chilly. There was no one out of place. Flappers and their boys clicked over the pavement in defiance of the cold. Gangsters' molls linked arms and strode down the street, their heads raised high as if they owned all of Harlem.

Louise needed a plan. She wrapped herself in her coat over her nightdress, shoved a hat on her head, and used the closest pay phone, a block away, to call Rafael.

She was going to need some help.

They spent a few minutes on the phone and Louise crawled back into bed. She had asked if Rafael could get Josie and keep her safe just in case, just until she got out. She had asked about Rosa Maria. She had made sure her friends were safe.

When she opened the door again, there was another letter waiting for her, addressed with her name in thin, slanted writing. A chill ran down her spine. The pay phone wasn't far from the house. She didn't see who had left it.

She threw both envelopes out.

When she woke up after hours that had passed like minutes, the sun low in the sky and her mouth dry and her throat parched, there was a little pile of letters at the door.

She threw them out.

They continued appearing every hour, materializing on the rug in front of the door until they stopped. Louise was sure to time it. When an hour passed, then another, with no new envelope, she was certain it was over.

She was never someone who was able to leave well enough alone. Louise rescued the crumpled paper from the waste bin. Thirty-nine envelopes in total, thirty-nine rhythmic thumps of a new envelope falling into its place.

Louise had watched for a couple of hours, camera posed at the ready to photograph whoever it might be. But she never saw the same person twice, lost in the throngs of people that passed by the door.

They attended church. Louise was made to sit in the front, next to her aunt and heavily pregnant second sister. Josie was still in the hospital. Minna made no mention of the photographs and didn't talk to her at all. Louise's cheeks were still burning with the embarrassment. She was counting down the minutes until she figured out a plan to leave.

Until then she had this.

Each envelope contained one letter. It took her a minute to figure out the correct order, and she lined each perfect square of paper—like an invitation to tea or luncheon that should have been sprayed with sweet perfume—up like a little soldier on the floor.

L O U I S E L L O Y D I S A M U R D E R E R
A N D I M C O M I N G F O R Y O U

The girlie writing did nothing to detract from the message. Who could've known where she was?

Louise's heart began to race. She looked around, fear inching its way up her skin. Who was watching her? Who would know?

At church, she had prayed, the old familiar routines coming back to her like an old friend. She had prayed for herself, for hope. For a way forward in a life she wasn't sure about.

Louise stared at the words in front of her now, unforgiving and angry. Anger clenched her lungs until she couldn't breathe. How could she explain it again?

She didn't have a choice.

Ultimately, she knew that it didn't matter what she said or how she tried to stand up for herself. There would always be someone speaking out over her, changing her story, and the changed version would be what was believed.

She looked at the square pieces of paper lying on the scuffed wood floor, taunting her.

She cleared her throat, breaking the tight and solid silence around her. She wasn't used to silence like this and it was uncomfortable. Louise cleaned the papers up, stacking them neatly and placing them in the box of her belongings.

She knew a couple of things. The first was that she had to get out of there, and the second was that she wasn't safe anywhere.

26

THE NOISES BEGAN shortly after the letters stopped. A fourteen-hour period of pure bliss, then the tapping, seeming as if it came from all sides. Louise was lying in the child-size bed she once shared with Josie and it felt as if the noises were right in her brain. She climbed up to the window. Louise had to stand on the bed to look out, and there was no one there.

Was she imagining it?

She didn't get much sleep that night. If she kept her eyes open or closed, she could hear it, a tapping at perfect two-second intervals.

By the time the sun had risen, Louise had decided she'd had enough. Her father spent the hours during and just after breakfast in his office. She opened the door and entered without knocking.

"You have to exit and knock to enter." Her father didn't raise his eyes from his papers as he spoke to her.

"Bullshit." Louise sat down and crossed her arms. She needed information and she was tired of playing his game.

"You know that language is inappropriate." He looked up at her with a frown.

"We need to talk about the week I was kidnapped," Louise said.

Her father stacked his papers in a neat pile on his desk, methodically and painstakingly slowly. "Why do you always want to talk about that?" His voice dripped with condescension.

She didn't know why he had to ask like that. She didn't know how to say it was still haunting her every time she closed her eyes.

Louise cleared her throat. She didn't even know what she wanted from him. She vividly remembered sitting in this exact chair, being told her mother had passed.

"I want to go through everything you have on me."

Like during the previous summer, her past was the key to figuring out this case. She was sure her father had more information on her in his files.

He paused at that. She raised an eyebrow. Louise had knocked him off guard. Her father was so in control, always three steps ahead, that this felt like a victory to her.

"Your private files. I know you have things on me and my sisters. I want it all."

"Do you really want to know? Know what I think of you? Know every way you've failed me and your family?"

She swallowed hard. She didn't want to know, but she nodded her head anyway. "I do."

Her life, in her father's eyes, filled one box. She took this box, marked only with her initials, and sat on the floor of her bedroom with it.

Did she really want to open it?

AT AROUND EIGHT in the evening, after Louise and her family had eaten dinner in tense silence, there was a knock on the door.

Louise was in the sitting room, listening to her aunt read Bible verses. Her father answered the door. She started when she heard him call her name.

At the door was a young Black man, younger than her. He had a smiling boyish face and his brown eyes were wide and twinkling in the evening sun. "Darling," he said, stretching out his arms to embrace her. Louise leaned in to kiss him on the cheek. "Play along. Rafael sent me." The words were whispered so fast, Louise almost missed them.

"Where have you been?" Louise asked. "I've been waiting. Father, Aunt Louise, this is my fiancé." She couldn't say the word with a straight face.

The stranger extended a hand and smiled a winning smile. "Michael Wallace, sir. It's lovely to meet you. Lovie here has told me all about you. I'm sure this is all a mistake." Michael talked so confidently that Louise almost believed him.

"Michael and I are busy setting up a life together," Louise said. She tried to be demure, tried to believe this lie so, in turn, her father would believe it as well.

"Why have you never mentioned him?" Joseph asked.

Louise cleared her throat.

"I've been working up my courage to talk to you, man to man, for Louise's hand in marriage." Michael was a convincing actor.

They were all standing in the front hallway, discussing Louise's intentions with this stranger. Her heart pounded. Trust Rafael to help her in the most dramatic way possible. But she had asked for help and she did trust him.

And if this worked, she would be in his debt for a very long time.

Michael stopped smiling, his face now all still. "Louise, go get your things. Mr. Lloyd, I would like to talk to you in private," he said in such a serious way that it made everyone obey him.

She retreated to her bedroom to wait. She hated the fact that her freedom had to be debated between men. She hated the fact that her father would probably believe this because he wanted to.

But if it worked, it worked.

She thought about Rosa Maria. This was all for her. All for them. Sure, there had been a misstep or two, but she had to keep her focus on the prize.

Once this was all over with, she could, if she wanted, resume her normal life. She thought about the tickets to Paris she had bought, purchased before her apartment had been robbed. They were the only valuable things that had not been taken when 3I was ransacked. She had nothing to pack; all she could do was wait.

Time slowed to a crawl. She sat on the floor cross-legged and waited. She was impatient with being a woman in this world. How was it legal or fair that she couldn't love another woman but her fate could be decided by two men over brandy and cigars?

Not that her father smoked cigars or drank brandy. It was the principle of the matter. She was twenty-seven years old and was still being treated like she was six. She felt as if she would never be free, never be able to live the life she wanted, if she was stuck in Harlem.

There was a knock on the door. Michael was there, grinning. "Let's go, Lovie."

THE MOMENT SHE was out of the house, Louise took a deep breath of fresh air, letting her whole body reset. Except for church, she hadn't been outside since her first night at her father's house.

Louise had almost forgotten how liberating it could be. She clutched her purse and her box and walked alongside this perfect stranger.

"Your father was very angry about those photographs."

"What did you tell him?" Louise asked.

Michael's smile was unreadable. "I told him they weren't real. All faked to destroy your reputation."

"And he believed you?"

"You're here, aren't you?"

Louise fell silent for a moment, unsure of what to say. She knew what she needed to do next. "I need to make sure my sister is okay."

"She's with Rafael. She's fine," Michael said.

"Who are you?" Louise asked the question she had wanted to ask for an hour now.

"I'm Mr. Schoonmaker's associate. He and Rafael came up with this plan. I was just the actor. Mr. Schoonmaker doesn't believe it's safe for you at your apartment. He would like to extend to you and your sister an invitation to stay with him until this is all sorted out."

Louise stopped walking, forcing Michael to break his stride. "Are you serious?"

"As a gunshot." He faced her and raised an eyebrow. He made a show of pulling out his pocket watch and checking the time.

She shifted the box in her arms; it was an awkward size and weight, which made it difficult to carry. He took it from her. She felt stiffness shoot down her arms.

"Why?"

"Mr. Schoonmaker is concerned for your safety, and I have to say, Miss Lloyd, I am too." He was so serious, he seemed older than she'd thought he was.

"Oh."

"I'm to take you to your apartment so you can pack. Miss Josie is already waiting." He reported all of this quickly, as if they didn't have time to waste.

Louise knew that time was ticking, and yet she was standing in the middle of the street, trying to process everything that was going on.

Louise raised an eyebrow. "Why would Schoonmaker do this?"

"Mr. Schoonmaker is an especially kind soul" was his only reply.

She would never be able to figure that man out. "We should keep moving, then."

There was a sinking feeling in her stomach. Her heart pattered. She looked around to make sure they weren't being watched as they moved as fast as they could down the street. They kept a quick pace, easily weaving their way around the people strolling along.

She was sure that this was only going to get worse.

27

SCHOONMAKER WAS QUICK to tell Louise that he did not live in a mansion. On the outskirts of New York City, with ten bedrooms and eight bathrooms, it felt like a mansion to her. Everything about it screamed new money, from the untarnished silverware to the slick mahogany of his furniture, all brand-new and unscratched. She and Schoonmaker sat across from each other in the rather lavish dining room. The table was grand and made for twelve.

Michael was helping Josie get settled. All Louise wanted was for Josie to be happy. She lit a cigarette and refused to eat, facing the man who had helped her.

"Are you sure you don't want anything? I've sent Anna home but I can whip something up."

"You've been so nice to me already. I don't need anything," Louise said.

It was her gut instinct not to trust someone who was nice to her. It always meant they wanted something. He had poured them both glasses of his special line of bootleg vodka; she immediately poured Coke into her glass. He didn't say anything to that, although she was sure he took it as an insult.

"Why are you so nice to me?" Louise asked.

"You're Rafael's friend. I protect my friends' friends."

"But why?" She couldn't get her head around it.

He raised an index finger to his slightly pursed lips as if he were thinking deeply about a very complicated subject. "That's what you do. Friends support each other."

Louise narrowed her eyes. In the short time since he had wormed his way into her life, he had been sort of supportive in his own way. "What do you want from me?"

"I want nothing from you." He winked. "This big house gets lonely sometimes."

That couldn't be it. She knew there had to be another reason, but she let the matter drop. "Well, thank you for taking me and my sister in." She sipped from her glass and inhaled from her cigarette.

Schoonmaker smiled. He relaxed into his seat. "You two are free to stay here for however long you need to. Please, put Anna through her paces. I'm sure she gets bored of my requests."

"You'll have to tell Josie that. The girl has an imagination." Louise leaned forward, pressing her elbows into the table.

Schoonmaker laughed. "I bet she does."

The two fell silent. Exhaustion hit Louise like a baseball bat to her ribs. She realized she hadn't really slept in three days. The days were all starting to blend together, and now she was so close to a bed. She could feel that she was collapsing into herself.

"I know you want to know what my story is," Schoonmaker said.

Of course she wanted to know the story behind Fox Schoonmaker, the Club King of Manhattan. She knew none of what he presented to the world could be real.

"Franklin Smith." He lifted his glass and smoothly dropped the New York accent he spoke with. Louise had been right: his speech had an unmistakable New Jersey twang. "I'm the first of six kids. Ma was poor. Dad was gone. I wanted to make something of myself, so I made myself into this."

Louise raised an eyebrow. "And you chose the name Fox Schoonmaker?"

He laughed. He seemed like a genuine person, someone real, now that she was learning about his roots.

"Seemed like a good idea at the time. I was twenty years old. I'm sure you did some things you regret."

He took a sip from his glass and he leaned on the table. Although she was sure that he was a decade and a half older than her, he had this air of mischievousness around him.

"I don't regret much in my life, but I do regret that name. I wanted to make something of myself and help my ma."

She had been thinking of Schoonmaker as a caricature instead of a real person, always ready with a stiff drink and a quick laugh. But now she could see the grooves in his face; he was finally showing his age.

"I think you and I have more in common than you want to admit, Lovie."

Louise rolled her eyes, but she could see it, if she thought about it.

"But do me a favor?" When he spoke again, Schoonmaker readopted the slick city accent Louise was accustomed to hearing him speak with. "Don't tell Rafael. He thinks Fox Schoonmaker is a real person."

Louise laughed and raised her glass. "Your secret is safe with me."

EVEN THOUGH THEY could have had separate rooms, Louise crawled in with Josie. The room the younger Lloyd sister had chosen was large, with a bed bigger than Louise had ever been in. Even knowing that Schoonmaker had made all this himself, that he had come from the same depths of impoverished life she had, she felt a stab of jealousy.

"How are you, Sunshine?" Louise asked gently.

Josie was still awake, lying on her back. "I think I'm going to be okay." The whispered reply came a minute after Louise's question.

Louise wrapped an arm around her sister, pulling her close. She needed to feel the quiet beat of her sister's heart.

The sisters didn't say much, or anything at all. It was going on two in the morning, and Louise was so tired. In her old life, her wild life, she'd have been out with Rafael and Rosa Maria, trying to conquer the world between glasses of gin and hastily smoked cigarettes. It had been so easy to feel like they were invincible.

Now she was old and tired.

"I'm sorry everything happened," Louise said.

She felt Josie turn on her side, burying her face in Louise's chest. Louise pulled her closer.

"I wanted to be there when you got out of the hospital."

"Rafael promised to teach me how to tell the future. It wasn't all bad."

"I'm glad you had fun."

Louise closed her eyes. Even with her pressing exhaustion and the fact that she knew she had a headache coming on, she couldn't sleep. What if something happened to her or Josie while they were lying in this bed? She supposed she was safe. Schoonmaker had had them change cars three times to make sure no one was following them.

But she couldn't be *sure.*

And if she couldn't be sure, she wouldn't sleep.

She made sure Josie was asleep, then slid on her dressing gown and shoes. She pulled the dressing gown close to herself, keeping the late-night or early-morning chill off of her skin. The house around her was silent; Schoonmaker had retired when she had. His private quarters comprised the third floor of the house. The dining room led out onto a backyard with a pool. She opened the door and stepped out, feeling the cool air break through the thin cloth of her dressing gown. Louise took a deep breath. It was still too early for the sun to rise. She sat on the stone steps, breathing in gulps of fresh air. She'd have to reset. Go over everything she knew again.

Nora had been murdered and the murderer was still out there somewhere. Watching her, waiting for a moment to strike.

Even if she was safe out here for now where the houses were bigger than anything she could ever have imagined, she didn't know how long that would last. It was a clever little ploy, getting her into her father's house. She knew that she had not outrun the rumors and stories about her.

Her name would still be in the paper. Her name would still be whispered through the streets of Harlem. She didn't think it was Martin. She didn't think he would put the time in.

No, the letters, the photographs, the phone calls, the writing on her apartment wall. This was a personal attack. This wasn't about Rosa Maria.

This was about her, and she knew it.

She swallowed hard. This was worse. Nora's death wasn't anything she had done. Nora had been a pawn in a game Louise didn't even know she was playing. There was something horrific about that. For all her faults, Nora had seemed like she was a good person. A kind person. And she had died because of Louise.

The count of people who had died because of her was going up. She was unsure how to settle with that.

Louise supposed that if she were going to do this to someone, she would have to stay close to her.

But who had come into her life around the time of Nora's murder?

Was it Schoonmaker? Had she walked herself and her sister into a trap? He was so kind to her, especially when he didn't have to be.

What about Harriet? Louise wished she had a cigarette; her pack and book of matches were upstairs in the bedroom.

She didn't know much about Harriet; the woman had shown up in her life in a cloud of mystery, a savior she had traded a favor for.

And Louise realized, as the cool early-morning wind brushed her face, that Harriet had all this information on her and she knew nothing about Harriet. Louise had done all the talking. Harriet had done all the writing. They had sat at the counter of the drugstore, Louise letting her story out to a woman she didn't know. She had been so grateful for the help, so happy to help, that she hadn't thought twice about it.

How could she have been so stupid?

It was so quiet here compared to Harlem. She was used to waking up to car horns and the other raucous sounds of the city. But here it was so still she could hear the chirping and swishing of insects in the grass before her. It was so quiet that she could hear the sound of her own heartbeat echoing loudly around her. It was very unnerving. The sky was the navy blue of the middle of the night. Louise had seen this color of the sky only on her way home from the Zodiac, and that felt like it was a lifetime ago. She could remember the seedy feel of the Zodiac, the way the music always blared, fast and loud. She missed that place, the one where she had grown up. It was a small loss in her life, but she felt it deeply.

Louise pulled herself up from her spot, reentered the house, and closed the door behind her. She was going to get some sleep.

It was really what she needed.

28

HOW DO YOU do it?"

Louise leaned back in her chair. It was breakfast time, and she knew that Schoonmaker was not a fan of talking to anyone except Anna until the clock ticked passed noon. Anna was from Germany and spoke with a thick accent. She was thirty and had been with Schoonmaker for years. She wore her dirty blond hair in a tight bun. Everything about her was strict.

Nevertheless, he was sitting across from her at the end of the table, slumped over a cup of coffee and some toast.

"What?" Schoonmaker asked.

She thought she had to raise her voice to have a conversation with him. She still wasn't used to the expanse of the slick mahogany table. She was sure that this table had it out for her, making her feel smaller than her five foot two.

"How do you do it? Or did? How did you fool people into thinking Fox Schoonmaker existed?"

The sun shone into the dining room. From there, Louise could see Michael and Josie sitting close to each other, having breakfast in the backyard, locked in a private conversation.

Schoonmaker loved to talk about himself. Louise had been in his house for less than twenty-four hours and this was the most important thing she had learned about him in this time.

He leaned back in his chair with the air of a distinguished teacher, someone whose opinion was respected. "I am so glad you asked, Lovie."

From the kitchen, she could hear Anna humming along with the radio. There was a certain sense of homeyness in the Schoonmaker manse. Louise realized that she wasn't different in this house, that she somehow belonged.

Schoonmaker took a sip from his coffee. He was always one for the dramatic. "There's really only one thing I can tell you: you have to believe the story you're telling, or you're gonna be caught so fast. And every mob man I've met hates being lied to."

"Illuminating. How did you *do* it?"

She wasn't going to stop until she got a satisfactory answer. She wondered what it would be like to essentially make yourself a new person. Schoonmaker had moved from New Jersey, dumping his humble farm origins for a man who was almost as rich as God. Louise often thought that if she had the chance to start over, really and truly start over, she would take it. She had spent so long being watched and scrutinized that she wanted the sweet release of anonymity. She wanted to be unknown. More than anything else, she wanted to be someone new. Louise had been thinking about Franklin Smith, who Schoonmaker had been. Was it easy to divide yourself into parts? Weren't there things in his old life that he missed? What about his mother and siblings?

Schoonmaker closed his eyes. Despite his height and his long limbs, he moved with a catlike grace that Louise was almost envious of. In the early-morning light, she could see that his face showed signs of his age that none of the rest of him did.

"You gotta commit to the story early." He raised his coffee cup to his lips again, this time without opening his eyes. "You have to figure out what you want and why you're doing it."

"What did you want?"

He lazily opened one brown eye, looking directly at her with a sardonic half smile. "To be rich." He closed his eye again. "To be clear, when I was your age or younger, I wasn't a good person. I did everything I could to make a quick buck."

He didn't elaborate and Louise wondered what he could have done that was so horrible.

"I did things I regret. But it got me all this, so it can't be all bad, huh?"

"Did you kill someone?"

Schoonmaker dodged the question, which made Louise think the answer was yes.

"I did con Harry and Marie Stevens out of cash, lots of it."

Harry and Marie Stevens were a shining young couple who were frequently in the papers, but Louise never knew why. She thought she had read that Harry Stevens was a big man in the horse racing business, but the papers always focused on where Marie Stevens got her clothes from.

"Did they know?" Louise asked.

"I'm here and not in prison, so no."

"What did you do with the money?"

"How do you think I was able to afford this place?" Schoonmaker leaned forward. He laughed. His question was supposed to be a joke.

She hadn't touched her breakfast. She realized that she was not a breakfast person, but Anna had put so much work into caring for them that she felt bad if she didn't try to eat a little, and it was slowly going cold in front of her.

Schoonmaker leaned back, suddenly more serious than she had ever seen him. "People will believe what you tell them as long as you dress the part and talk the talk. People aren't going to pry into your background as long as you seem like you fit in. All it is is confidence, which I have in spades." He winked at her. "Are you planning on faking your death and going to live a long life elsewhere?"

"That was on my to-do list for today." Louise took a sip of her coffee. She loved how Anna made it, just sweet enough that she had already drunk multiple cups. "I was just curious."

"Ah, Rafael told me you're curious about a lot of things."

"Why would someone fake their own death if they didn't want to get rich?" Louise asked.

Schoonmaker's lips turned down. "Is there a reason to do anything that isn't money?"

Louise's eyes flicked to the window. Michael and Josie were still in the backyard. She watched as her sister girlishly turned her head to the side, allowing him to kiss her on the cheek. "Family?"

Schoonmaker considered this. "I think people have a lot of reasons for the things they do. Why do you want to know?"

Louise shrugged. She didn't have a good answer for that one, and maybe she didn't need one. She picked up her coffee cup and smiled at him. "No reason."

LOUISE STRUCK A match and lit a cigarette. She was sitting in Morningside Park, a place that used to be a calming spot for her. She could feel stares from people burning into her skin, whispers behind their hands, dirty looks. Schoonmaker had insisted on her being driven in his least ostentatious car, a black Ford Model T, in which Louise had sat in the back and stared out of the window. She had been right. She managed to pick up a copy of the *Tribune* before walking to the park. Her name wasn't on the front page, but she was in there.

She deserved this.

She didn't know what was being said about her. She could imagine the slurs and the insults. She sat straight and still. It felt as if all of Harlem had been waiting for this to happen. She was Harlem's Hero, after all. She was a savior. She had sacrificed her own safety for the care of others. And now the tides were turning on her.

Harriet dropped onto the bench on her left, then lit her own cigarette. She was daringly wearing a pair of crimson trousers with such wide legs they looked like a skirt. With her black blouse, the look was dangerous and effortless. It was much different from what Louise had seen Harriet wear. They didn't say anything for a moment, sorting through their own thoughts.

"Did you . . . ?" Louise couldn't even finish her sentence.

"Are you okay?" Harriet asked, ignoring Louise's question. She leaned back on the bench, staring up at the cloudy sky.

"Yeah, I'm gonna be okay." How many times had Louise told that lie? How many times had she said it and hoped it would be true? She wondered if it would ever be true.

"I can't believe a paper would print those lies about you."

"Harriet, we . . ." Louise didn't know how to explain it. She wasn't sure exactly how to say it. "You're the blonde in that photo of me."

"I know. But we shouldn't say anything about it, darling."

Harriet shifted her body so that they were a tiny bit closer. If Louise could have removed her eyes from Harriet's opal-shaped face, she would have been able to see a couple of Schoonmaker's men watching them and their every move.

If Harriet was Nora's killer, then Louise was safe for now. She didn't think Harriet would stage an attack on her in public in the middle of the day.

"I'm almost done writing about you." Harriet pulled Louise back to the present. She smiled shyly, and Louise had never known Harriet to be shy about anything. "I think it'll do a lot of good." Harriet pulled out two more cigarettes, lit one for Louise. It was as if Harriet knew exactly what Louise needed.

She accepted the offered cigarette. "I think I have a plan for that." Discussing this in the open was a gamble. She knew anyone could overhear her. Louise looked over her shoulder. Luckily, as she talked to Harriet, people began to ignore them. "If you could hold on to that—"

"I really would like to take this to the papers soon."

"I know. I have a plan. I promise, I just need a little time."

Harriet raised an eyebrow. Her eyes didn't leave Louise's face. Just a week ago, the eye contact would have given Louise pause, a little flutter of anticipation.

"I don't like surprises, Louise."

"I know." Louise removed the cigarette from between her lips. "I'm just asking for a little bit of time, okay?"

Harriet pursed her lips. Sometimes talking to her felt like a battle Louise was two steps behind in. She looked into Harriet's eyes. Was she Nora's killer?

"A little more time."

In the end, Harriet acquiesced like Louise thought she would.

Louise took a long drag on her cigarette. "Soon, I promise."

She had no intention of keeping her promise to Harriet. It was the first lie she had told that she didn't feel very guilty about. If she was sitting next to a murderer, she would have to play it cool. Do some research.

She knew that Schoonmaker's men, her security detail, were close. She could see one a few paces away, pretending to read a copy of the *Tribune*.

She had never wanted to be famous. She had never wanted to be a household name. The Black papers had moved on, but the *Tribune* was like a dog with a bone, obsessed with wringing every bit of her dry. They would be relentless and she thought there was only one way to make them stop.

"Where have you been?" Harriet asked. The question was so subtle, so quiet, it was as if Harriet was just thinking about it now. "No one answered at your apartment."

"I'm shuffling around some things," Louise said. "I'll have to get you an address when I get one." She had never given Harriet her address. Louise had been quite careful not to give that information away. "I didn't feel safe in my apartment. There were multiple break-ins." Louise searched the other woman's face for anything, any sign of guilt or recognition

"Oh," Harriet said. She dropped the butt of her cigarette and ground it under the heel of her shoe. "How awful."

"Yes, it is." Louise agreed. "But I'm going to get to the bottom of it. I always do."

IF LOUISE FELT out of place in Harlem, she could count on blending back in with the faceless masses in Midtown. Still, even though she had been to the *Tribune* offices before, even on a Saturday like this when they ran a skeleton crew, the idea of going there made her nervous.

She didn't pause to talk to the receptionist, the same one who had been at the desk a year ago and was probably reading the same book. She descended the stairs to the bullpen, where a few reporters wrote, a couple women typed, and another woman was on the phone.

Walter Hart was sitting alone at his desk, furiously scribbling something. He looked up as she approached. He didn't look surprised to see her standing in front of him. In fact, he smiled as if this were a lovely luncheon.

"Miss Lloyd, welcome."

"Let's get to this," she said.

She didn't have that much time to wait. She could have chosen any one of the Black papers, but her attack was two pronged. The *Tribune* had a much bigger reach, and her story had run in these very pages.

"I knew you'd show up."

He was smug as he spoke. He was younger than she was. The weekend crew at the *Tribune* was made up of the reporters who needed to prove themselves. Hart had Bernard Thomas' old desk.

"If I do something for you, you have to do something for me," Louise said.

"Intriguing. What?"

"I need the name of the person who delivered the photos you printed."

Walter raised an eyebrow. "Interview first. Information after."

He escorted her and a clever-looking redheaded girl named Gina to an empty private office. Walter and Louise sat at the ends of the table with Gina in between them. She had glasses of water, cigarettes, and a notepad ready to take Louise's story.

It was chilly in the room. Louise was glad for her cardigan. Hart took his time lighting a cigarette, fancying himself the award-winning writer when it was Louise and Gina who were about to do the majority of the work.

Louise knew that she had to tell her whole story and keep nothing hidden. If she wanted the public on her side, she had to give them what they wanted.

There were so many better things she could have been doing. She needed to get back to the investigation and make everything right.

But she didn't know how to do that without first doing this.

"Let's start at the beginning, shall we?" Walter said.

He leaned back in his seat. Gina picked up her pen, ready to write. They both looked at Louise intensely—their eyes were almost the same color—and Louise swallowed hard.

"Nothing is off the table," she said. "Ask me anything."

Telling a stranger—two strangers if she counted Gina—about her entire life was less nerve-racking than she thought it would be. She had already told Harriet most of it. Walter leaned away from the facts and more toward the sensational, asking about her love life, the way she was raised, the horrors of the last summer. She reiterated the story of the faked photographs, saying again that she wasn't a deviant.

Hart lobbed questions at her in a quick and brusque way, trying to get the most out of her that was possible. She maintained her composure. It was the least she could do.

They finally finished, after an hour and a half in the little room, tearing through Louise's life. When it was over, Louise followed the journalist to his desk. Gina disappeared to begin typing everything up.

"What do you want from me?" Walter asked. He paused to light a cigar.

Louise thought that there was no better way to look disgustingly pretentious and new money than smoking a cigar in public.

This was a power play. He wanted to look intimidating. Luckily, Louise didn't find a baby-faced white man with a too-big cigar between his thin lips in any way intimidating. "I need to know who sent you the photos of me."

He reached into his desk, pulled out an envelope. "Hand delivered to my desk."

"By who?"

"The courier." He looked at her as if she should have known the *Tribune* had a courier.

Louise suppressed the urge to roll her eyes. "Did the courier say from who?"

He sat back down at his desk, taking a moment to go through his papers as if this was an inconvenience to him. "No, but you can go ahead and ask. He doesn't come back till tomorrow, though."

Louise cleared her throat. "Do you know a Harriet Sinclair?" she asked. She didn't know what she wanted him to say.

"I've never heard of anyone with that name." He rushed his sentence.

"Why did you print them?" Louise asked.

"I thought they weren't real." He wasn't moved by anything she asked him.

"But you still printed them." Louise wanted to know why. She wanted to know what type of person tried to destroy someone else's life. "You thought they were falsified. Did you even check?"

He tilted his head to look up at her. He considered her, taking his time. Every look was deliberate, as if he was trying to hold the power in this conversation. "It was a good story. You were a good story. That's why."

Louise felt pangs in her stomach, one of anger, one of confusion. “You printed it without talking to me because you thought it was a good story?”

“Everyone loves when a hero falls, Louise. Be more careful next time.”

He winked and she knew she had been dismissed in the most insulting way.

EVEN THOUGH SHE insisted she was fine, Louise’s security detail escorted her up to the Bed-Stuy apartment. She wasn’t used to having two people follow her around to make sure that she was safe.

She knocked on the door of Rafael’s unit. Eugene opened the door. “Hey, boss.”

“Eugene, we aren’t behind the bar right now.” Rafael gave the men behind Louise a wary look.

Louise turned to them. “Can you wait in the car? This won’t take a moment.”

The two men were unoriginally identical, both in crisp, expensive black suits with unamused looks on their faces. They hadn’t bothered introducing themselves. Louise hadn’t asked their names. She hadn’t known what to say to them. Once they left, after sharing a quick look that said a thousand words, Louise turned back to Eugene.

“Is Rosa Maria in? I need to talk to her.” She hadn’t seen, much less talked to, the woman in days. She remembered how hurt Rosa Maria had been over the newspaper.

“Yeah. Why?” Eugene asked as if Louise had asked just because she was curious.

Louise had been dreading this, but she had no greater ally than the woman she loved.

"Can I talk to her?" Louise asked. She tried to keep her sentences short and clear. No way Eugene could misunderstand.

"Come in." He pulled the door open. She sat on the couch, falling into it as she waited.

Rosa Maria appeared, partially dressed in a half slip and a brassiere that formed a diamond in the center of her chest; her hair was unbrushed. She stopped when she saw Louise. "What do you want?"

Was this a bad choice? Was this a wrong move? When Louise looked at Rosa Maria, her mouth ran dry. "I need a favor."

"Why should I help you?"

Rosa Maria was fiery, bold, and passionate. It was something Louise loved about her. She knew it would take some time for Rosa Maria to get over everything. Louise knew Rosa Maria was furious—in fact, she herself was furious—after seeing their intimate business printed in the paper like that.

Louise cleared her throat, changed the subject. "I am so sorry. I never meant for any of this to happen. I never meant to lie to you."

Rosa Maria rolled her eyes. "Why should I help you?" she asked again.

"I think I know who tried to frame you but I need information on someone."

Rosa Maria sat down at the coffee table. She ran a hand through her hair. "I don't work at a newspaper anymore."

"But you know people who do, right? All you have to do is ask."

Rosa Maria was silent for a moment. Louise waited, watched her turn over the idea in her mind.

"Who is it?"

"Harriet Sinclair. Your height, red-brown hair, blue eyes. She's always dressed beautifully and she's not from here."

"Is she the girl in the photograph?" Rosa Maria asked. She lit a cigarette, anything not to look at Louise.

"Yes," Louise said. Guilt settled on her skin. "She said she was trying to get a job writing at a paper."

At that, Rosa Maria snorted her derision. "I'll ask around."

"That would be wonderful. Thanks." Louise breathed a sigh of relief.

"I'll get my brother to tell you what I find."

Rosa Maria rose from her seat and disappeared into her bedroom. Louise sat on the couch for a moment, then exited.

The backseat of the car was a lonely place. She pressed her face to the glass of the window as they glided down the road in an uncomfortable silence. She understood where Rosa Maria was coming from, that her life had been turned upside down because of Louise. Louise didn't realize it was possible to miss someone as much as she missed having Rosa Maria by her side. They had been together for almost all of Louise's adult life. And one thing had changed that.

She didn't know how to explain. She didn't know how to say something to change the other woman's mind.

Louise closed her eyes, letting the motion of the car lull her to sleep. The drive to Schoonmaker's mansion was a fast one, all things considered. She hoped that Rosa Maria would be able to find something on Harriet. She hoped that she was right, that she hadn't wasted her time following bad leads.

She hoped for a lot of things, and mostly, she just wanted this to be over.

The car lurched to a stop. Louise looked up. There was smoke coming from the engine. "Miss Lloyd, you're going to need to get out of the car." The driver looked at her. "Mr. Norris will stay with you while I work on it."

Louise did as she was told. The moment she was out of the car, another came careening down the road, slamming into the Ford. Mr. Norris tackled Louise, throwing her out of the way.

She remained on the ground until the dust around her settled. Until everything was still and quiet. Cars passed without stopping. Louise pulled herself to her knees and then her feet, blood rushing through her body. Mr. Norris was leaning over in the street. His partner had been killed instantly. The cars had crumpled like they were paper, wrinkled and creased.

How many times could she narrowly escape death? Was this a dream? Louise pinched herself. No, she was awake, but it was a nightmare.

"Change of plans, Miss Lloyd." Mr. Norris was collecting himself. He turned to her, his square face grim. "I'm going to get you back into the city. Then I'll make contact with Mr. Schoonmaker from there."

He talked quickly, keeping his eyes on her face. She nodded, unable to say anything. She was barely able to conjure up a coherent thought, let alone say something out loud.

"Are you all right?" Mr. Norris asked.

"Yes. Thank you," Louise said.

He had acted quickly, getting her out of the way just before anything happened.

She exhaled, feeling her heartbeat slow down. And she knew then that she wouldn't be safe anywhere.

29

LOUISE PUT HER foot down. After walking from the middle of nowhere to the Schoonmaker residence, Louise had taken her shoes off within ten minutes, preferring ripped stockings to bloody feet. Schoonmaker and Mr. Norris had taken it upon themselves to discuss her fate in front of her.

"Stop."

Louise was drowned out by the two men sitting at opposite ends of the table, talking rapidly over each other. She picked up a knife and tapped it against her glass. The chiming silenced both men and Louise cleared her throat.

"I am very grateful for the help you have given me over the past couple of days, but I'm not leaving this place. I am not being run out. This is what they want. I don't want to go to any safe house. And I'm not separating me and Josie."

Now she stared at the two men on either side of her; she was sitting in the center of the table. "I'm not changing my life any more than I have to." She had already given up a lot. She had lost her girlfriend, her apartment, her life as she knew it. She wasn't going to lose anything or anyone else.

She paused to light a cigarette. "I can get to the bottom of all of this, but you have to promise to trust me." She didn't know if these two white men could do that, these men who had so much more than she had, who were so much more well-off. "I am not putting my sister's life in any more upheaval."

Everything she did, she had to ask herself if it was worth it. Every choice she made had to be a conscious one. She had Josie to think about.

Schoonmaker started to protest but she held up a finger before he could say anything. "I am so close. I think I have it all figured out. You just have to trust me."

"And if someone attacks you in my house?" Schoonmaker asked.

Louise raised her skirt under the table, removing her little pistol from her garter strap. Not the best place to keep it, but until her dresses came with pockets as deep as those in men's clothes, it would have to do. She placed her gun on the table, receiving raised eyebrows from both men. "I can handle myself."

Schoonmaker laughed, and the tension in the room dissolved. Sure, she still had a lot of work to do, but she felt as if staying in one place was the best.

She sipped from her glass; she was drinking some abominable concoction of alcohol with Coke and a cherry on top. It was just enough to deal with the brutalities of the day. She leaned back in her seat full and calm now. Anna had made several dishes, even though there were only three people constantly in the house. They had already had dinner. Every moment she spent in this mansion was, somehow, more luxurious than the one before it. She didn't know how Schoonmaker stood it, every moment of this existence in this pretty little house, indulging every whim and thought he had. Actually, as she thought about it, it didn't sound so bad. Louise exhaled. She was tired of being a nervous wreck.

"What a Sheba, huh?" Schoonmaker asked.

"She's a bearcat," Mr. Norris said.

For the first time since Louise had met him, he smiled, a crooked smile that betrayed no real emotion.

Louise wondered if he was grieving his partner.

"It's a shame Mr. Rollins died." Louise was twenty-seven and she had already seen enough death to last her a lifetime. He had died for her.

Schoonmaker nodded. His mood turned somber. "I'll have to contact his family."

Louise drained her glass, picked up her gun, and rose from the table. "If you don't mind," she said, "I'm going to retire now. I've had quite the day." That was the understatement of the year.

The men rose when she did—good manners could be learned—and she allowed both men to kiss her cheek before she left.

Josie was sitting on the bed, writing in a journal. This was a new habit for her, one she kept just as private as the rest of her life. Louise climbed into bed without changing out of her dress and lay on her back, nudging Josie in her side.

"Leave me alone," Josie said.

"Is that any way to talk to your favorite older sister?" Louise asked.

Josie closed her little notebook. It was small, easily concealed in a purse. She put her pen down. "You know, I've always preferred Minna."

"Liar." Louise looked up at her sister.

Josie smiled. She no longer wore bandages on her wrists, but wore sleeves to cover the scars. The scars were something she would never outgrow.

"Are you happy?" Louise asked.

"I like it here." Josie did everything thoughtfully, quietly. She never lied and Louise knew she was telling the truth, but there was something Josie wasn't saying.

"I'm sorry this didn't work out the way I planned for it."

Louise had to give up the idea of cozy mornings with Josie in 3I, give up the idea of walks in Morningside Park, staying up late and doing all the things they hadn't been allowed to do as children.

But this big room with its navy walls and scarlet sheets, this was as close as they could get to perfection.

She just knew it wouldn't last long.

LOUISE OVERSLEPT. WHEN she'd awoken, bathed, and dressed, it was almost noon; she hadn't slept so late in a while. She made sure to keep her gun on her at all times. She descended the stairs to find Josie and Michael sitting at the table, looking very close. She paused and turned before they could see her.

She was not about to ruin a romantic dalliance for her sister.

It had been a couple of days since she had been in the city, a couple of days since the accident, and the whole house seemed to be nervous. She had had to ask specifically for a copy of the *Tribune*, and when she received that morning's copy, a photograph of her, hazel eyes narrowed and a frown on her lips, was on the front page. She had never seen herself look that actively angry.

LOUISE LLOYD IN HER OWN WORDS

More like her own words twisted to match a story that already had been written. Louise exited to the backyard, lit a cigarette, and began to read.

The *Tribune* in the past year or so had become more slanted toward yellow journalism. She understood that she was on the front page. It was the least she deserved.

She scanned her words, scanned her interview, her life altered to fit a story. She read about her upbringing, her kidnapping, and her brief stint as a "consultant," to the NYPD the previous summer.

A lot of the piece was filled with Walter's own observations, mostly about her looks. Apparently she could be rather attractive if she didn't dress so dowdily.

That was news to her.

"Miss Lloyd." It was Anna who broke into her thoughts. The maid stood a few paces away from her, a strict frown on her face. "You have a visitor. Mr. Moreno is waiting for you in the drawing room."

Louise folded her paper and rose.

"If you would be kind enough as to follow me," Anna said, and turned on the heel of her sensible shoe.

The drawing room was different from the living room, which was different from the parlor. When Anna opened the door, Rafael was seated on the new couch, boater hat in hands. It was the first time in her life she had seen him look grim.

"Ah, lady of the house?" Rafael asked.

"Only for a little while." Louise sat across from him, leaning forward on her elbows.

Rafael looked her over. "Old Schoonmaker's taking care of you and Sunshine?"

"He has been the perfect gentleman."

Rafael laughed. "Doesn't sound like Schoonmaker."

Louise wished this could be a congenial chat between old friends. She didn't ask after Rosa Maria, although that was the only thing she wanted to do.

He lit cigarettes for both him and her, and when Louise accepted, he began. "I've got good news and bad news."

"What's the bad news?"

"Rosa Maria dug as much as she could. She doesn't think anyone named Harriet Sinclair exists at all." Rafael leaned back in his chair, puffed on his cigarette. He was silent and totally still in a way that was unnerving to Louise.

"What's the good news?" She was hesitant to ask.

Rafael smiled. "You look very pretty today."

She rolled her eyes at his attempt at charm and wit. "Who is Harriet Sinclair?"

"She doesn't know. Just knows that no one with that name has applied to basically any paper in the city."

"How could she have found this out?" Louise tapped her cigarette in a nearby ashtray.

"My sister, bless her, has a type of magic no one can explain. Or, I assume, she just asked around. She spent a lot of time on the phone yesterday." Rafael raised an eyebrow. He was unbothered by the workings of his sister. "I, in case you were wondering, have decided to write a show. I think you'd be perfect for the lead."

"Can you please focus?" Louise asked. She bounced her right leg impatiently. She wanted answers and she wanted them now. "Harriet said she was new in town, trying to be a real reporter."

"Have you considered the possibility she was lying to you?" Rafael smirked, pleased with himself for coming up with the obvious conclusion.

"No," Louise said, deadpan. "Thank you for raising this option." She used the butt of her cigarette to light a new one, then dropped the spent one into the ashtray. "I know this isn't about Nora or about Rosa Maria, but how exactly could this be about me?"

"Have you gotten into any trouble in the past year or so, Lovie?" Rafael didn't need to say anything more. "I know you've been thinking about your past, but what about Gilbert?"

Nora was one of the kidnappees. Louise had killed Gilbert. It all led back to him.

But she was sure he was dead.

So who else?

Rafael rose, dusting off his trousers. He clutched his hat in his hand. "I gotta go find Schoonmaker. Any idea where he may be?"

"No," Louise said.

"Pretty bad lady of the house," Rafael said.

"I'm working on it." Louise rose with him, collecting her paper.

Rafael slid the paper, the angry photo of her, toward her. "Interesting article this morning."

"You read it?" Louise asked.

Rafael put his cigarette back between his lips. "I looked at the picture. Same thing, right?"

Louise rolled her eyes. He left her there in the drawing room, holding her newspaper with a story about her life.

She couldn't believe that things had gone so wrong so quickly.

Louise returned to the backyard porch, settling herself in the weak spring sun. She opened the paper and resumed reading.

She had to know what was being said about her.

THE LAST TIME Louise had seen Minna's son was when he was a squealing infant. Now he was over a year old, and hiding behind his mother's skirt as Louise faced them at their doorstep.

"Louise," Minna said.

She was bigger now than she had been the last time Louise had seen her. This was supposed to be a quick trip, and now Louise was unsure of why she had come here in the first place. Getting out of her father's house, letting Michael escort her and Josie to the Schoonmaker mansion: it had all happened fast and her head was still reeling.

"Why are you here?" Minna asked.

"I want to talk to you, but it couldn't be over the phone," Louise said.

"Come in, then," Minna said, pushing the door open.

They settled in the kitchen, sitting across from each other. Minna leaned back and sighed, rubbing a hand on her stomach. Benny, the toddler, tugged on Louise's skirt. She picked him up and placed him on her lap. He immediately began to crawl around, trying to reach for her hat.

"It's about Josie," Louise said. "I want you to know that she is safe and she is with me for the time being."

"Where is that?" Minna said. She closed her eyes for a moment, her hand still on her stomach.

"I'll give you the phone number. We're staying with a friend."

Louise shifted the toddler so he was sitting again. She looked into his open, trusting eyes and big smile. He was so little, so small and defenseless. She ran a finger over his cheek and he tried to bite her.

"What friend, Louise?" Minna asked.

She looked around. She knew that no one could be watching her in Minna's house, but she still felt eyes on her. "A friend. He lives outside of the city. What's important is that we're safe."

"What's going on?" Minna asked. "I saw you in the *Tribune*. Can you please tell me what is happening?"

Louise inhaled, trying to keep herself steady. "It's better if I don't tell you too much, okay? It's better if you don't know." She realized that this might be her last time seeing and talking to her middle sister.

Minna was frowning, displeasure crossing her face. "Your life isn't that mysterious, Louise. Tell me what's going on right now."

Her voice was low and cool. She was angry. Benny stopped shifting in Louise's arms, momentarily stunned into behaving.

Louise knew that she should try to relate to her sister. She should try to be honest. So swallowing hard, Louise told her the whole story. She told it as they drank coffee, Louise eventually setting the toddler down so she could reach for her cup. And when she was finished, Minna nodded, taking it all in.

"And the photographs?"

"All lies. Someone is trying to really mess with me." The resentment was acid on her tongue.

"And the friend you're staying with?" This was typical Minna. She needed all of the facts.

"A friend of a friend who can take us in for the time being," Louise said.

Even though Louise was the eldest, it was Minna who tried to domineer. "What if she wanted to stay with me?"

"She doesn't," Louise said.

"How do you know?" Minna asked.

Louise was craving a cigarette but Minna didn't allow her to smoke in the house. Visiting her sister always made Louise tense. She wondered how they could be a result of the same set of parents.

"I know because she told me. She loves it there. Don't pull her away from it."

Minna narrowed her eyes and inspected Louise closely for a lie.

"You wanted me to help her. This is how I'm helping her. Look, she is happy and that's what we need right now." Louise shouldn't have been discussing Josie's life without Josie. It felt wrong, but she needed Minna to know this. "You can call anytime you want. I'm sure she'd be happy to talk to you."

Minna nodded with a snort. "Right. Because why would she talk to me when she has you, the fun sister? The sister who indulges every one of her whims. She doesn't need structure or anything when she has Louise!"

"Why are you angry at me? You're the one who asked me to talk to her."

"And set her straight. Not let her go gallivanting off wherever. She needs to be serious. She's seventeen. If she doesn't settle down now, she'll—"

"I'm twenty-seven and I haven't settled down. Just because you got married and had a kid doesn't mean everyone else wants to. She should be able to explore the world if that is what she wants." Louise was yelling. She stopped when the baby started to cry.

Minna kissed her teeth, rolled her eyes. She moved to pick up her crying child and disappeared farther into the house without saying anything else.

Louise waited until she was outside to light a cigarette. Her anger was bundled up inside of her, and as she stormed down the street, she realized she'd forgotten to give Minna the phone number for the manse.

It didn't matter now. She could call after both of them had had some time to cool off.

Louise had always known that Minna didn't exactly agree with her choice of a lifestyle. Like their father, Minna believed there was one real way to live a life.

Louise stomped down the street and smoked, bumping into

people as she passed them. Minna was so set in her own life, she couldn't see anything different. And it made Louise angry, knowing that Minna would never understand what her life was like. Maybe it was better if they lived their lives apart. Just because they were siblings didn't mean they had to talk or see each other. They had tried to mend their relationship, but maybe they were too different after all.

Louise exhaled, and seamlessly lit a new cigarette with the butt of her old one. She dropped the butt to the ground as she walked.

She and Minna would never see eye to eye and that was fine.

Or she wanted it to be fine.

30

LOUISE STILL HADN'T given up the key to her apartment. She was the rightful tenant of apartment 3I for a few more days. She was going to clear out her last few belongings. The envelope she received the photos in was still in the drawer. She hadn't thought about taking them out now that the entire neighborhood of Harlem and most of Midtown had seen them, but she pulled them from the drawer.

Louise turned on the kitchen light, sat down at the table. She pulled the photographs out of the envelope, the things that had come to ruin her life, and spread them out on the table, looking over them. They weren't pieces of art; they were quick and dirty. She picked up one that showed Rosa Maria's arm around her waist, Rosa Maria's lips near her neck, an intimate portrait of climbing into bed after the Dove and a late night.

She held the photograph up, trying to figure out where it had been taken. The building next to hers had windows that faced into 3I. She couldn't recall ever seeing anyone in those windows. The thing about apartments, though, was that you never really had any type of privacy. Louise picked up her purse, then slid the photograph into the pocket of her coat, right next to her gun.

Getting into the building next door was easy. There was no one watching the door, and she used a hatpin to unlock the front doors. She climbed the stairs, craving some exercise, a feeling she got when she had been lying around the Schoonmaker manse all day. Louise felt her shoes click on every step, old and unsteady under her slight weight.

She had to guess; that was the hard part. Louise paused at every door, pressing her ear to it, trying to find out which apartments were empty. She heard children crying, men and women yelling, and then she got to one that was quiet. . . .

She hoped she was right, or she was breaking and entering for no reason.

Louise got on her knees to pick the lock. She pushed open the door with her fingertips. She was expecting something similar to her unit, but this was smaller, shabbier than her apartment. There was no room for a separate bedroom, and one small bathroom was hidden in the corner.

It was neat but empty. It was clearly lived in, with a small cot, a chair in the corner. It was the most basic of living, making it seem as if this apartment wasn't being rented, but borrowed. Louise took the photograph from her pocket. She held it up toward the window. This was it. This was the angle used to take that photograph. Whoever was spying on her had taken the photos from this unit. She didn't know why she hadn't noticed sooner.

Louise pulled the chair toward her and sat down. She drew her pistol from her pocket and aimed it at the door. She was going to wait all night if she had to, but she was going to find out who had taken the photos.

THE PERSON LOUISE faced when the door opened again, the man of average height and build wearing an average brown suit with common dark hair and dark eyes, was not who she was expecting. He stopped short when he realized he was on the wrong side of her pistol.

"Who are you?" Louise asked, trying to keep the fear from her voice.

"Who are you?" He adjusted the bag he had slung on his shoulder.

Louise assumed that was where the camera was. "I'm asking the questions here," Louise said. "Who are you?"

He took his hat off, keeping his muddy brown eyes on the pistol in front of him. "My name is Philip."

"Who do you work for?" Louise asked.

"No one . . ." He trailed off.

Louise raised an eyebrow. She could do this all night if she had to. She was going to get the answers she wanted.

"Wait. You're her. You're Louise Lloyd."

"From the photos, yes. Who do you work for?"

"No one. Please, lower the gun. I'm not going to hurt you."

Louise rose from her chair, keeping her gun between them. "How do you not know who hired you?"

She wasn't going to let him think that he was in charge here. She stepped toward him. With her heels, she was only a little shorter than he was.

"I work freelance. People hire me to take pictures. I run ads in all the papers."

"And who hired you for this?" Louise asked.

She kept her voice level, trying to hide all emotion away. But he had had an active part in ruining her life. She was furious, but she wasn't going to show it. She thought she was always taken less seriously when she exploded in anger. No, she had to remain calm to get the answers she needed.

"I don't know. The letter came with a key to this apartment. I was told to take photos and send them away after I developed them. Please, don't shoot me." His voice shook.

Louise frowned. "Where did you send them to?"

"I just sent them off to an address. I don't know who wanted me to do this. I am so sorry." He seemed repentant but Louise didn't believe him.

"You ruined my life with those photos. You ruined everything." She couldn't stop her voice from quaking as she spoke. "How much did you make?"

"Ten dollars a photo."

"A hundred dollars?" Louise asked. The ten photos that had been sent to her and to the *Tribune* were worth that much. "That's what my privacy is worth to you."

"I am so sorry. I didn't know what would happen with them. I thought it was an angry wife looking for something. I thought it was a marital thing. I didn't know."

"But you did it anyway," Louise said.

He didn't look at her. The remarkably average Philip stared at the floor beneath his dull brown shoes.

"I am so sorry."

"You wouldn't have done it if you were sorry," Louise said.

He was silent for a moment.

Louise glared at him. "If you knew what my life was like."

"I saw you in the *Tribune*. Front page. I didn't ruin your life." There was an edge to his voice now. An unrepentant one, an angry one.

What had she gotten herself into?

"That was damage control. You made one hundred dollars and I had to save myself from the gutter."

"Girls like you deserve to be in the gutter."

He knocked the pistol from her hand, shoving her down before she could react. She fought back, arms flailing and legs kicking in ungraceful self-defense. She managed to get her gun back, a bullet firing errantly in the melee, and she ended up with her legs straddled over his chest, the gun near his temple.

"Give me the address." Louise's breath came out in heaves. "Give it to me now."

"Let me up," he said. "I'll give it to you."

She slowly rose and allowed him to his feet. He reached into his pocket and pulled out his wallet. He drew out a scrap of paper and handed it to her. His hand shook as she took it from him.

Louise left the unit. Stopping in the hallway, she unfolded the paper. The ink was black and thin, giving an address on the Lower East Side. She put the piece of paper in her pocket and collected her things.

It was going to be a long night.

31

KEEPING HER CAMERA close, Louise walked down the street, following the rush of people until she found the address she was looking for. The Pryce Hotel was on Delancey Street and was, from what Louise could tell, a hotel for young women who were trying to make something of themselves.

The slip of paper gave a number, 533, and that was all. No name, nothing. She assumed that the mail would go to a single room, then be handed out to the guests. Louise climbed up to the door and pushed it open.

A stern woman with glasses on the bridge of her nose stood behind a reception desk. "May I help you?" she asked, raising an eyebrow.

"Yes, I need to talk to a tenant of yours." Louise had decided on the subway not to lie. She was going to tell the truth and that was going to get her where she needed to go. "Room 533?"

"Who are you looking for?"

"Is there more than one young woman per room?"

Louise regretted having not dressed nicer. She wore a rather old skirt and blouse, with her worn-out coat over them. This woman was never going to take her seriously dressed like that. Louise straightened out her posture, pulling her shoulders back. The woman stared at her.

"I'm afraid there is. Are you looking to rent a bed?"

"I am not," Louise said. "I would just like to speak to whoever is in room 533."

"Why?"

Louise didn't know how to say what she wanted to say. She cleared her throat. "I think my sister lives there, but I can't be sure. She ran away and we just want her back."

The lie slipped from her, and even though she'd decided she was going to tell the truth, she was grateful it had. The woman appraised her, looking her up and down. Louise held her gaze.

"I can't let you in to see any of my girls. I don't know who you are and I have a feeling you're lying to me." The woman pursed her lips, all of her distrust in Louise showing in those lips. "I'm going to have to ask you to leave now."

"Mrs. Rutherford, I believe I have a package."

The voice interrupted the battle between Louise and the woman. The woman instantly smiled and turned toward her ward.

"Louise Lloyd?"

Louise turned toward the voice. The young woman was Black, brilliantly dressed in a red suit and a matching hat. Her oval face seemed to glow. She was strikingly beautiful in a very odd way. She toyed with her gloves as she stared.

"I can't believe it."

"Miss Haynes, do you know this woman?" Mrs. Rutherford asked.

"I do, in fact. She's an old friend. Mrs. Rutherford, if you would be so good as to get me my package, I think my guest and I will go to my room. Thank you."

The parcel was given quickly and Louise followed this woman, who seemed familiar, to the elevator.

The moment they were inside, alone and away from prying eyes, Miss Haynes turned to her. "I know you don't remember me." Her voice came out in a rush. "I was one of the girls you saved."

32

Once situated in the room, which Louise noted was 533 as Miss Haynes unlocked the door, the two women faced each other. Miss Haynes was smiling brilliantly.

"Lottie Haynes." She extended a hand, which Louise shook. "This is quite the surprise. Are you thinking of moving here? Mrs. Rutherford can be a beast if she likes—just a warning."

"No, I . . . uh . . . no. You live here?"

"In this very room. Alone now, thank God, and everything is wonderful in the world."

Lottie busied herself by opening the closet door and shoving aside clothes on hangers, then throwing single shoes over her shoulder until she came up with two cloudy glasses and a bottle of brown alcohol. She set the glasses on an end table that was covered with makeup, and poured. Louise took one, but didn't drink.

"I've been living here for years. I work in a jewelry store. Do you want anything? It's the least I could do. Oh, did you hear about Nora? She got bumped off a couple weeks ago, real tragic."

"Uh, yes, I actually want to ask you about something," Louise said. Lottie talked so much, so quickly, changing topics so easily, that it was hard to keep up. "There were these photographs printed of me in the paper. The photographer said that he mailed them here."

"Photographs of what?" Lottie asked. She leaned toward Louise, her eyebrows going up and her voice going down. "Sensitive material?"

"You could say that," Louise said.

Lottie smiled. "I haven't heard of anything of the sort. My roommate was strange, though. Pity she moved out."

"When did she move out?" Louise asked.

"Few days ago, I guess. She left in a hurry, real fast. Left me all alone. Are you sure you don't want to move in?"

Lottie lit a cigarette, pulled her feet under her. She had taken off her hat and her shoes and her coat, settling into the small apartment.

"Yes. Who was your roommate?" Louise asked.

"Here's the thing. We worked opposite schedules. Mrs. Rutherford requires us to have a respectable job, you know? References. And one day this girl just appears in my room. Says she's my roommate. I work nights, and she works during the day. I talked to her twice."

"You work at a jewelry store open at night?" Louise asked.

Lottie laughed. "No! I pretend to work at a jewelry store. I'm a cigarette girl. Nice work if you can get it."

Louise blinked twice, trying to keep up with the hurricane that was the woman sitting across from her. She placed her glass on the end table. "Could you describe her? Did you know her name?"

"She introduced herself as Harriet, but she had this letter that said Emily. She threw it away real quick. I saw it in the trash. I don't think she meant to throw it out. I saved it."

"Emily?" Louise asked.

Lottie nodded. Then she rose and rifled through a half-open

drawer that was stuffed with clothes. She turned with a piece of paper in her hands. She handed it to Louise. The writing, thin and slanted, was writing she knew all too well.

"Here. I don't know why I saved it. Felt important. I was gonna give it back to her but then she left, so then I kept it. I was gonna throw it out, but if it means so much to you . . ."

"Did she know you have this?"

Lottie shrugged. "I dunno. We never really talked." She finished her glass and poured herself a new one. "What's her story? Mrs. Rutherford was blazing mad, but she paid through three months, so I have a single until then, I guess."

"I don't know," Louise said.

She felt bile rise in her throat. She swallowed hard and let her eyes drift to the signature.

That too she recognized.

MAYBE IT WAS Schoonmaker who got sick of Louise's moping. Maybe it was Louise who got sick of being in the house. In any case, they, with Josie, Michael, and Rafael, went out. Louise wore a burgundy velvet dress with lace insets in the front, forming the straps, and in the back. She placed a starry jeweled headband across her forehead. She felt more like herself than she had in ages.

Josie was excited. Louise had dressed her in a red dress with a royal blue lining. The skirt hem rose in the front, fell in the back. By the time Louise had dabbed lipstick onto her sister's lips, Josie had been transformed.

The club they went to was a dinner club, serving dinner from eight until midnight, then transforming to a club where Upper West Siders got their kicks until three in the morning. It was Schoonmaker's second-favorite holding.

He really was the Club King of Manhattan.

They arrived just as the club was transforming. Schoonmaker waved them in with a wink to his doorman. The band was already onstage; the tables were being cleared away. They were seated in a booth with heavy velvet curtains, the only things that didn't move when the club was transformed. It was simply called the Dinner Club and Louise loved it from the moment she walked into it.

The band began by playing a Charleston. Louise allowed Rafael to whisk her onto the dance floor with all the other dancers.

"Ready?" Louise asked.

"Let's show them something."

Rafael pulled her close as the music began. She trusted him to lead. That was their entire relationship on the dance floor: he led and she followed. He started something and she ended it.

They hadn't danced together in weeks, maybe months. She had barely been on the dance floor in weeks, and when she had been, it had been with Rosa Maria.

But the quick tempo brought back the steps that were ingrained in her memory. Right foot front, then back, then left foot front, then back, letting Rafael twirl her and lift her easily into the air. They were known to be good, and Louise had forgotten just how good they could be.

By the time the song ended, Louise was flushed with sweat and craving a drink. But the band started up a foxtrot and Rafael looked at her, raising an eyebrow.

And off they went. The foxtrot was a closer dance, and the step was a gentle walk across the floor. It was the first dance she had really learned how to do. Louise rested her head on Rafael's shoulder, letting him guide her across the floor.

"You good, Lovie?"

"Everything's jake."

She meant it. She really meant it. This was the first night in weeks when she felt like herself. On the dance floor of this swanky club, surrounded by the brightest possible bright young things, the shiny floor beneath them, the music around them.

She never felt more herself than when she was on the dance floor.

When the band slowed to a waltz, Louise's most despised dance style, they returned to their table as Michael and Josie exited the booth. On the table there was already a round of drinks with the bottle next to them. Louise eyed them warily. She picked up the bottle and sniffed it; smelling nothing but aromatic bitters, she poured a glass.

"Do you approve?" Schoonmaker asked. He had already confessed in the car, a red Ford exactly like the one Louise had nearly died in, that he was not a dancer. He was just grateful to open a space for people to have fun.

"I suppose I do. It's nothing like the Dove."

They kept one of the red velvet curtains closed, for privacy's sake. Louise had to lean forward to watch Josie and Michael fumble their way across the dance floor in a display of shy affection.

"How did the Dove get its name?" Schoonmaker asked.

"I told him to ask you." Rafael leaned back in his seat, taking a moment to light a cigarette.

The Dinner Club had the same energy as the Dove and the Zodiac before it, even if its attendees were the young men and women of high society trying to get their kicks in at night before returning to their lives and marriages in the morning. It was less frenzied, more polite and refined, but it still had the same mood Louise saw in her clubs: desperation for something bigger than themselves.

"Josie had a twin. Celia. She was killed last summer." Saying the words still made Louise's heart hurt. "I called Celia 'Dove' and

Josie 'Sunshine,' silly little nicknames, but she would have loved to have a club named for her."

Schoonmaker raised a glass. "To Celia."

Louise and Rafael copied him; then they all drank from their glasses. Louise was determined not to get too tipsy, which was her worst habit. Sitting in the velvet booth, almost invisible to the patrons who saw Schoonmaker and whispered, she was having the time of her life.

Schoonmaker enjoyed the attention. He posed for photographs, gave kisses, and was genuinely loving every moment. It was easy to get swept up into the life that he had built for himself—one of parties and big houses and constant happy-go-lucky optimism. It was like being next to the sun in every way, being blinded by happiness in life.

Even still, she was sure she caught Schoonmaker giving Rafael a longing look over the crowds. Rafael didn't notice. Of course he didn't.

It was strange to Louise, but after everything she had been through just in the past month, she wanted to take in every possible moment she could in his presence.

She lit a cigarette, her body sighing and resetting, and she was ready to go when the band kicked into something faster, something she could really dance to.

Louise looked forward, snatching a glance at Josie in Michael's arms.

Young romance. How beautiful it was.

STUMBLING HOME FROM the Dinner Club was much more refined than coming home from the Dove or the Zodiac. The car sped from Manhattan back to the Schoonmaker manse, a considerable drive. Enough time for them to fall asleep and sober up.

But Josie was a lightweight who refused to sober up. As Louise hauled her up the stairs, she kept humming a waltz.

"I get it now," Josie sighed as Louise undressed her.

"What do you get?"

"Why you dance. Why you snuck out of the house. Why you left. I get it." Josie raised her arms over her head as if she were a practiced ballerina. "It's magic," she murmured. "Such magic." She twirled around and Louise caught her.

"Right," Louise said with a good-natured roll of her eyes.

She was glad Josie was happy and was having fun. Most of all, Louise was very glad she had been able to get her sister help when she needed it, or she might never have experienced a night like this one. Louise made sure to place a glass of water next to her sister. Then Louise changed from her dance dress—the lace insets had gotten rather itchy on her shoulders—and into a nightgown. Then she wrapped her dressing gown around her. She picked up the box she had taken from her father and went downstairs. Josie snored as Louise shut the door.

Louise knew Schoonmaker had an office, but it was on the third floor, the man's private quarters, which Louise wouldn't enter. She settled in the kitchen, pouring herself a glass of water and sitting under the dull electric light. She placed the box on the table.

Harriet.

Emily.

Louise had to stand to take the lid off. There were several different files, all outlining Louise's life from an outsider's point of view. She combed through them until she found the years she needed: ages fourteen to sixteen. It was odd seeing how her father treated her as something to be studied rather than as a human being.

Being that age, not really a child and definitely not an adult, being a mother to three girls, being primed for a life as a pastor's wife, as someone who would serve, hadn't been easy. Louise closed her eyes, swallowing back tears. Those years had made her who she was.

As she'd expected, her father had copious notes on her kidnapping and the months surrounding it. He had paper coverage, the stories that he made her do to raise the church's visibility. Everything she did in that year, aside from leaving, was to support him.

Some of these she had seen before. She had seen her face, young and shocked. She had seen a then-young Officer Gilbert behind her. She had stared at these papers so much that they had started to lose all meaning. She had never wanted to go back to this. But it defined her as much as her childhood had.

It was too early in the morning to really go over any of this. After a night of dancing, all she wanted was a cigarette and to sleep for hours. But she had to keep her mind on this. In the sleepy hours of the silent house, where Rafael was crashing in a guest bedroom, she had to stay focused.

She stared at a grainy photograph of herself, dirty from being in a basement. Scared witless. She distinctly remembered never wanting to be that girl again.

And there she was. She was sitting at this table, going over things she might have missed in her past. It was funny how memories worked. There were some things she remembered like they had happened yesterday. There were others that she was sure she had been told about but couldn't remember.

And there were a few things Louise would have to find out for herself.

33

THERE WAS A time when everyone in the precinct would have stopped everything and looked at Louise when she entered. It always made her feel like a bug under a microscope, made her feel very other in a room full of white men and the white women who served them.

She was very grateful that that did not happen now.

It wasn't lost on Louise that when Martin became a detective there seemed to be only one free office.

She crossed to it now, then knocked on the closed door. She waited ten whole seconds and then opened it. It was empty but unlocked.

"How odd," Louise said to herself.

She looked around to make sure that no one was watching her and entered, closing the door behind her. The entire layout of the office had been changed. The desk was across the room from where it had been, the board against the wrong wall. It was smaller than she remembered, or maybe the space wasn't being used properly now. She thought about the afternoons spent in this very office, the bottles of Coke drunk, the murders discussed with the murderer. Louise shivered. She remembered how stupid she had been the previous summer. Sure, it was all obvious when she looked back but she should have been smarter.

Although she didn't know what exactly she could have done. All she knew was that she should have done something, anything, differently.

Because of the new setup, she didn't know where to start searching. It took a moment for her to try to figure out if Martin's predecessor had left anything of use. She hoped it hadn't all been thrown out. Louise had briefly considered going to the old apartment, but she didn't want to surprise anyone who was living there now.

Louise kneeled down. The way the desk was positioned meant that she was hidden from view should the door open. There was a photograph on the desk, the lone personal effect. Louise recognized the woman in the photo: redheaded, Irish, always ready for a fun time, Maeve Walsh. Louise hadn't spoken to her former housemates since she moved out. She was surprised that this was still happening. Louise should have told Maeve the man had been cheating on her.

Shaking that thought off, Louise began with the bottom drawers, totally inconvenient. She hoped that they hadn't been cleaned out.

She pulled the left one open. There was a scrap of paper and a broken fountain pen. Very disappointing. She closed the drawer, and as she did, the door opened. Louise froze. She didn't pull her gun, although she wanted to. She stayed put, hidden, holding her breath, and hoped the person would leave soon.

The door closed. "Have you come to turn yourself in for the murder of Nora Davies, Miss Lloyd?"

Louise exhaled and then rose to her feet. Martin was standing by the door, arms crossed. She leaned on the desk.

"I don't like the changes you've made. Makes this place look tiny."

"What are you doing here?"

"I have some questions," Louise said. She stopped and lit a cigarette, as if this were her office. She exhaled. "I know you're so busy trying to frame people for murder, though, so I'll just keep poking around until I find something. Thank you."

"I'd watch how you speak to me," Martin said. "You know I could make your life complete hell. I could ruin you."

Louise laughed, really laughed, in his face, watching his stony features turn crimson. It was the greatest feeling in the world. "As if my life hasn't been ruined already. You can't make my life hell. I'm living in it every day."

"What do you want, Miss Lloyd? Here to make a case for your little girlfriend's freedom?" He was sneering.

"I was just thinking I should give Maeve a call. Let her know her sweet detective is a serial cheater."

"You have no proof." Martin kept his eyes trained on her. She could see the wheels in his head turning.

"I know Annie Taylor broke up with you when she moved, but that doesn't mean that you aren't currently cheating on Maeve," Louise said.

She smiled as innocently as she could. Annie Taylor had nearly been a casualty of the Girl Killer the summer before. Over the winter, she had broken up with her illicit boyfriend and moved from the city. Louise wrote her sometimes, but not lately. Annie seemed happy enough. Louise was glad of that.

"Maeve and I are happy," Martin said.

She doubted that.

"Your predecessor—" Louise began.

"Detective Theodore Gilbert," Martin intoned.

"The cold-blooded murderer who tried to kill me," Louise continued as if the man had not spoken. "I want to know if you threw out any of his things."

"Most of it was NYPD property. It all went into storage, I believe. Why?"

Louise smiled. "You know, I do sometimes tire of doing your job for you."

"You're not doing my job for me."

"You were ready to arrest someone for a crime she didn't do just because she was covered in blood." She was needling him. She should stop. "Where is the storage?"

Martin exhaled through his nostrils, rage barely held back. "If I show you, will you never bother me again?"

"I'm not sure that is a promise I can keep," Louise said.

They eyed each other for a moment. She knew that she was again trapped in a small room with a man who could do anything to her and face no repercussions. Despite her breezy, casual tone, she was nervous that he would try something.

And if she fought back, that would be the end of her.

Martin rolled his eyes. "Keep walking down this hallway. It's the last door on your left." He opened the door and waved her out.

"Much obliged," Louise said. She dusted off her skirt and then passed him at the door.

He caught her by the wrist, holding her in place for a moment. "Never do this again, Miss Lloyd. You would not believe the things I could do to you. Do your business and then leave. I never want to see you again." His voice was cold near her ear.

She pulled away from him. That suited her. She never wanted to see him again either.

HE HAD A flat-faced officer accompany her to the storage area. Louise stood by as the door was unlocked. The boy—he really was just a child in a too-big uniform—opened the door and allowed Louise to enter first. She scanned the boxes, the shelves, the cabinets, for an inkling of where to start.

"Officer . . . ?" Louise turned to him.

"Wilson?" he said as if his name was a mystery to him as well.

"Officer Wilson," Louise said. "Were you here last summer?"

"I hadn't started yet."

He refused to meet her eye in the most curious way. She was used to that. She always found it an insecure move.

"So you never met Detective Gilbert?" she asked as casually as she could.

"Never, ma'am." The answer was stone-cold.

Louise realized that she was not going to get anywhere with him. The cabinets were to the front, shelves to the back. She bypassed the cabinets, not wanting to rifle through papers that didn't interest her anyway.

"Did you know he was a killer?" Louise asked.

"I heard someone framed him." Wilson's eyes followed her as she moved toward the back.

The shelves were chronologically sorted, and she moved past the early years.

"He tried to kill me," Louise said.

She didn't know why she was insisting on this line of conversation. He didn't say anything to that; she didn't think he wanted to. She scanned through the boxes until she found exactly what she was looking for. She pulled one box from the shelf: belongings of a dead man no one thought to throw away. She placed the box on the floor and then sat in front of it. Wilson hovered, watching her as she moved. She ignored him.

There were a few artifacts, a few personal things of his. She didn't like doing this, didn't like having to remember the man she'd thought had been good to her. She'd tried in vain to keep the memories away and now she had to face them head-on.

Why would anyone save any of this? Who would want to be reminded? He was a black stain on the entirety of the police department.

She wondered what there was to hide.

She began to sift through the items. Papers made up the first layer. Nothing case related, just personal schedules, letters. She stared at the handwriting she knew so well. She picked up one page, which wasn't about her but it could have been. It outlined a daily schedule: wake up, have breakfast, go to work. The bigger items were toward the bottom of the box. Louise riffled through the leftover papers, past the embroidered handkerchief, until she found what she was looking for.

Her fingers felt the picture frame. Before she could pull it out, she closed her eyes, hoping and praying. She opened her eyes and stared at the long-forgotten photograph.

The woman was younger, just a girl. An oval face framed with dark ringlets, and even in the faded black-and-white of the photograph, Louise could tell her eyes were cool and blue. She knew she was looking at Harriet, but younger.

She pried the photograph from its frame, turned it over.

On the back was written *Emily Gilbert, 1915.*

34

LOUISE NO LONGER slept. She had always been a night owl, but now the exhaustion was a different breed. She was awake because she was worried, because she was scared, because she felt she couldn't sleep and let Harriet get her.

She was sure that Harriet wasn't in the manse, but now Louise was nervous she was seeing things in every corner of the house.

Schoonmaker stayed awake with her until one or two, probably sensing the fact that she needed someone around. It was nicer with someone with her. They sat at opposite ends of the table, smoked, played cards. Louise was very good at playing cards, a hidden talent from her show days. They were in the midst of a poker tournament in which Louise was fleecing him.

"I think I figured it out today."

He raised an eyebrow, cigarette between his lips. "Figured out everything?"

"Just Nora's murderer and who's been watching me. Incidentally, they are one and the same."

Louise searched through her cards. Her hand was not that

good, no high cards and only two in the diamond suite. But it was something she could work with. In the center of the table was the current pot, composed of a hodgepodge of cigarettes, loose bills, and a wayward lipstick Louise had found in her purse.

She didn't know the last time she had used that lipstick; now she was partial to the deep red that had come with her camera, but she didn't want to lose this one.

"I'm not very surprised at that," Schoonmaker said.

They had spent their late nights talking, just talking. It was nice to be able to compare stories. He told her about his early days as Fox Schoonmaker and about his mother. Louise had in turn told him about the Girl Killer investigation, every moment of it. He hadn't asked about her kidnapping. She was relieved at that.

Louise kept her face still and stony, trying to trick him into thinking she had better cards than she did. "The only thing is, I think it makes me sound insane."

Schoonmaker met her eyes from across the giant table. He had discarded his waistcoat and rolled up the sleeves of his shirt, and he looked like the all-American farm boy he should have been. "Tell me anyway."

"I think the reporter I met is actually Theodore Gilbert's little sister come to take revenge on me for killing her brother."

Schoonmaker let out a low whistle. "Can you prove it in a court of law?"

Louise was briefly reminded of the summer night when she, Rosa Maria, and Rafael had faked a séance. That had enraged Gilbert so much, he had killed her sister.

If she had been more careful, more discreet, Celia would still be alive.

Louise would never make a mistake like that again.

"Not yet, but I think I'll be able to." She shoved her pot of roughly four single dollars and her last three cigarettes into the center of the table. “All in.”

“How do you plan to prove it?” Schoonmaker asked.

“I don’t know yet.”

Louise had been racking her brain. The moment she got home, she had tried calling Rosa Maria, then had spent an hour trying to make any type of contact. The phone in the Bed-Stuy apartment had rung and rung until the ringing of the phone had given her a headache and the phone operator had seemed a little sad for her.

And she still didn’t know what she was going to do or how she was going to do it.

“Why are you so nice to me?” Louise asked.

She asked him this frequently. And that night, he was too tired to make a joke as a response.

Schoonmaker lit a new cigarette. “Rafael has gotten me out of a scrape or two. There was a small incident with the mob in Chicago, and he helped me get out of it. Now anything I can do for him, I will do.”

There was something he wasn’t saying. She could see it; he was avoiding her gaze.

“What else?” Louise asked.

“There’s nothing else,” Schoonmaker said. He tossed down his cards. “I’m out. You play too rich for my blood, Lovie. I should get you against my men. You could teach them a thing or two.”

“I would be glad to teach them a lesson,” Louise said, showing him her dismal cards.

He laughed, a delayed reaction to his own misfortune. He pushed Louise’s winnings toward her. Louise realized that he consistently put in ten times the cash she did, and now she had a solid little nest egg, to be counted later.

Schoonmaker drained his glass, a ghost of a smile still on his lips. "Go again?" he asked.

She could see he was getting tired and trying to hide it for her sake. She knew he was awake and losing at cards to keep her company.

"I've taken enough of your money for one night, I think." Louise picked up one of her cigarettes and placed it between her lips but didn't light it.

Schoonmaker rose, barely resisting the urge to rub his eyes like a child. "Good night, Lovie."

They always parted like this. Louise had the stamina to stay awake way longer than he did, a superiority she felt childishly proud of.

"Don't stay up too late."

When she was alone, when he'd dragged himself up the two flights of stairs to his private quarters, she exited through to the backyard, as she was wont to do during these late hours. She sat on the concrete path, stretching out on her back, tipping her face to the sky.

She always felt most at home in the early hours of the morning, and she knew that she had to start formulating a plan.

35

THE LITTLE CAFÉ was the one where she and Harriet had first met. The one where she had agreed to being Harriet's interviewee. Now, as Louise sat there, five minutes early, and banking on the fact that Harriet would be late, she was nervous.

Louise had had to use a pay phone from the city to arrange this meeting; she didn't want Harriet knowing where she was.

"Louise, my lovely Louise."

Harriet's greeting was breathless as she rushed toward the table in the center of the little café. Harriet was pink cheeked and dressed in a shade of blue that complemented the rich tones of her dark hair and the brightness of her eyes perfectly. Louise reminded herself that the woman across from her was a murderer. The woman across from her was cold and ruthless.

Louise had thought this was a good idea, but as Harriet sat there, placing gloved hands daintily on the table, her throat went dry. She took a sip from her water glass.

A public place. Harriet wouldn't hurt her in a public place.

"You are a liar," Harriet said. Her face remained pleasant but her tone was cold. It was unnerving.

"What do you mean?"

Louise knew exactly what she meant. She didn't know where Harriet was staying now that she had left the Pryce, but there was no way she could have escaped the *Tribune* and Louise's face on the front page a couple of days ago.

"You said you'd let me tell your story. You lied, and I can't stand liars."

Harriet raised an eyebrow, still acting as if she were talking about tea or the weather or a stage play. Her voice was cheery as a waitress came to serve them. Harriet's blue eyes remained on Louise until the waitress left.

"I didn't lie about anything." Another lie, and Harriet knew it. Louise was going to play dumb. "I don't know how they got that story about me. I think I'm going to sue."

The smile that jumped onto Harriet's lips was a delayed reaction. Louise watched her carefully, trying to predict what move Harriet would make next. Harriet gracefully lifted her teacup to her lips.

"You're just a common dinge, you know. Your word is all you have." She talked quickly and quietly, getting the insult out before she was interrupted by something. "You lied."

"I didn't lie," Louise said.

She was certainly uneasy. She sipped her tea, although she hated drinking tea. She tried not to show it. She wasn't going to show this woman, whoever she was, any weakness or any fear. She wasn't going to make the same mistakes she had made last time.

There were so many things Louise could have countered with, but she held her tongue. Patience was a virtue.

"I asked you here to apologize." She hated saying it. "I truly didn't know at all. And I think I need your help with something." The words were flowing before she could really think about them. "Then I'll give you exclusive access, I promise. I won't talk to anyone else."

As she lowered her teacup Harriet's blue eyes narrowed over it, boring into Louise with sharp accuracy.

"It's a good story. Harlem's Hero solved another case," Louise said.

There was one thing Louise knew about Harriet: she would never be able to resist a story. Not many people would, especially about Louise and her business. Louise didn't know if she liked that.

It didn't matter that Harriet wasn't a real person, wasn't an aspiring writer, wasn't someone with the normal desires for success.

Louise had to keep her where she wanted her.

"Exclusive access?" Harriet asked.

"Of course."

Louise sipped from her teacup. She wondered if this was how powerful men felt making clandestine deals over cards. As Louise looked at Harriet now, it was clear that she was the same girl in the photograph, only twelve years older. Harriet had grown into her features, her eyes and lips, had grown a little taller, carried herself better, but it was the same person.

Louise recalled Gilbert's mentioning a sister once or twice, and now that Louise realized who Harriet was, she saw the similarities between brother and sister.

"Do you promise?" Harriet asked.

She extended a hand. Every move she made bled money and social standing. Louise had wondered why Harriet was even interested in her. But she knew now. And she knew better.

"Of course," Louise said.

She shook Harriet's hand. She could feel her stomach in knots, anxiety choking her until she could focus only on how she could barely breathe. She took a small breath, trying to inhale as much as she could.

"Where are you staying now?" Harriet asked innocently as she finished off her cup of tea.

Louise blinked and finished her own cup of tea. How funny that was. She had never mentioned moving to Harriet. In fact, she had been careful not to.

"I haven't moved." The lies were spilling like rain from a cloud. Louise said a quick prayer and hoped she wasn't headed to hell for it. "I'm still at the same place."

"How odd. I called but no one answered."

"The phone was disconnected," Louise said. She'd have to, eventually, remember all of this. That was more nerve-racking than the actual lying. "I'll call you when I'm all settled."

Harriet smiled her ray-of-sunshine smile, "Please do, darling love." She placed bills on the table and chirped the pet name as if this were a date. "I'm looking forward to it."

"So am I," Louise said. She still had some work to do.

THE WOMAN KNOCKED on the door of the Schoonmaker manse while they were all eating dinner. Anna answered the door and reappeared at the dinner table. "Visitor for Miss Lloyd."

"Which one?" Josie asked as if the visitor could be for her.

"The elder one, Miss Josie." Anna turned to the girl with a hint of a smile.

Like her twin sister, Josie could charm anyone effortlessly. It was a power the younger Lloyd chose not to exercise. Louise placed her napkin on the table. She wasn't doing much eating these days anyway.

"Did you ask who it was, Anna?" Schoonmaker asked. His eyes rested on his maid.

"She says Rafael Moreno gave her this address," Anna said. "I can turn her away."

"No," Louise said. "Don't do it." She rose from the table. "Anna, I'll receive her in the parlor."

She thought it was odd that someone existed in the house to do her bidding. It was uncomfortable, but Anna never showed displeasure at having to take orders from a Black woman. She was grateful the manse's maid wasn't Black like her. Louise wasn't sure she'd be able to take it.

"Of course, miss." Anna turned on her heel and silently disappeared.

Louise picked up her napkin and dabbed at her face in the most ladylike manner she could manage.

"Lovie, are you sure?" Schoonmaker asked.

"I'll be fine," Louise said.

Truthfully, she was dying of curiosity. She wanted to know who was waiting for her. She should have been more careful, but sometimes curiosity was more important than being careful.

"If I scream, come help." She had her gun on her. She'd be able to protect herself.

Louise made her way to the parlor, where Anna opened the door for her. The visitor, the woman, was sitting on the same velvet couch Rafael had. She was in her late forties, a woman who wore her age beautifully. Her skin showed lines at the edges of her eyes and her mouth, but she didn't seem like a woman who ran from aging. She wore a crisp blue dress and held her hat in her lap. She had a twinkling jewel clip in her hair. She looked up with liquid brown pools for eyes, deep and arresting.

"Louise Lloyd? I tried to call earlier but you weren't home. I'm sorry to just show up like this. I saw you in the paper."

Her voice was low and throaty, like nothing Louise had ever heard before. She sat down across from the woman. She looked so familiar, but Louise couldn't place her finger on why.

"You took a moment to hunt down. Your friend Rafael said you wouldn't mind if I stopped by."

"It's no trouble," Louise said. "Who are you?"

"I am so sorry. My name is Laura Cameron."

The woman extended a hand. Louise couldn't do anything; she was frozen to her spot.

"I believe we have someone in common."

That was an understatement. "I thought you were dead," Louise said. She blinked twice, trying to make her thoughts start again.

"He tried," Laura said. "I've wanted to meet you for a while."

The woman in front of her was the woman Theodore Gilbert had been in love with. The sunny afternoon in the park when he had confessed this secret of his seemed so long ago.

"I am so sorry for everything he put you through, but I also want to thank you. I was so scared he would find me."

"Where did you go?" Louise asked, breathless. This woman's sitting in front of her felt like fate, felt like something bigger than both of them.

"To Boston for a while. I came back here just as the murders started last summer. I stayed away from Harlem. I didn't want him to find me. When I found out about you . . ." She paused to light a cigarette. Laura was everything Louise wanted to be when she was Laura's age: graceful, eloquent, and beautiful. "I can't explain it. I wanted to meet you."

"I can't believe this," Louise said. It was the only thing that came to her lips.

"Me neither. What did he tell you about me?"

"He said that you died in a fire. I found the letter you wrote him when you ended the relationship. But I couldn't find any notice of a fire in Harlem when he said it was."

Louise had searched the *Tribune* archives. She had assumed the woman lived in Harlem.

"I lived on the Lower West Side then," Laura said thoughtfully. "He did set my home on fire, but I got out." Laura rose from her spot, crossing the small space between them. She kneeled in front of Louise and placed her hands on top of hers. "I am so sorry for everything you had to go through, everything he put you through. Living with it couldn't have been easy."

She squeezed Louise's hands in a maternal gesture. Louise surprised herself by bursting into tears, something she hadn't done in years.

"Come here, darling," Laura said, pulling Louise's head into her chest.

Whatever happened next, Louise would always remember this moment.

36

LOUISE KNEW SHE was right. She knew that Harriet was Emily, that Emily had killed Nora and set up Rosa Maria to take the fall.

Rafael and Eugene had been picked up and brought over for dinner.

"How is Rosa Maria?" Louise asked. It was the first thing out of her mouth after they arrived.

Rafael smiled sadly. "I asked if she wanted to come, but she had a date."

"With who?" Louise asked.

"Some guy our parents set her up with," Rafael said.

"Real sheikh, that one," Eugene told her.

She watched the other man, noted his sweet doe eyes. She didn't appreciate this information.

Louise's heart sank into her stomach. She knew the Moreno parents, far away in Mexico, still had ideas about how their daughter's life should be led while letting their son run wild. She knew Rosa Maria was meant to have married by now. She knew that

Rosa Maria loved men and women; her world was a lot more flexible than Louise's.

And they were broken up. Rosa Maria was free to do what she liked.

And if she wanted to date a good-looking stranger, she could.

But Louise missed her. It was like a significant part of her was just gone. Her heart panged with loneliness every waking minute.

"Good for her."

"You don't have to pretend to be brave for us, Lovie," Rafael said. "How much does Schoonmaker know?"

"Not everything."

Although they had become close friends, which surprised her, Louise couldn't come clean about her sexuality to Schoonmaker. He had been accepting of many things, like her race and her sex, but she drew the line at his knowing her sexuality. It did dawn on her that he had probably picked up a copy of the *Tribune* and seen the photographs printed of her, or that Rafael might have told him why she couldn't stay in the city. He had never pressed her about her love life or anything else Louise didn't raise.

"Right. Where is the old man anyway?" Rafael asked.

"Dining room," Louise said.

"Lead the way, Lovie," Rafael said.

Having her friends around the dining table made the whole room seem smaller than when it was just Schoonmaker, Josie, Michael, and Louise. It was funny how the addition of two people could change the room.

She was quiet through the first course—Schoonmaker insisted on having four courses every evening—and through half of the second.

"You okay, Lovie?" Rafael asked.

She had missed him. She was used to being close to him and his sister constantly, at one apartment or another, playing piano, dancing, living their lives. The Schoonmaker manse was too far away from her normal life, but that was the point.

Louise looked up at Rafael. For a moment she had forgotten that there was a lively conversation going on around her. She was playing with her spoon, dipping it into the soup and stirring it around.

"Everything's jake."

"Can you try that again?" Rafael asked. "Once more with feeling."

Louise rolled her eyes. "Everything's jake. I'm just thinking."

Rafael's dark eyes stayed on her, and she knew he didn't believe her. All Louise could focus on was proving it, proving her theory. She knew that if she didn't have solid proof, all of it would be for naught.

She forced a smile on her face. "Later."

Later was after Josie went to bed, Michael a step behind her. Schoonmaker brought out bottles of vodka, which Louise faithfully mixed with Coke.

Once Schoonmaker, Rafael, Louise, and Eugene were all settled around the table, cards dealt and the pot started, Rafael asked, "What is going on with you, Lovie?" He turned to Schoonmaker. "Has she always been like this?"

"Yes," Schoonmaker said. He was focused on his cards.

Louise stared at him. He had a tell. His nostrils flared whenever he tried to lie.

"I'm lost," Louise said.

They sat, making a rough square at the table, Schoonmaker at one end and Louise at the other, with Rafael to Louise's left and

Eugene to Louise's right. She scanned the table, taking a moment to size up her competition.

Then she launched into everything she knew about Harriet and about Nora's death.

Once she finished talking, Rafael let out a low whistle. "Impressive."

"I know." Louise lit a cigarette. "But I can't prove it."

It was going to haunt her. She was going to lose it if she couldn't figure it out.

"Won't the police handle it?" Eugene asked.

She could always count on him for being very sweet while asking incredibly stupid questions.

"I doubt it," Louise said, "as they want to send me or Rosa Maria up the river."

"What are you going to do?" Eugene asked.

"First, I'm going to win tonight," Louise said. "Then I am going to figure it out."

"SHE'S HAPPY, YOU know," Rafael said.

The group had dwindled down when Louise won, and Eugene and Schoonmaker decided to retire. Now Louise and Rafael faced each other, smoking cigarettes. It was getting to be two in the morning.

"Rosa Maria is happier than I've seen her in a while."

"Oh," Louise said. She didn't know how she felt about that.

"I think she needs more time," Rafael said.

She thought he was trying to make her feel better; it wasn't working.

"I think by winter, you two will be back together."

Louise leaned back in her seat, closing her eyes and tipping her face toward the ceiling. "I don't know."

She cleared her throat. The last thing she wanted to do was talk about her ex-girlfriend with her ex-girlfriend's twin brother.

"What am I going to do?" She was whining, and she hadn't whined since she was a child.

"I think you always do exactly what you set your mind to," Rafael said.

She took a sip from her glass. "This means you'll get the Dove back."

That was what she was fighting for. Rosa Maria's freedom. Rafael's livelihood. It wasn't about her. It could never be about just her. It was hard to focus while she was missing Rosa Maria so much.

"I'm glad. You'll have a job again."

"I don't think so." She opened one eye. She took a drag on her cigarette. "But I'm glad it'll be open."

She didn't like thinking of the Dove locked up and cold, full of lost revenue. The place had been theirs, and it was like a friend they missed.

"Are you sure?" Rafael asked.

Louise sat up, pushing stray hairs from her eyes. "Am I sure what?"

"It sounds unbelievable. Did Theodore Gilbert's little sister kill Nora and set Rosa Maria up for the murder? Is this some wild revenge scheme?"

Louise sat forward, leaning an arm on the mahogany table between them. "I think so."

"I could never be that patient." Rafael lit another cigarette. He was quite at ease at the manse, as if it were his world.

“I know. You do have a problem with waiting for things,” Louise said. Rafael wrinkled his nose. “But Nora’s murder was so clean that I’m not sure I’d be able to prove it unless Harriet admitted it.”

“So get her to admit it.”

“How?”

Rafael smiled. “That’s the best thing about you, Lovie. You never give up. You are possibly the smartest woman I know.”

“Keep complimenting me,” Louise said.

“No,” Rafael said. He got up, stretching for a moment before he leaned down and kissed her forehead. “I’ve got to go to bed. Eugene worries if I stay up too late.”

“You two seem happy,” Louise said. That was something she could say sincerely.

Rafael smiled again. “I think I’m a man in love. Did you ever think you’d see the day?”

Before Eugene, the last man Louise knew Rafael had a crush on had been Theodore Gilbert. Louise could safely say she never thought she’d see the day. Rafael had changed, whether he knew it or not.

“I never did,” Louise said.

He left her at the table, smoking a cigarette and trying to figure out what to do.

37

HER TIME AT the Schoonmaker manse was coming to an end. Louise knew that and was determined to milk every moment of it. She was awake early. Rafael and Eugene were in the spare room across the hallway. When she woke up, Josie wasn't lying next to her.

The sisters met up on the stairs. Josie was wearing a dressing gown wrapped around her body and nothing else, her dark hair mussed and a distinct aura around her.

"Josephine Sylvia Lloyd," Louise said, raising a hand to her mouth.

"It's not what it looks like," Josie said quickly. She refused to meet Louise's eyes.

"It looks like you've been making whoopee with a near perfect stranger," Louise said.

Josie didn't say anything. She just pulled her dressing gown closer to her body.

"Hey, Sunshine. Does he make you happy?" Louise asked.

When Josie looked up, there were tears in her eyes. "Yeah, he does."

She had always been the more sensitive twin. She felt deeply. Louise had always been more protective of her.

"We didn't even do anything," Josie said. "We just lay there and talked and it was so perfect."

Louise doubted that, but she let her little sister keep her dignity intact. She had seen how Josie and Michael were with each other and she didn't want to mess with that.

"Sure, Sunshine. Go get some sleep. I'll send Anna up with some breakfast later."

"There's something else," Josie said.

She seemed nervous about mentioning it.

"What?"

Josie took a deep breath as if she was steeling herself for Louise's reaction. "This isn't how I wanted to tell you and you have to promise not to get mad. We're moving. We're gonna go to California. It's where Celia wanted to go. I think it would be nice."

Louise pulled her sister into a tight hug. "I think that would be nice too."

She knew her sister was going to turn eighteen. That by almost every measure, Josie was an adult and she could do what she wanted, but it was still strange to think about. Louise had almost single-handedly raised Josie and Celia. She couldn't follow Josie to the ends of the earth to keep her safe, no matter how much she wanted to. And she did want to. But Josie was happy, even if she was still fragile. Louise just hoped her sister would keep her balance.

"I'm glad you're happy, Sunshine. That's all I've ever wanted."

"Me too," Josie said.

Louise kissed her on the forehead and let her go, watching as her sister climbed the stairs to their shared bedroom.

SHE WAS WAITING for Rafael and Eugene before going back into the city, where she would make a plan. She was going to trap Harriet in her lies.

As the smallest, Louise was placed in the middle of the backseat, a position she did not like and complained about for the entire ride.

They were dropped off outside of the Bed-Stuy apartment building. The apartment was empty when they got in. Rafael checked the second bedroom.

"She said she'd be home by now."

"I can leave," Louise said.

"No," Rafael said. "She's not here. She said she'd be home."

They kept calm. Rafael got on the phone, calling Rosa Maria's friends, former coworkers, the people she would spend a night with. One by one, these people reported that they hadn't seen her.

When Rafael hung up the phone for the last time, Louise felt panic grip her chest. This was a singular type of panic that she had felt only once before in her life: the morning Josie came to her boardinghouse to tell her Celia was missing.

"Do you know the name of the man she was out with last night?" Louise asked. She concentrated on breathing: deep breath in, hold for five seconds, and release.

"Philip something," Eugene said.

"Philip . . . Where did they go?" Louise asked.

She couldn't fight the panic's cold fingers on her lungs and heart. Rafael disappeared for a moment, then returned with Rosa Maria's social calendar. Louise took it. She adored the fact that Rosa Maria was a busy enough woman to keep a social calendar; Rosa Maria had always been more social than Louise had been. It was something that had originally endeared Rosa Maria to her.

"There is no need to panic. Louise will find her. She'll be fine. She always is," Eugene was saying quietly.

He had wrapped Rafael in his rather large wingspan, holding him close. Louise averted her eyes, as if she wasn't meant to see this tender moment.

She flicked through the pages until she found April. She read through Rosa Maria's diary of lunches, job interviews, and other plans. And then she came across *Philip—The Black Cat* with a phone number. Louise breathed a sigh of relief. She knew where that was. It was a quasi speakeasy in Harlem that had sprouted up in the shuttered Maggie's Café. Maggie Lister had decided to retire, letting her grandson, Frank, transform the place.

"I'm going to sort this out. Stay here in case she calls or comes back. Check out that phone number. I will sort this out," Louise promised.

She exited the apartment, closing the door behind her. She should have known that some promises were impossible to keep.

IT WAS QUICKER to take the train than to drive in the city. She left Mr. Norris and the Ford back in Bed-Stuy as she raced down the street, barreling past people trying to enjoy their morning. She knew that this had to be Harriet. This had to be something she was cooking up.

The train ride seemed to take an hour longer than it should have. Louise sat still, keeping her eyes on the window as she moved toward the destination.

When she got to the Black Cat, a place that advertised itself as a restaurant, totally on the up-and-up, the police were waiting there for her. Detective Martin was dressed cleanly and he could not keep the smug look off of his face.

"Miss Lloyd. We meet again."

"How did you know I would be here?" Louise asked.

"Good guess." Martin's face was totally unreadable.

"I want a lawyer," Louise said.

She didn't know if she would be allowed to have one. She didn't really know her rights.

"Too bad." Martin lit a cigarette. "We are going to stay here until you tell me everything."

"Then we're going to be here a long time," Louise said. "I've already told you everything I know."

She was eager to see if he could be as patient as she was. She doubted it; he had never had to dress squalling twins who wanted to match but didn't want to match.

She crossed her arms over her chest. The idea was not to speak first. She kept her eyes trained on his, saying nothing, keeping her face still and stony. She knew that he could play this little game too, but she was better at it, as she was at most things.

"We can do this all day," Martin said.

"If you're not arresting me, I want to go." For all of Louise's bravado, her mouth had gone dry, making it hard to talk.

"You can't always get what you want," Martin said. "Now tell me."

His voice had gone dangerously cold. She had played him too much. He could kill her in front of this place, in broad daylight, and he would get away scot-free. The crushing realization that she had made a mistake flooded over her.

She swallowed hard.

What could she do?

Louise exhaled. She would be wrong no matter what she said. "I didn't kill Nora Davies. Rosa Maria Moreno did not kill Nora Davies. I believe I know who did."

"Who?"

"Detective."

A young officer pulled Martin's attention away. They had a quick conversation Louise couldn't quite hear. She leaned forward to glean anything she could from the conversation.

"Fine," Martin said, and turned toward her. "You are free to go, Miss Lloyd. But one more thing. Who do you think killed Nora Davies?"

Should she spill it? Should she tell him and have him laugh at her? She weighed the options as quickly as she could, trying to see into the future for both answers. She settled into a smile that didn't tell him anything.

"I suppose you'll have to do your job."

38

LOUISE RAN INTO Harriet a couple of blocks from the Black Cat. To her surprise, Harriet had a car.

"I want to show you something," Harriet said.

The car was a slick red Ford Model T. Louise had never learned to drive, never needed to, but seeing that car made her want to learn.

"Get in." Harriet opened the passenger door for her.

Louise knew that this was risky, letting Harriet take her somewhere. She shouldn't get into the car; she should run, get help.

But this was her only chance at finding Rosa Maria.

And that was a risk she had to take. Louise climbed into the passenger seat.

Harriet was gripping the steering wheel with gorgeous leather gloves. "Got yourself into some trouble, dear?" she asked as she took off.

"Just a spot," Louise said.

Harriet drove at a pace that was dangerous and uncomfortable.

She had no care for anyone else on the road as they sped away from the city.

"I thought we could take a lunch, talk about the story you want me to write," Harriet said.

She almost had to yell over the spring wind whipping through the car. Louise had never been in a convertible and she decided that this was not a particularly fun experience. That and her life was in the hands of a murderer. If the car crashed, Louise would be dead.

"Sounds lovely," Louise said. She had to keep it together. "I can't wait."

"I'm taking you to this darling little place I know," Harriet said. "You have been so hard to find lately. I'm glad we can do this."

Louise kept a smile on her face, trying to pretend to be excited. "Me too," she said. "It'll be nice to get away."

"Oh, lovely," Harriet said, turning her eyes to Louise while maintaining her breakneck pace. "It will be to die for."

Louise was not expecting the house they arrived at to be their destination. It was modest, three floors, one of many like it on its street. Harriet parked the car and Louise felt her stomach shift back into position. The drive had been nearly deadly.

"Coming?" Harriet asked. "I want to show you something."

Harriet got out of the car. She was again immaculately dressed, in a dress and a coat of petal pink with a black hat and black shoes.

Louise did as she was told, trying to figure out where she was. There was something about this quaint little neighborhood that seemed so familiar to her. She looked around as Harriet marched toward the front door.

"Louise, come on!"

Louise had to get a message to Rafael. That was the only thing on her mind as she followed Harriet into the house. She had to save Rosa Maria. She was following a killer into the belly of the beast.

"So," Harriet said, "this house has been in my family forever."

The house hadn't been updated for decades. Louise followed her inside, watching as Harriet took off her coat, then tossed it to the floor. The only sound in the house was the click of their heels on the hardwood.

"I haven't visited in a while, you know? Things just got busy, but I thought we could have a picnic in the backyard while we talked. And you can tell me why you were arrested."

Louise turned, looking out the window. The streets were silent around them. She blinked up at the moody afternoon sky.

"Are you okay?" Harriet asked.

Every fiber of her being was telling her to get out, to leave, that nothing good would happen if she stayed. But she ignored her gut instinct and turned to Harriet.

"Of course," she said with a smile. "I just have to iron my shoelaces."

"Upstairs," Harriet said.

Louise knew that she shouldn't leave Harriet alone, but Louise headed up the stairs, gripping tightly to the wooden banister.

THE UPSTAIRS WAS dark, a shocking contrast to the sunny lower floor. She found the bathroom, bypassed it, and went into what seemed to be a bedroom. She was looking for a phone; she needed to find a phone. She closed the door behind her and shoved an old trunk in front of it so it couldn't open. The air was musty in the bedroom. There was no bed, although there was an outline of one in the rug on the floor. Louise took off her shoes and held them in one hand so she didn't make any noise. She knew that she was at a disadvantage in this place. There was an old wardrobe and a desk. There was a phone on the desk. Louise picked it up and heard nothing. The phone was dead. She was trapped.

She opened the wardrobe. It was empty, save for scraps of letters someone must have forgotten to throw out when they cleaned. Louise kneeled down, putting her shoes on the floor. Louise recognized, in the faded ink, Theodore Gilbert's writing. Louise looked over her shoulder, getting the sense that someone was watching her.

She was not getting anywhere new. She didn't know where she was. All she could really say was that she was outside the city, in the suburbs. Louise knew she should run. She removed the trunk from in front of the door and stepped out. She did go into the bathroom, and ran the water in the sink for a moment. She put her shoes back on and descended the stairs. She could hear Harriet humming in the kitchen.

Her heart was in her throat. What had she gotten herself into? What had she done? Why hadn't she asked for help when she needed it? Her stomach was in knots and her thoughts were racing.

Harriett had procured an apron and had put it on over her dress. She had poured two glasses of what Louise thought was gin.

"Come on in. I just need to finish something up." Harriet never lost her cheery tone, as if this were just a normal day among friends. "It is so nice to be out of the city, isn't it? I love it there, but sometimes it can be so stifling. I really am glad you're here."

If Harriet noticed that Louise wasn't saying anything, she didn't mention it. Harriet took a sip from her glass. Louise didn't touch hers. Harriet narrowed her eyes. Louise forced a smile on her face. She pretended to take a sip from her glass. She was sure it was drugged, and she was never going to let anyone drug her again.

There was no way Harriet was this stupid. She must have known Louise was onto her. Louise put the glass down.

"You know, I was thinking: it was so lucky we met when we did. If you hadn't shown up right then, who knows what that man would have done to me?" Louise was wondering if their first meeting had been engineered. There was nothing that Harriet would leave to chance.

Harriet smiled. She leaned on the countertop. "Who knew that Louise Lloyd would be my first friend in the city?" She was doing a very good job of keeping up this charade.

"Where are you from?" Louise asked.

Harriet frowned, her face darkening for just a moment. "I thought I told you."

"No," Louise said. "In fact, you've never told me anything about yourself. If you have any siblings, maybe?"

"None. I had a brother who died in the war."

Harriet turned away from her. Louise took a step away from the counter.

Another opportunity. Louise could run, sprint to the next house, ask for help, and call Rafael. But she was rooted to the spot. She had to follow her first instinct and find Rosa Maria. Harriet turned back around.

"I had another brother," she said. Louise realized Harriet was on the verge of tears. "And I loved him. He was my best friend, my hero. All I wanted was to come here and spend time with my brother."

She stepped toward Louise. Louise took another small step back. She could see the rage in Harriet's eyes; she could see the hatred. Louise took a deep breath, trying to remain calm. Harriet swung at her. Louise moved before the other woman could make impact. Harriet grabbed Louise; she was quite strong for a woman of her stature, willowy thin. She grabbed a cloth from the counter and pressed it to Louise's face.

Louise fought. She tried, but she was no match for the world going black around her.

39

A HEAVY SENSE OF déjà vu settled over Louise as she opened her eyes. She was sitting on a chair, wrists bound behind her and ankles bound below her, raw rope digging into her skin and stockings. Her heart began to beat fast. It was dark and a little warmer than it had been, but she knew this place.

This was the exact cellar she had woken up in over a decade ago.

Her head throbbed. Her mouth filled with saliva. She wasn't alone.

"Louise."

It was Rosa Maria. Louise would have recognized her voice anywhere. Their backs were together, and if Louise twisted her wrist, they could just very gently brush fingertips.

"Are you okay?" Rosa Maria asked.

"I'm okay." Louise could feel tears welling up in her eyes. "How are you?"

"Been better," Rosa Maria deadpanned.

"Do you know how you got here?" Louise asked.

"I don't know." Rosa Maria was breathless. "I just went out with this man Philip, and I—"

"I think I know who he is," Louise said. "He's the one who took the photos of us that were in the *Tribune*. He works for Harriet. You were set up."

She felt the tips of Rosa Maria's fingers grasp hers. The subtle touch calmed her down. She had to keep her senses. She had to keep her nerve. She had broken out of here before. She knew that she could do it again.

"I know who drugged us, I know who killed Nora, and I know who set us all up." She should have seen this coming from a mile away. "When you didn't come home last night, I knew I had to act. I am so sorry. I should have known better."

Rosa Maria didn't say anything. She was crying, quiet little sobs that shook her shoulders. "Why didn't she just kill me? How are we going to get out of here?"

"I'm gonna get us free. Just stay still."

Louise closed her eyes, trying to figure out how to undo the knot without seeing it. It was akin to picking a lock. She took a deep breath. Her only goal was to get them out of there.

That place had haunted her nightmares for years on end. She couldn't count the times she had woken up in a cold sweat, convinced that she was going to be taken again, that this basement was where she was going to die.

But she wasn't going to focus on that. Louise was going to focus only on what she could do right now.

"Rosa Maria, if we don't get out of this, I need you to know I didn't plan any of this." The words fell from her lips as she struggled with the complicated knot. "I love you so much. I am so, so sorry."

"Louise, just concentrate."

Classic Rosa Maria. And she was right. Louise opened one eye.

She was facing the wall with the small window. Light filtered through it, the dark and duskiness of the evening. Her hands were going numb and it was harder and harder to move her fingers.

"What if we don't make it out of here?" Rosa Maria asked.

Louise's fingers slipped over the rope. She closed her eyes, taking a deep breath.

"I'm going to untie us, and then we will figure it out."

Easier said than done when Louise couldn't even begin to undo the knots; then she had to contend with her ankle bindings as well. One thing at a time. She could do that. One thing at a time, and then they could focus on getting out of there.

Louise considered that another Gilbert sibling might have to die at her hands. How many times would she have to take someone's life? Would this make her a murderer? She didn't want to do it. She didn't have her gun on her. Foolishly, she had left it at the Schoonmaker manse.

"I tried to call Rafael and Eugene. The phone here is disconnected, but I'll get you free. I'll distract her and you run for help, okay?" Talking through a plan always helped Louise make sense of everything.

"I'm not leaving without you."

"Rosa Maria, you have to. If there is any chance of either of us getting out of here alive, you have to."

Louise could barely breathe. She was losing feeling in her fingers. She stretched them out, trying to wake them up.

"I am not leaving without you," Rosa Maria repeated.

"I love you so much."

What wouldn't she give to kiss Rosa Maria one more time, feel her body against her own as their heartbeats synchronized? Louise could picture their life together: growing old, celebrating birthdays and holidays and anniversaries together. She wanted to be there for the publication of Rosa Maria's first book. She wanted to be there when the world realized what she already knew: Rosa Maria was a force to be reckoned with. Louise blinked back tears. She couldn't get emotional now.

"You have to do this. For us. Okay? I'll distract her. You run. We can take her."

"Okay," Rosa Maria said.

Louise moved to grasp Rosa Maria's fingers in hers. Then she continued fiddling with the knot. She could feel it starting to loosen.

"What about you?" Rosa Maria asked.

"Don't worry about me. Go get help." Louise tried to keep her breathing even as she worked on the rope that bound them. "This house is at the end of the street. You'll have to go to your left when you exit. Run and keep knocking until you find someone who will let you in, okay?"

"Louise, if you die and I'm not there, I will never be able to live with myself."

"You're in this because of me. Let me save you, please," Louise said.

This was the woman she would always care about. She would always love her. She pulled the rope away. Rosa Maria leaned forward, beginning to fiddle with the knot around her ankles.

Then the door opened. Harriet stepped in, a frown on her face. "You're not going anywhere."

HARRIET CROSSED OVER to kneel in front of Louise. In her right hand was a pearl-handled gun. "You know, you are the root of all of my problems." Harriet laughed a girlish little laugh. "My name is Emily Gilbert. Do you recognize me?"

"You're his sister." Louise tried to keep her voice even and steady.

"His only sister. And you took him away from me." Emily's eyes narrowed. Her American accent melted away, replaced with a brisk British one. "You trusted me. You told me everything. All it took was one chance encounter. The man on the street that day? I hired him." She looked very proud of herself. "I have made this past month of your life hell, and it's only going to get worse, Miss Lloyd." She stood up, and without letting go of her gun, turned the chairs so they were facing each other.

Emily kneeled down next to Rosa Maria, running the backs of her fingers over Rosa Maria's face. Rosa Maria closed her eyes. Louise could see that she was sobbing, her lips moving in a silent prayer.

"You ruined my life, Louise. You took my brother away from me. I loved him and you took him away from me. And I don't know why you thought you could get away with that. Everything has a price. You'd do well to remember that."

Rosa Maria wasn't free; her ankles were still bound. Before Emily did anything else, she made sure that Rosa Maria's arms were tied behind her again.

"Sure, I killed Nora. I drugged you and your stupid little friends."

Emily began to pace in front of them. Louise didn't watch her. She kept her eyes on Rosa Maria.

"You know what? I found you two disgusting. Lying on the gross floor of that club, faces inches apart. You two are depraved. I almost shot you then and there. But I didn't. I thought it would be so much more fun to play with you."

Emily stepped back to Rosa Maria. She kneeled down. "You know how easy it was to get your little girlfriend to kiss me? I didn't even like her. Louise was just so starved for affection, she'd do anything for anyone."

"Let her go." Louise was not going to let this woman get to her. "You have a problem with me. Let her go."

Emily looked at Louise. She was smiling coldly, maliciously. "You think I would do that? Just half the fun? I've put so much work into this. I had to watch you and hire someone to take photos of you and steer you in the wrong direction. I had to trash your apartment. I even had to call your father and tell him I was concerned about you. Do you think this is easy for me?" Emily exhaled, pouting. "Think about me. I would much rather do anything else, but you needed to learn a lesson, Miss Lloyd. You mess with the Gilbert family and we will mess with you right back. I'm just finishing what he started."

Emily had done it all. It was what Louise had suspected, but the time and energy and money Emily had invested in taking her down was shocking. She had had to be so patient.

"I want to have my fun now, Louise. And you're going to let me. I worked so hard to make sure all of this was in place. I called the police on the Dove, saying one of you had murdered Nora and I saw the body. I sat with your father, pretending to *really* be concerned about you. I called the police on the Black Cat. I have never worked so hard in my life and you tell me to let her go?" Emily moved so she was kneeling in front of Louise. She reached a gloved hand out, brushing her fingertips over Louise's cheeks. "I bet you fantasized about me. I fantasized about taking you down, you disgusting dinge bulldagger. You're so stupid, you'll trust anyone who asks. Think about that."

Louise's heart was in her throat. She couldn't undo her own knots. This was it. This was how she was going to die. She had no idea how to get out.

Emily rose to her feet and paced a large circle around the chairs. She toyed with the gun in her hands, as if this was just a little bit of fun for her. She stopped pacing and tapped a finger against her lips.

"You know what I can't decide? Which of you I should kill first. Maybe I should just kill her and let you live in the pain."

Louise had made her peace with dying young a long time ago. "Kill me. If you're going to kill anyone here, it should be me."

Emily stopped moving. Louise refused to look at her, focusing only on Rosa Maria.

This was the end. She was sure of it. Louise felt a sort of calm wash over her. There was no way she was going to get out of this alive.

"Wrong answer," Emily said.

She pressed the gun to Rosa Maria's temple. Rosa Maria closed her eyes, tears streaming down her cheeks, waiting for the pull of the trigger and her quick death. Emily counted to five.

"I win, Miss Lloyd."

"Let her go. She didn't do anything to you. Kill me. Kill! Me!" Louise was screaming, her voice rising octaves.

Emily looked at her, steel in her cool blue eyes. "An eye for an eye, Miss Lloyd. You take someone I love, and I'll take someone you love."

Time seemed to slow down. Louise fought against the bindings keeping her in her chair. She was screaming at the top of her lungs.

"Emily Gilbert, drop the weapon." The voice was cool, clear. It was Detective Martin.

Emily froze. Martin, four officers, and Rafael of all people flooded into the basement. Weapons were drawn, all trained on Emily. Emily dropped the gun only when she knew it was over.

The little pistol clattered to the floor. Louise could move her foot just enough to kick it away.

She never thought she would be so relieved to see Andrew Martin. He pulled Emily away from her, and officers began to untie Louise and Rosa Maria. Louise began to cry true tears of relief as she fell onto Rosa Maria's lap.

Emily was quiet as she was arrested. She didn't say anything, just glared at Louise, her lips tight with fury.

As the fear of losing her life dissipated and she realized she wasn't, in fact, ready to die, Louise realized something else: she was going to leave this basement, this city, and never return.

40

AFTER BEING CHECKED by a doctor, after repeating their statements to police several times, after watching Emily Gilbert be arrested and taken away, they went dancing.

Schoonmaker, Eugene, Josie, Michael, Rafael, Rosa Maria, and Louise all arrived at the Dinner Club as it changed from the restaurant to a nightclub. Louise wore a beaded blue dress with a deep V-neck and a feathered skirt—a dress she had seen in a shopwindow and she'd had to have. She felt glamorous; she felt beautiful. Rosa Maria was wearing a spangled red dress that managed to complement her perfectly. Louise did one Charleston at the beginning of the night, letting the light reflect off the beads on her dress, making her glow as she went through the steps. She and Rosa Maria danced right next to each other, just like old times, holding court on the floor and making everyone else watch.

Truthfully, Louise didn't feel much like dancing that night. An hour had passed and she was trapped in Schoonmaker's booth by Rafael on her left and Rosa Maria on her right, making it impossible for her to move. The band was playing a waltz. They had been playing a lot of slow songs and Louise was keeping an eye on Josie and Michael on the dance floor. They had danced every song together. Louise couldn't help but find it adorable, the way Josie looked up at him with all the care and the trust in the world.

Louise had cried herself out. She felt raw now. Her makeup was doing a bad job of hiding the redness of her eyes. At least her lips were red to match.

"How did you find us?" Louise asked Rafael. She took a sip from her glass, feeling relief swell into every pore of her being.

"Well, it took a little detective work." Rafael preened. He was grinning and he was going to hold it over their heads for the rest of their lives that he had helped save them. "I called the number Rosa Maria had in her date book but it was disconnected. I thought it was the Black Cat, but I guess it was the house. Then I asked the cable girl to give me the nearest available number. Then I called them, and they told me their address and . . . then I called the police."

He had had to tell the story several times. Rafael loved to repeat it. He loved feeling like a hero. He was going to try to bask in the glory of it for as long as he lived.

"I have never been more grateful to have a baby brother," Rosa Maria said.

Rafael wrinkled his nose, annoyed at being referred to as her baby brother. "I had to tell Martin everything you told me," he continued. "I didn't think he'd believe me, but he did."

It didn't matter how it had happened. The case was closed. Nora's murder had been solved. The Dove would be able to open up again soon.

Rosa Maria lit a cigarette, then exhaled before leaning back in the booth. She hadn't been saying much. Louise understood how she was feeling.

Going dancing was supposed to help them celebrate, but for the first time in a while, Louise did not want to be there.

Schoonmaker left them early, intent on flirting a pretty blonde into his bed. Louise could see him by the bar, his tall, languid body leaning down toward her, as he tried every charming move he had. For her part, the pretty blonde didn't seem too moved. Michael and Josie were still on the dance floor, ignoring everyone else but each other. Louise drained her glass, then filled it again. The band changed, speeding the tempo up a little bit.

Eugene leaned into Rosa Maria. "Dance?"

Rosa Maria nodded. She and Louise had to be careful about dancing together in public in places like this. Louise, especially, didn't need any more attention than she'd had. She watched as Eugene led Rosa Maria to the floor and began a solid foxtrot. She loved watching Rosa Maria dance. There was a fluidity to her movements that was easy and graceful. She made it all look effortless, like everything else she did.

Rafael watched them go and nudged Louise gently. "You all right, Lovie?"

Louise took a sip from her glass. What a loaded question. She should be fine, and she was fine. But her heart was still stuttering in her chest as if Emily were somehow still right behind her. She was eager to go back to the manse and sleep through the night.

"Everything's copacetic, babe."

"You're lying to me."

"No, I'm not."

Louise finished her drink and turned to him. That was her fourth drink and she was now past slightly tipsy and on her way to buzzy drunk, right where she wanted to be. Rafael looked into her eyes. He was wearing a suit of inky green, a lazy and typical fashion choice that would have had women falling all over him if he'd wanted a woman. She blinked, trying to hold eye contact.

"I can read your thoughts, Lovie. And I'll say it again: you're lying to me."

He was teasing her but, at the same time, she knew he was totally serious. There was a part of her that couldn't believe it. The nightmare from her youth, the past summer, and now this spring. It had all led her to this.

"I'm just not good company tonight," Louise said.

Rafael raised an eyebrow. He sipped from his glass. He didn't say anything. Louise opened her mouth to say something, and when she did, she began to cry.

EMILY GILBERT GAVE a full confession. Louise was at the manse when she heard, and when the phone call came in, she cried again.

Martin asked both her and Rosa Maria to come down to the station. When they arrived, they were escorted into his office. He regarded them both. It had been a day since Emily was arrested. Louise's name didn't make the papers so much this time around. She hoped that Nora's friends would be able to find some closure.

"I believe I owe you an apology," Martin said. He practically choked on the words as he said them.

Louise and Rosa Maria shared a look.

"To who?" Louise asked.

"Both of you."

Martin didn't look at Louise. His eyes were on his desk. He was hating every moment of this and she was going to milk it for all that it was worth. She was reveling in the feeling of a case finished and closed, the long exhale after which she imagined that her life would get back to normal. She would be able to move on, and that was what she wanted.

"Why don't you apologize to her first?" Louise asked.

Martin glared at her. He cleared his throat. "Miss Moreno, on behalf of the New York City Police Department, I apologize for falsely suspecting you of murder."

"Apology accepted," Rosa Maria said.

Martin turned to Louise. She could not keep the smile off of her face. This was all she ever wanted in her life and she was so excited that it was finally happening. "Miss Lloyd, although you are a pain in my side, on behalf of the New York City Police Department, I apologize for falsely suspecting you for the murder of Nora Davies." He exhaled, as if that had been a Herculean task that was the hardest thing for him to do.

"Thank you," Louise said haughtily. She and Rosa Maria shared another look.

"I very much appreciate it," Rosa Maria said.

He was trying to make sure they didn't sue the police department, but all Louise wanted was to leave.

"If that's all, I think we're finished here," Martin said.

Louise didn't move from her spot. She wanted to say something else but she wasn't sure what. She felt as if she could sleep for three days and still be tired. "What is going to happen to her?"

Martin had turned back to his paperwork, already trying to forget who was sitting in his office. "She'll probably hang."

"Right," Louise said.

That didn't come as a surprise. Louise would have liked to be there to watch her be executed. She wondered how many women had been executed in the state of New York.

"If that is all," Martin repeated, "I hope the two of you have a pleasant rest of your day."

Louise and Rosa Maria shared one last look and left the small office.

Once they were outside, Louise turned to Rosa Maria. It was a cool spring afternoon and they stood in the middle of the street, facing each other as people rushed past them. Louise didn't mind being anonymous in the swarms of people on the Harlem streets.

"Do you want to go back to Schoonmaker's? I think we need to talk about some things."

Rosa Maria considered Louise's suggestion for a moment, lighting a cigarette as she did. She looked so beautiful in the afternoon light, dressed seriously in black. Her brown eyes glinted in the sun. Her black dress made her look taller than she was. She still had marks on her wrists from the ties. Louise did too. They were still sore from being bound up so tightly. Louise had dressed similarly, not wanting to stick out or draw attention to herself in any way.

She hoped that the Harlem's Hero part of her life was over now. She hoped that she was free to be whoever she wanted now without the prying eyes of newspapermen or police or people who wanted to change her or make her do things she didn't particularly want to do.

"Why not?" Rosa Maria said. "It's not like I have much to do today anyway."

41

ROSA MARIA HAD never been to the Schoonmaker manse. While Schoonmaker still insisted it was a normal house where normal people lived, Louise and Rosa Maria agreed that it was definitely a mansion. Louise gave her a quick tour, showing her the parlor and sitting room and living room, and taking her out to the backyard.

They ended up in the blue room, where Louise was in the middle of cleaning and making sure she was ready to leave. Packing up the large room was easy because Louise had barely unpacked. It was Josie who had made the initial mess, but Anna had come in every day after breakfast to tidy up. Louise would miss living with Anna, who was efficient and quiet. There were a lot of luxuries that Louise had gotten used to while living at the Schoonmaker manse, and she didn't know how she would adjust after she was gone. Trying to get out of 3I as fast as she could, Louise had thrown her things into her trunk haphazardly. Now all she was doing was moving one article of clothing at a time from one spot to another. Josie had already packed her things in anticipation of her own move. Louise couldn't believe that her youngest sister was going to move away from the place they had called home for the entirety of their lives.

But Louise figured that if Josie could do it, she could do it too. Her tickets to Paris were now secreted in her trunk along with her passport. The ship departed in two days and she was going to have to soak up every minute of living at the Schoonmaker manse until then.

"This is just like old times," Rosa Maria said.

Louise laughed. In the boardinghouse they had lived in together, Louise's bedroom had been pink. They had spent hours in that room, getting ready for nights out, sneaking back in, having a life together.

Rosa Maria sat on Louise's bed, crossing her legs underneath her, watching as Louise rearranged her things. She lit a cigarette, then moved so she was lying down on her stomach.

"I have two tickets to Paris," Louise said.

At the same time, Rosa Maria said, "I think we have to talk."

"You go," Louise said.

Rosa Maria pulled herself up so she was sitting on her knees. Louise could see her working through exactly what she wanted to say, making sure she had the right words. "You're my first love. I will always love you, but I think it's best if we stay apart."

"Oh," Louise said.

She moved so she was sitting on the bed. They faced each other. Sitting across from Rosa Maria was something that felt strange now. They had been so close, and that closeness was so easily undone.

"I guess you don't want to come to Paris with me, then?"

Louise had some money to get herself over there and contacts in her new city, all thanks to Schoonmaker. She had been hesitant to take it. Louise liked being a self-made woman, but she remembered that Emily had torn 3I apart, taking almost every cent she had. She was grateful for everything Schoonmaker had done for her. Louise had to be careful, but she was set.

"I think I should stay here. Someone needs to manage the Dove," Rosa Maria said.

The Dove was scheduled to reopen that Friday. Everything was back to the way it should have been. Rafael was probably in the club right now making sure it was sparkling clean. He had offered to give Louise back her old job, and while she had wanted to take it, she knew she had to move on.

"That's nice. I'm glad." Louise didn't know why she felt she had to be so formal.

"Do you need help packing?" Rosa Maria asked.

Louise sensed that Rosa Maria didn't really know what to say.

"No, I'm almost done," Louise said.

She was glad not to have so many things. She was going through the things she used to wear, the makeup she used to use. It was like seeing herself through a different set of eyes. She had removed some things to give to Josie, who was always happy to take Louise's clothes. She was trying to pack light. She didn't want to move across an ocean feeling weighed down. The two women were caught in silence for a moment.

Rosa Maria cleared her throat. "I am so sorry for how I handled things. I should have stood by you."

"You don't need to apologize," Louise said. "I was wrong." She leaned on the table.

"I shouldn't have left," Rosa Maria said.

"I shouldn't have let you," Louise said.

Would she miss this? She would miss waking up next to Rosa Maria, sharing dances and a life. Moving into 3I had been the best thing they had ever done. There had been so many times, so many nights, when Louise had thought that she and Rosa Maria were invincible. But they were so young when they got together.

And now they were broken up and awkwardly sitting on a bed. Louise was still holding a dress in her hands. She put it down, freeing herself. She wanted to cry, but she had cried herself out.

"I'm going to miss you so much," Louise said.

Rosa Maria dabbed at her eyes with the sleeve of her cardigan. She didn't usually get emotional, unless her life was in danger. She nodded. "Me too."

This was the best thing for both of them. They both knew that now. They couldn't maintain a romantic relationship. Louise knew that Rosa Maria wanted to get married, have children. There had to be some universe where they would end up together. Rosa Maria took Louise's hand in hers, kissing Louise's knuckles.

On some level, Louise had always known that this would happen. But she hadn't realized how much it would hurt.

42

THE DRIVE TO the pier is a long one. It's just her and Schoonmaker. She sits in the front of the Ford for the first time ever and watches the city go by from the window, the beautiful spring day accenting the people on the street living their lives.

Her heart is beating wildly in her chest. This is the place where she has lived her whole life. She doesn't know how she can leave it behind.

She saw her sister off yesterday at Grand Central Station. Josie was wearing a rather fashionable traveling suit of emerald green with a matching hat. She was excited to start her new life. Louise hugged her baby sister tightly, kissing both her cheeks and then her forehead. She watched until the train pulled away, Josie sticking her head out of the window and waving until Louise couldn't see her anymore.

And now it is her turn. Schoonmaker drives with care, keeping his eyes on the road as he talks about everything. She has gotten used to his presence over the past several days.

The days have blurred together, which is probably because she has barely slept at all.

But now nervous energy is keeping her awake. She has her passport and money in her purse. Schoonmaker wanted to upgrade her to first class. She didn't decline. She wants to have every experience possible.

When Schoonmaker parks and Louise gets out of the car, Rafael and Rosa Maria are waiting for her. She shouldn't be surprised, but she is. The twins are standing side by side, eagerly looking for her, watching for her.

She crosses to them and Rosa Maria pulls her into a hug first. Rosa Maria is wearing her signature perfume. Louise inhales the sharp floral scent and feels the other woman's body against her. She's giving up her first love, the first person who truly made her feel alive.

Their breakup will be less painful if she's an ocean away.

Rafael is next, picking her up and twirling her around. He was the first person Louise ever met at the Zodiac. He's one of her closest friends, the reason why she met Rosa Maria, a part of her life for the past decade.

She can't imagine her life without them, and yet she must.

She has to move on.

Rosa Maria hugs her again and then loops her arm through Louise's. She's smiling, but her eyes are filling with tears. "I'll miss you so much."

Louise boards the ship, becoming one of many, invisible in the crowd. Louise leans on the railing, trying to spot Rafael, Rosa Maria, and Schoonmaker.

The Statue of Liberty is behind her. She watches it until she can't see it anymore, a tiny mark in the distance. She leans over the rail of the ship, letting the spray hit her face.

It's her first time on a ship like this; it's her first time leaving the States. With everything that's happened over the last year, she's eager to leave it all behind.

The ship is quiet around her. Most people have gone inside. Dinner is being served. She doesn't feel like sitting among people she doesn't know who will judge her for the color of her skin. She's eager to be a stranger among people; she's no longer Harlem's Hero.

But she feels a tear fall down her face. Everything about who she is is about Harlem. She knows she'll miss it. She'll miss being close to her friends. She'll miss being part of something bigger than herself.

But she can't take it anymore. The murder, the police, constantly being watched. Everyone always wants something from her, something she can't give. They want her to be someone she can't be.

It's stifling, being stuck under the weight of other people's expectations.

The sun is setting and she's watching it go down, a brilliant shock of color. The water is still and quiet. She didn't think she'd like traveling on the water; she thought it would be less stable, more shaky.

But she's used to it, and at least she isn't sick.

She's saying good-bye to the Louise Lloyd she used to be. She's only twenty-seven and she's lived enough lives for three people, she thinks. She's spent her youth changing who she is overnight, flitting from one person to another.

And she's not sure that any of those people are really her.

Who has she been? She's been a chorus girl, a waitress, a manager, a detective. All of these roles have filled her with pride, but it's the detective she likes being the best.

She's able to bring justice to people who deserve it. She's able to help the people who need it. Even though she's been shoved into it every time, that doesn't mean she doesn't love it.

Louise braces herself against the rails, gripping them tightly. New York City is nothing but a memory now. And she's excited to see what comes next.

AUTHOR'S NOTE

Every murder is driven by love, money, or pride. At least, that's what Josh Mankiewicz told me on his podcast *Motive for Murder*. The case in *Dead Dead Girls* revolved around love, and the one in *Harlem Sunset* revolves around pride.

The unsolved murders of Jack the Ripper inspired the case at the heart of *Dead Dead Girls*, but the case in *Harlem Sunset* isn't wholly inspired by any one event. I wanted to play with the subject of memory and lean into the Prohibition-era love of the occult.

Harlem Sunset was a different beast from *Dead Dead Girls*. The action kicks off on Louise's twenty-seventh birthday, and she is very cautiously optimistic about her future. When sitting down to plan this novel, I had to think of how I wanted Louise to grow. A blessing and a curse of writing books that follow the same main character is that she can't be static. Everything has to teach her a lesson. I've already pushed her to her limits and she thrived, but at what cost?

It made sense that Louise would want nothing more than a quiet life with her girlfriend. She wants anonymity, and she also wants to see the world. Putting her in her comfort zone and then removing her from it is going to help her grow, even if that growth is painful.

Another major topic of this novel is identity. Many of the characters have to hide parts of themselves to fit into the world they live in. They have to make small concessions every day about who they are and who they love. Being any orientation other than straight was illegal in New York in 1927, and Louise has some very close calls in this one. Standing up for, and clearing, Rosa Maria brings to light some significant, life-altering realizations for Louise.

Fox Schoonmaker is my *Gatsby* character, although not based on anyone in particular. I wanted to introduce a character who is living the exact opposite of Louise's life. Schoonmaker's riches didn't come easily—he made a fortune profiting off of illegal liquor sales and nightclubs. Now everything in his world is opulent, a stark contrast to Louise's, as she still has to fight for everything she has. He's almost the perfect embodiment of the American Dream, changing who he was in order to be who he wants.

As Louise embarks on a new journey, she too will have to change. . . .

HARLEM SUNSET

NEKESA AFIA

QUESTIONS FOR DISCUSSION

1. At the start of *Harlem Sunset*, Louise Lloyd has made a new life for herself. How has Detective Gilbert's legacy affected Louise? How has it affected Detective Martin?

2. Have the events Louise, Rosa Maria, and Rafael experienced together changed their friendship and the course of their lives? If so, how?

3. Louise's family has a strong presence in *Harlem Sunset*. How would you describe Louise's relationships with sisters Minna and Josie? How have Louise, Minna, and Josie handled the loss of Celia? Do you think Louise is satisfied with how their relationships evolve throughout the course of the novel?

4. Louise and her father, Joseph, don't see eye to eye. How has this shaped Louise's life and how she sees the world?

5. Joseph reveals something significant to Louise about her mother. How does this revelation challenge Louise's perceptions of herself and her family? Do you think Joseph was justified in keeping this information from her? Why or why not?

6. Is Louise too trusting? Does her tendency to trust people change throughout the course of the novel?

7. Louise and Rosa Maria encounter several challenges to their relationship. How do they cope with these challenges individually and as a couple?

8. Louise and Rosa Maria's relationship has changed a great deal by the end of the novel. How do you feel they each contributed to these changes?

9. Schoonmaker is an intriguing and mysterious character. Why do you think he offered to host Louise and Josie? What do Louise and Rafael see in Schoonmaker?

10. Louise's past as a kidnapping victim has affected every facet of her life. How does she come to terms with that past in *Harlem Sunset*? Do you think she will ever be at peace with what she experienced?

ACKNOWLEDGMENTS

Writing a novel during a WHOLE ASS PANDY is hard.

Doing it alone in a tiny apartment is even harder.

First I'd like to thank myself for writing a novel alone in a tiny apartment during a whole ass pandy.

Thanks and love to:

Agent: Travis Pennington

Editor: Michelle Vega

Marketing and publicity teams: Natalie Sellars, Dache Rogers, Stephanie Felty, and Jessica Plummer

Cover artist: Emma Leonard

Book designer: Alison Cnockaert

Copy editors, typesetters, and proofreaders

All the love in the world also goes to:

My family

The Berkletes

Fury Road

Sarah Strange

Lora Maroney
Allan Perkins
Molly Clark
Chloé Maxwell
Vincent Briggs
Black girls everywhere
and
You

Photo by FizCo Photography

NEKESA (Nuh-kes-ah) AFIA (Ah-fee-ah) is a Canadian millennial who is doing her best. When she isn't writing, she is either sewing, swing dancing, or actively trying to pet every dog she sees. The Harlem Renaissance Mysteries is her debut series.

CONNECT ONLINE

NekesaAfia.com

NekesaAfia

NekesaAfia